SECOND TIME'S THE CHARM

VANESSA M KNIGHT

To the men in my life—my husband and my son. Without you both, I never would have had the courage to write word one. You are my heart and soul.

I love you both.

ACKNOWLEDGMENTS

I want to thank my editors. You made the story stronger and better, and I'm grateful for that.

I also want to thank Nicole Leiren for the fabulous book title and for dedicating hours and hours to reading and rereading. You are an awesome critique partner.

Thank you to Windy City RWA for the insight and friendship. And to all my critique partners who read the early drafts and didn't laugh: Cici Edwards, Jackie Powers, and Kathy Korbal.

Last but not least, thank you, thank you, thank you to my mom, my family and my friends for your unrelenting support. Your encouragement and belief in me made all of this possible.

CHAPTER ONE

ALLISON SOUTHBY STILL HAD TIME. No one had seen her. She could jump in her car and disappear before anyone knew she'd ever pulled up to the house. She'd heard Mexico was beautiful this time of year.

But then reality slapped her in the face. No matter how much she wanted to run away, she couldn't. Loraine had asked her to attend, and Herb would have wanted her here.

Her stomach churned, and her hand grasped the gold Celtic knot that hung around her neck. Calm washed over her as the familiar texture of the rope design slid through her fingers. She stared at the entrance of Loraine's massive house in the Chicago suburbs, where Allison had received the necklace so many Christmases ago. In fact, it was where she'd spent every Christmas for more than ten years.

She could do this— handle seeing him—handle whatever was behind that door. She could handle anything.

Drawing in a deep breath, she rang the bell next to the double wooden doors. A hay-like scent wafted from the fall crocus lining the portico. The only sound, the music of finches and sparrows cutting through the tranquil morning. Maybe it was canceled, and no one was home. Hope flowed through her like a boat along the Nile—then capsized as the house shot to life.

Noise erupted from behind the door, right before it swung open. Instead of the butler Allison expected, Adam Byrnes stood before her, his short, brown hair disheveled. His chiseled cheekbones and angular face were the perfect backdrop to his green eyes.

Her gaze moved down his strong neck to his form-fitting black sweater. The rolled sleeves gave her a perfect view of his bulging forearms. His dark straight-leg denim jeans hugged his hips, and—heaven help her—other parts of his anatomy. Her mouth watered in appreciation. Apparently, a cop's life agreed with the man. He looked amazing. *Dammit.*

Was it too much to hope for a paunch and receding hairline?

Her eyes held their position until she heard an amused, "See anything you like?" from the sex-on-a-stick trance-inducer before her.

Damn. She blinked as mortification crawled up her neck. "Not at all." She prayed she spoke with conviction. She might like what she saw, but she would slowly roast in the fiery pits of hell before she'd admit that to him.

A cleansing breath left her lungs as she raised her eyes, set her chin, and met his stare. "Do I...know you?

You kind of look like Loraine's son, but I haven't seen him in years. Wait." She snapped her fingers. "I know. You're the new butler."

Adam's amused gaze burned right through her. She hated that about him. He had this annoying way of seeing everything she was thinking, especially her main weakness—him. But this time, she was ready. She wasn't about to let him affect her. She was way too strong and smart for that now.

That wayward sex-on-a-stick thought was a momentary lapse, but easily overcome. After all, it didn't count since she didn't say it out loud. *Yeah.* No matter how flimsy, that was the story she was sticking to.

"How was your drive out?"

"Fine." She looked past his shoulders into the house. A strong desire to run far, far away overtook her. But her feet wouldn't move. They were plastered to the ground, which was probably best. She needed to be here.

She had this. After all, she was a successful busi-nesswoman. She could be an adult and have a civilized conversation. She managed to pull that off in spades as the Vice President of Byrnes and Company.

"How's your sister?"

"Fine." Why wouldn't he just move out of the way and let her in? Just because she could have a civilized conversation didn't mean she wanted to.

His face fell as he reached for her arm. Sadness crept into his eyes as he asked. "How are you?"

The muscles in her jaw ticked as she fought them

down. The relaxed-no-worries smile would not leave her lips. She wouldn't let it. She was fine. Well, she *would* be fine. No one needed to know the extent of her sadness, especially him. She did not want—nor need—his pity. "Fine."

"That's a lot of 'fine'." His eyebrows furrowed in concern. She should have known that emotion was temporary, and sure enough, the concern left his eyes, and a mischievous glint took its place. "Perhaps you know a different word?"

A different word. There were so many words she would have liked to call this man, share with this man over the years, and yet there were so few appropriate places to say them out loud. In fact, the day his father's will was read was definitely not the place to share those words. Jerk, joker, jackass...and those were just the Js. There were so many more letters in the alphabet.

"Since you're not going to answer me, would you like to come in, or should I have everyone move outside?" He motioned her into the foyer. Despite her annoyance, Allison found herself following him through the ornate hallways to the Byrnes' family library. She could practically taste the blood from biting her tongue. The man drove her crazy.

Allison now remembered why she'd managed to evade Adam over the years, which wasn't easy since she worked for his father. But, somehow, she'd done it. She'd avoided dealing with the arrogant, pompous, annoying, cocky assh— Oops. She was thinking all of those non-sharable words, again.

Unfortunately, he didn't act like those nonsharables all the time. Sometimes, he was sweet and kind and caring. Of course, those momentary lapses in assholism had led her to drop her guard, and ultimately her panties, before he ran away screaming for the hills. She'd known he wasn't the staying kind, yet she fell for his charm. The man exemplified her idiocy.

She hated reliving that painful betrayal over and over again. So, anytime she'd been faced with an opportunity to see him, to dredge all that up, she'd find something—anything—more important to do, which usually included her sister and ice cream.

It helped that he lived in Phoenix.

She pulled her attention away from the broad-shouldered man walking in front of her. She reminded herself, yet again, that she was not here for him; she was here for his mother.

That fact hit home as she walked into the library and melancholy lodged in her throat. Herb's desk was empty. Desolate. Adam moved into the room, and his brother, Dale, and Dale's girlfriend, Nadia, huddled together and whispered. Their mother, Loraine, sat on the other side of the dark mahogany conference table.

Allison walked past the small seating area, adorned with a loveseat, chair, and coffee table, to where Loraine was hunched down in her leather seat. Her designer suit looked too big on her small, delicate frame.

When had she lost so much weight? Allison's thoughts played back the last few days, to the funeral and the times she'd sat with the woman as she cried following Herb's death. Had Allison been so out of sorts that she hadn't noticed the woman fading away? No. That couldn't be it. All of her attention had been focused on Loraine when she was with her. This weight loss was new, and it needed to be rectified immediately. She refused to let her wither away.

A small smile lit up Loraine's face, warming Allison's heart. Yes. She belonged here. Loraine had asked her to be here, and Allison refused to let the woman down, no matter how much she wanted to throttle her son.

Edward Connolly, Herb's longtime friend and lawyer, cleared his throat. "We should begin."

He shuffled the papers in front of him, his voice booming as he began. "First of all, I must request there be no interruptions. Please mute all cell phones. Observe silence. I will answer all your questions at the end. I am here to address the high points of Herb's last will and testament. I will not read it word for word. I'm presupposing you all are capable of reading"— Edward's eyes landed on Dale and Nadia— "and therefore, you may read the rest of the will on your own. I have a copy for each of you to take home. I'll begin with the condo at Braelind Towers in Chicago. Herb states that the Chicago condo and all of its contents are hereby bequeathed to Allison Southby, in recognition of all of her hard work over the years. He also asked me to deliver this note."

"Note?" He died so suddenly, how would he have known to write a note?

"He has written you all notes. He penned them after the heart arrhythmia a few years back."

Allison lifted the satiny white envelope from the table, shifting in her seat as she checked the faces in the room. Dale leaned his head on Nadia's shoulder while the woman twirled her long red fingernails through his blond curls. Adam and Loraine smiled, and Allison breathed a sigh of relief. No one appeared to feel shafted at the generous gift. Despite that, discomfort tickled her neck as she forced her fingers to open the envelope.

She knew this was too much. The condo must have cost a few million dollars. There was no way she could accept it. Maybe she could talk Loraine into taking it back. She could do that. There were so many things Herb's widow could do with the property—rent it out, keep it for trips to Chicago, or sell it and use the money for the animal shelter in the barn behind their home. Loraine wouldn't turn down such a charitable offer.

Although she loved the condo, Allison didn't need anything so extravagant. What would she do with five thousand square feet? Over half the condo would go to waste.

She slid her finger under the envelope flap and pulled out a handwritten note.

ALLY-GATOR,

You have always been like a daughter to me. Over the years, you talked constantly about leaving your ghastly apartment. However, you spent so many hours working, you never had a chance to find a suitable place.

I hope you will enjoy the condo as much as I did. Redecorate it. Enjoy it. It's yours.

Love,

Herb

P.S. Please throw out all the chocolate mints before you invite Loraine over. There is a stash in the hall closet and in the safe. I don't want her to know I ate that crap when she wasn't around.

ALLISON SHOOK her head and smiled. He'd loved those sweets. The harder Loraine had pushed to feed him healthy, low-fat food, the harder he'd pushed to eat the high-fat, low-nutrition alternative. It had been a fight built on love. Loraine loved Herb and wanted him to be around for a while. He'd loved her, but couldn't get over his mistress—chocolate mints.

Allison read the beginning of the note again. A suitable home. Ha! She'd made the mistake of inviting Herb and Loraine to her apartment once. And only once.

You would've thought she lived in a hut with dirt floors in the real Ukraine, not a third-floor walk-up in Chicago's Ukrainian Village. A barrage of real estate information had flown from that point forward.

They had always worried about her. Worried too much. But she couldn't complain. Wouldn't complain. When she had first met Herb, she was at a low point. Her parents were gone, she'd quit school to care for her sister, Brook, and the bank had been foreclosing on the family home. She thought she'd never recover financially, socially, or emotionally, but with Herb's help, she'd managed to get through. He'd always been a wonderful friend and father figure.

She closed her eyes and saw the faces of the two great men of her life. Her mentor, Herb Byrnes, and her father, David Southby. A longing ache grabbed hold of her chest as she realized they were both gone. *Gone.* Taken unexpectedly and quickly before she could blink. Her breath stuttered as the past played in a movie reel across the inside of her eyelids.

Herb's blue eyes sparkling when he'd watched her finally graduate from college, and her father's smile when she'd run for high school class president.

Gone.

Her strangled heart throbbed. Herb's faith that she could run the company in six months, and her father's love that never had wavered.

Gone.

Tears sprang to her traitorous eyes, and she barely felt the gentle weight of Loraine's hand on her arm.

"Are you okay, dear?" Loraine sounded so very far away, as if the whole room was underwater.

Allison struggled to control herself. Today wasn't about her. "I'm fine. I just need a minute."

"Edward, can we take a break?" Loraine handed Allison a tissue.

The lawyer gave Allison a sympathetic smile. "Of course. I need to check in with my office, anyway." He reached for his cell phone and headed out into the hallway.

Allison rubbed her temples, her elbows resting on

the table. Get a grip. What the hell was wrong with her? Loraine needed her to be strong. Today was about helping this woman who was always there for her, not dwelling on her own issues of loss.

Allison gave one final exhalation and drew her shoulders back. She found strength as she wrapped her fingers around the necklace at her throat. She had this. Her eyes scanned the room. The distraught look darkening Adam's face almost sent her back into despair. Instead, she turned to Loraine and smiled. "I'm sorry. I got a little choked up. It was nice to be remembered."

"Of course, he remembered you. The daughter we always wanted." Loraine took the tissue from Allison's trembling hand and reached over to wipe a tear from her cheek. "Now, no more crying. This is a happy day. I'm finally getting you out of that horrible apartment. I hope you're ready to shop. You'll need some new furniture, linens, decor. We'll design a color palette, and maybe add a cornice to the dining area. I've always wanted to do that."

The genuine smile that snuck onto Loraine's lips as she talked about the condo told Allison the older woman would never let her return the gift. If only talking about the redecoration made Loraine this happy, the actual shopping and designing would keep her mind off the loss of her husband for months. Allison refused to take that joy away from her. She deserved a little happiness right now. She *needed* a little happiness right now.

As Allison wrapped her fingers around the woman's maternal hand, she knew she'd be living in that monstrosity soon. But somehow, looking at the small spark lighting Loraine's eyes, she found she didn't mind. She didn't even mind that she had no idea what a cornice was.

She squeezed Loraine's hand and focused her attention on the impending move. Although the thought of packing up all her worldly possessions and lugging them across town was as appealing as a root canal, it was much easier to dwell on that than think about how much she would miss Herb.

CHAPTER TWO

ADAM SHIFTED in his seat as he stared at Allison. His throat tightened at the sadness in her eyes. He would give anything to take away that haunted look. The misery. The grief. He would give anything to wrap his arms around her. But given the way she was avoiding eye contact, that would go over like a Drug Enforcement Agent in a crack house.

He leaned back in his father's leather armchair and studied the warm sun glistening in Allison's dark-blonde hair. The rays brought out the golden shades of the strands, making her appear practically angelic. It almost made him feel guilty for giving her such a hard time outside. Almost. It was way too much fun to watch her indignation when he pushed all the right buttons. She made it so satisfyingly easy.

Edward strolled back into the office and returned to the head of the table. "Are you all right to proceed?"

"Yes, thank you." Allison mangled the note on the table with her left hand. Adam almost called her out on her bullshit. Her white knuckles and teary eyes said she was anything but *all right*. "I'm fine." Or *fine*.

That was the same crap she'd tried selling outside earlier. He knew better. Add in the fact that she thought he was dumb enough to buy it, and he didn't know if he was offended or just angry.

"Then let's proceed. I have an appointment in Chicago, and I shan't be tardy, so I must be brief." Edward rearranged the papers in front of him, frowning down at them. "Here we are. To his sons, Dale and Adam, he leaves Byrnes and Company. Each is entitled to 50 percent of the business and all its assets. He has left the remainder of the estate, including this house and all monies and holdings to Loraine. I have a note for each of you." Edward thumbed through the envelopes on the table and placed one in front of each recipient.

His mother picked up her note and held it to her chest, the sadness washing through her eyes and falling down her cheeks. Adam's heart wrenched, and his throat tightened with every tear sliding down his mother's face. He didn't know which was worse, losing his father or watching as his mother hung onto the last shred of her husband.

Her breakdown long forgotten, Allison rested her arm on the back of his mother's chair rubbing her wrist with her other hand. The two women shared a look. Adam's throat opened as he realized his mother would be all right. Allison would always be there for her.

"Are you kidding?" Dale whined, interrupting Adam's reverie. "What am I supposed to do with Dad's business?" Apparently, the bittersweet moment unfolding between Allison and his mother was lost on Dale. Not that Adam was all that surprised. Dale did live in his own Dale-centric world.

"Just relax. We'll figure it out," Adam soothed, trying to stop the conversation from progressing. He just wanted to get his mom through the reading. They'd deal with the fallout later.

"Even though I'm not happy to convey this information, I have an obligation to tell you that Ben Mooring has contacted my office. He wants to talk about buying the company." Edward began stacking and tapping his paperwork, placing part of the pile into his briefcase.

"Ben Mooring?" Blood boiled and pulsed beneath Adam's skin. "That jackass isn't getting within five feet of my father's company. Tell him to go slither back under that rock he calls home."

So much for dealing with the fallout later.

"Don't," Dale yelled at Edward before turning to Adam. "Are you crazy? Do you want to come back home and run the company? I didn't think so. Dad forgave him, and you know he's our only option. Who's going to buy a dying jewelry business in this economy?"

"I wouldn't call it dying, Dale," Adam argued, and realized he believed it. Even though the jewelry business had taken a hit over the past few years, they still had a few large contracts, including one with the Professional Hockey League, making rings for Championship Cup winners and necklaces for their wives.

No matter how successful the business was or

could be, Dale was right. Adam had no intention of staying in Chicago and managing the company. But what were the other options? He liked the life he'd built in Phoenix. He liked his home, his job, and his friends. He was comfortable there.

It didn't matter that lately he'd felt restless. He couldn't put his finger on what exactly was missing, but he was positive that his dad's company was not it.

"Well, it seems you boys have some decisions to make. I have to get back to the office," Edward said as he packed the rest of his paperwork into his briefcase. "Loraine, you call if you need anything. Anything at all. Boys, Herb was like a brother to me, so there is always a special place in my heart for you."

"Thank you, Edward. You are a good friend." Loraine dabbed at her tears.

Edward rested his hand on Adam's shoulder. "Your father was very proud of you."

Adam smiled as Edward's words struck at his core. His father had always said how proud he was, but it was still nice to hear. Over the years, Adam had always thought Edward was a little shady, always thought something was off. But over the past few weeks, the lawyer had proven his loyalty as he helped in the planning and execution of Adam's father's last wishes. Herb couldn't have asked for a better friend to see his family through all of this.

The friendly, paternal hand dropped away as Dale shouldered into Adam and grasped Edward's arm. "If we were interested in selling, how much do you think we'd get?"

Edward glared at Dale's death grip.

"Enough," Adam said. Hell, he wanted to yell it, but yelling had never seemed to help when it came to his brother. Anyway, he was so tired of fighting with Dale. It seemed like that's all they ever did.

He should be thankful his younger brother showed up at all today. Dale had been late or nonexistent for every appointment that meant anything to Adam or his parents. When Herb won Chicago's Man of the Year, Dale had been late. When Adam graduated college, Dale wasn't just late, he plain hadn't shown up.

Instead of feeling thankful, Adam was pissed, annoyed, fed up, and just done.

"Come on," Dale pleaded. "You don't want this dinosaur company any more than I do. This is not my path to spiritual enlightenment."

"What are you talking about?" Adam ran his hand over the large knot that had shanghaied the back of his neck. Spiritual enlightenment?

"You really want to leave the good life in Phoenix to manage Dad's company?" Silence squeezed the oxygen from the room. Adam took a long gulp of the thick, tension-ridden air and slowly let it out. He didn't speak for fear he'd say something to upset his mother, but the anger simmered just below the surface, his thumping heart rate pulsing in his ears. He'd never understand it. He worked with druggies and murderers, never once getting flustered or showing his cards. He was an expert in playing it close to the vest when on the street. However, get him in the same room with his brother, and he was ready to go to the mat in mere seconds.

Edward's phone buzzed, deflating the vacuum-sealed room. Edward looked at the screen and turned to Adam. "I should take this. Call me if there's anything I can do."

Adam's eyes never left Edward's retreating figure, even though Dale's glare was boring holes into his skin. He had a feeling Dale was looking for something from him, but as usual, Adam had no clue what that might be. Did he want to talk about Dad's company? Did he want some sort of resolution? Probably, but this was neither the time nor the place.

Dale threw up his hands. "I give up. I'm outta here," he mumbled as he clutched Nadia's hand. She smiled nervously and rose from the chair.

"Dale, relax. You're practically living here. You don't have to leave." Adam tried to hide his annoyance, but he had a feeling he wasn't successful. His brother had showed up at his parents' house a few weeks ago, girlfriend in tow, and he didn't show any signs of leaving anytime soon. Well except to storm off, but he always came back. "Nadia, please sit down," he requested as she straightened her miniskirt.

She dragged her long nails along the dark fabric of Dale's shirt as her eyes implored his for direction. Adam almost felt bad for the poor woman, but after more than ten years on the force, he'd learned to read people pretty well. That look told him she wasn't turning to Dale because she was scared—she wanted to please him. Although he couldn't understand her desire, he couldn't help but notice the love in her eyes. He would have been happy for the jackass if he didn't want to strangle him.

"Baby, let's go." Dale glared at Adam. He pulled Nadia toward the door, and she stumbled in an attempt to keep up in her high heels.

A few moments later, the roar of a motorcycle engine spurred Adam to walk toward the window.

Nadia climbed on the back of the monstrosity darkening his parents' quiet suburban driveway. The trees lining the driveway practically gasped for air as smoke billowed from the retreating pipes.

He hated that his brother left in a huff, but he didn't know what else to do for the man. Adam watched his mother bow her head, defeat rolling off her slumped figure. Adam hoisted his hand onto her shoulder, sorrow and exhaustion draining his last shred of energy. He thought the day of the funeral was going to be the worst of it, but today turned out to suck just as bad. They sat in silence until the shrill clang of the doorbell resonated through the house.

"Edward must have forgotten something," Adam muttered as he left the library and headed to the house's entrance. He heard footsteps behind him as he opened the front door.

A dark-haired woman with light brown skin stood on the porch, and behind her, a man slowly approached the stairs. Their sunglasses and impeccably pressed black pants looked both professional and casual. Cops, Adam deduced from the rigid postures and serious expressions. He knew that particular expression well. He wore it quite often in his dealings with the public.

"Lieutenant Adam Byrnes?" the woman on the front porch asked, and then continued when he nodded. "I'm Detective Shay Washington with the Chicago Police Department." She smiled and held up her badge. Her partner made his way up the stairs, obviously assessing the situation around him. "And this is my partner, Detective Joe Perretti."

"It's nice to meet you, Detective Washington, Detective Perretti." Adam shook their hands and then leaned against the doorframe.

Detective Washington adjusted her sweater to clip her star back onto her black chinos. "May we come in, Lieutenant Byrnes?"

"Yeah, but please call me Adam." He glanced back inside the house at his mom. She didn't need this today. She'd had enough heartache the past few days. He'd do anything to keep her out of this.

"We weren't sure if you'd still be in the area. The Phoenix Police Department must miss you."

"I'm sure they're getting on without me." Adam smirked. The only reason they brought up Phoenix was to show they'd done their homework. It was a common tool used to throw people off-kilter. *The police know things about me...what all do they know?* He did it all the time. He just wasn't accustomed to having it used on him.

"We'd like to offer our condolences," Detective Washington said.

"I met your father a few years ago at a charity auction. He was a good man," Detective Perretti added.

"He was. Thank you. I'm assuming this isn't a social call."

"No. Due to your father's high-profile status, and the conditions surrounding his demise—he was alone at the time—we have been assigned to investigate his death. May we speak to you and your mother for a moment?"

"Yeah." Adam stepped outside, closing the front door behind him. "But please go easy on her. My father's passing hit her pretty hard."

They nodded, and Adam opened the door. He held it for the entering officers and then led them through the foyer to the sitting room.

The large room held two sitting areas, and large windows allowed morning light to fill the one that faced the backyard. The simple, comfortable furniture there was ideal for a lazy day of relaxation. The other area was formal, perfect for a meeting with the police. The areas were separated by a five-foot-wide fireplace complete with an ornate stone mantel.

Adam turned to the visitors. "Officer Washington and Perretti, this is my mother, Loraine Byrnes, and the vice president of Byrnes and Company, Allison Southby."

"It's nice to meet you both. Is there a problem?" Loraine's voice rose as her fingers twisted, worrying the tissue in her hand.

"No problems, Mrs. Byrnes. This is standard procedure. May we ask you a few questions?" Detective Washington asked.

Adam placed an arm around his mother's waist and kissed her temple, and Allison lowered herself onto the loveseat.

"Can I get you or your partner anything? Tea or coffee? Water?" Loraine focused on their guests as Detective Washington sat on the couch. Adam's mother was never one to let simple pleasantries go unspoken. No one would go thirsty, even though her world was falling apart.

"No, thanks." Washington pulled a notebook and pen from her pocket as her partner propped himself against the wall behind the sofa. Adam took a seat in his mother's Queen Anne chair, facing the officers. The room was coated in silence as he waited for the onslaught of questions. But before they began, he realized he had a question of his own.

"Have they begun the autopsy?" He'd heard rumors of the backlog that plagued the Cook County Medical Examiner's office. He was hoping this case wouldn't get lost in the county's great abyss of paperwork.

"Yes, the Medical Examiner is working on it."

"Wait. Herb was buried yesterday," Allison stuttered as the color drained from her face. Hurt and confusion tumbled across her features. He probably should have mentioned the details to her, but he'd wanted to avoid worrying her needlessly. She was going to have enough on her plate with the company, and he didn't want to draw her attention to something that might be nothing. From the daggers in her eyes, he realized he'd chosen wrong.

"The burial was a show for the well-wishers to say their good-byes. I wanted the police involved to ease my mind." Adam tried to explain, but the hurt and anger weren't receding from Allison's face.

"While the coroner's office does their investigation, we wanted to ask you a few questions." Detective Washington allowed her gaze to rest on each person while she spoke in calming tones. She really was good at talking with people and putting them at ease. Adam was impressed. Police officer "bedside manner" was not something that was easily taught, so those who had it were at a premium.

"Mr. Byrnes was at work the night he died. Did he normally work that late?"

"Sometimes. He was planning on staying at the condo, so I didn't question when he didn't make it home." Tears slid down his mother's cheek, each tear another spike through Adam's heart.

"The initial diagnosis was a heart attack. Did your husband have a history of heart problems?"

"He was on beta blockers for a heart arrhythmia, but my mother put him on a hardcore diet when they found out about his condition." Adam walked into the kitchen to grab his father's medication and returned with the bottle. He handed it to Detective Washington.

Adam's lips curled up as he recalled the phone conversations he'd had with his father over the past few months. Herb had complained over and over that Loraine was "trying to kill him" with tasteless food.

His least favorite had been the puffed rice coasters she tried to pass off as snacks. His father had started bragging about his hidden treasure troves of food throughout the city of Chicago. He would purposely spend time at the Braelind condo, not so he didn't have to endure the stress of driving fifty miles in heavy Chicagoland traffic, like he'd told his wife, but so he could eat "normal" food.

Guilt lodged in Adam's stomach. He should have told his mother about the stashes of junk food. Maybe his dad would be around today if he had told her about the food hoarding.

"Any other conditions?" Detective Washington asked his mother.

"No, although I know he wasn't sticking to the diet I laid out for him. I knew those damn chocolate mints would be the end of him." She plastered a small attempt at a smile on her lips, and Adam's guilt subsided. He should have known that nothing got by his mother.

"Does this bottle have your husband's doctor's information?" Detective Washington asked as she searched for the doctor's name on the pill bottle.

"Yes. Dr. Schmidt."

The detective began to scribble in her notepad as she stared at the bottle. "You can keep the bottle. We don't need it."

"Thanks." The detective stood and walked to the fireplace mantel. She inspected the array of photos adorning the family shrine, pausing at each frame. "Beautiful pictures. It must be nice to have so many loved ones at a time like this. Who are all of these people?"

Adam attempted to help his mother to her feet. She slapped his hand away, and he fought back a grin. Now, this was the mother he remembered, feisty and independent.

His mother made her way to the detective's side. "Well, this is Adam, when he played football in high school, and this is my younger son, Dale, at his graduation. This one is Allison and her sister, Brook, at Christmas a few years ago, and that's my husband's assistant, Julie Connolly, and her son, Cody." She clasped the frame in both hands and looked dreamily at the picture. "He is an amazing bundle of joy. I just adore him."

The dreamy look dissipated as she grimaced. "After all, it's not like my sons have given me my own grandchildren to spoil. So, I have taken it upon myself to spoil Julie's."

Detective Washington smiled, and Adam ran a hand through his hair and tried not to make a face. Even after the day his mother had just had, she managed to find an opportunity to sprinkle in grandchildren and marriage guilt. She'd taken up the new hobby over the past year. He was hoping she'd get bored with the ineffectiveness, but so far, that hadn't dissuaded her from laying down a thick coat whenever they talked. Whenever he had a few minutes to call home, the conversation started with the wife-and-child inquisition. That was probably why he'd tended to call his father more often than his mother.

That wasn't exactly true. Adam had called the old man because he was a great sounding board and an excellent advisor. Police work had never been an issue for Adam, but supervising employees was. Every week, unbeknownst to everyone, Adam talked through employee problems he was having at the department. Even though his father hadn't been well versed in the ins-and-outs of a police department, he'd worked with some of the largest organizations in the country. He'd known all about circumventing the political backstabbing inherent in government work and fostering positive employee relations. All things Adam had needed ongoing guidance to navigate.

Hell. He still needed that guidance.

Longing squeezed his heart. His father. Was gone. If Adam decided to have children, his dad would never know them. His children would never know what a wonderful grandfather they had. All the guilt his mom had piled at Adam's feet now wrapped around his throat and made it impossible to breathe. He always thought they had more time. He knew he'd lose his dad someday, but that was always some elusive future date. Not now. Not today.

He watched the detectives make their way to the front door. Crap. Apparently, the meeting was over. What exactly had he missed while he was stumbling down memory lane? Adam quickly walked up behind them and reached around them for the door handle, getting the front door open just ahead of the detectives.

Detective Washington handed Adam a business

card. "We'll contact you with any new developments. Thank you for your time."

"I'm sorry for your loss," Detective Perretti told Adam. He paused at the end of the walkway to look back. "If you need anything, please give me a call."

CHAPTER THREE

"WHERE THE HELL HAVE YOU BEEN?" His boss, Paul Mörder, growled into the phone. The man didn't have the patience for incompetence. Neither did he.

"Not that it's any of your concern, but I was at the will reading."

"Everything is my concern." Paul used to be an asshole; now, there weren't words for his disposition. The Feds were breathing down his neck on trumped-up charges of racketeering and bribery. They claimed they were cracking down on organized crime. Paul liked to call it harassing hard-working Americans.

Like Paul had ever worked a day in his life.

"You don't sound all that thrilled. The old man must not have left you anything good." Paul laughed. "I hope this isn't going to interfere with our plans."

"No. It's all under control."

"It better be. I'd hate to see what you did to Herb happen to you," Paul threatened.

"I know where all of the evidence is. Don't worry."

"Bring it to me. I'm not going to jail again."

"I will as soon as I can. You're under a microscope with all of this media attention."

Paul's voice raised an octave, probably with his blood pressure. The fat fuck was one aneurysm away from oblivion. "I don't give a shit about the media. I want that account information in my possession by the end of the week. If I don't have it, I will have no problem sending you to hell. But it won't be pain-free. I will shove my fist so far up your ass I'll be tickling your tonsils. Don't put me in this position again."

Paul slammed the phone down, leaving an echo.

He placed his head in his hands and sighed. Paul wasn't going to stop. His blood pressure boomed in his ears as the heat traveled to his balding head. This was not what he needed right now. If Paul told the Russian mob what happened, he was as good as dead.

AFTER THE DETECTIVES LEFT, Allison patted Loraine's hand and gave a small smile. She slowly made her way to the door. It was silly, but she somehow felt betrayed. It was just a simple heart attack. Why the drama? Why hadn't Loraine told her about it? Or Adam? Granted, Loraine had been overwhelmed the past few days, and Allison avoided Adam like an STD.

Adam walked at her side as she headed toward the rental car of the day. She really needed to get her car fixed before someone noticed. She always had the worst luck with cars, which, of course, gave everyone a good laugh.

"Rental?" Adam asked. He noticed everything. Dammit. The rental agency's name was plastered on the license plate holder. Even if he weren't a cop, he would have to be a moron not to notice. "So, what happened to your car this time?"

"Flat."

"Did you drive over a pothole? Porcupine? Your sister?"

"That only happened once, and I didn't run her over, it was her foot."

Any other person joking about the foot-squashing incident would've been funny. Any other day, she might have laughed. But this man, on this day? Not going to happen. Her humor was saved for someone who didn't drive her crazy.

"Do you need help putting on the spare?" His eyebrows shot up.

Allison stopped, stared. A warm current slithered through her at the return of concern in his voice. She sometimes forgot how thoughtful and caring the man could be—the times he'd driven her home, so she didn't have to take public transportation late at night, or the food he'd deliver when she was sick...

Whoa. Allison mentally slapped herself for thinking about the virtuous side of the man before her. Those noble traits were what sucked her in the first time. No more.

The annoying crap back in the house, now, that was the Adam Byrnes she was coming to know and avoid. Whenever she saw him behave like a compassionate, helpful human being, she needed to remember that he was an ass and every other word she decided not to use to describe him today. Those damn non-sharable words kept popping up. Thank God he was leaving soon. Hell, maybe he'd even catch the first flight to Phoenix so she could get back to her life.

"No. Brook's boyfriend is taking care of it while I'm here. Apparently, he worked as a mechanic to pay for law school."

"Multi-talented. Your sister always knew how to pick them." His smile was forced, but the sentiment seemed sincere. "Well, I'll see you tomorrow."

"Tomorrow?" She scowled. So much for him flying out tonight.

"I'm sticking around for a while. I want to make sure your transition is easy. We need to formally announce your promotion to CEO."

So much for him leaving any time soon. "Great, thanks," she snipped and turned her back on him. He reached out and wrapped a hand around her arm. Although she tried to fight it, an electric current prickled where his hand touched her skin. Somehow, the warmth of his skin felt so good, even when she felt an overwhelming urge to smack him.

"Is there a problem?" Adam had the audacity to sound concerned.

Problem? So many problems—the loss of her parents, and now Herb, Loraine's grief, moving, an unexpected autopsy. Where would she start, if she even wanted to? The only problem she didn't have was her job, and now he was going to invade that space. Her life was one big problem. But she refused to let it show. She just needed to make a clean getaway. "Nope."

"Allison, talk to me," he pleaded. She heard the dejection, sadness, exhaustion, and heartbreak in each word. She wanted to feel bad for him. She should feel sorry. She should be consoling him. She should...shit. Despite all the things she should be doing, she couldn't get past the anger, the hurt, the...betrayal.

"Why would there be a problem?" she said abruptly and spun toward him. "It's not like I feel like a fool, or anything. I mean, I stood over his casket thinking it was going to be lowered. Why the charade? Do you enjoy making others feel ridiculous?" She rambled on, not quite sure why she was blathering about the lowering of the casket. In fact, she wasn't quite sure what she was talking about at all. *Ugh.* She just needed to take it out on someone, anyone. And Adam Byrnes was the closest anyone around.

"I'm sorry. We didn't think it was a big deal. I wanted to do an autopsy because it seemed like a good idea. We decided to keep it quiet because we didn't want to alarm anyone."

"Fine, but why didn't you tell me?"

"Only family knew..."

"Oh. I understand." Of course. She angled her face away, trying to hide the hurt in her eyes. She knew she wasn't really part of the family, but she thought she was more than just some outsider. Somehow Adam managed to treat her like an outcast every chance he got.

Herb had always found a way to invite her and her sister to family gatherings. He'd known they had nowhere else to go. He beamed as he talked about his whole family being there to enjoy whatever holiday was upon them. He'd told the men to be nice to "the daughters he never had," or "the daughters he always wanted."

Where Herb had been inviting and accommodating, Adam was disobliging and cold. He'd made sure everyone understood that she wasn't really his sister. He'd dropped little hints and taunted her incessantly. At first, she thought Adam harbored feelings for her, stuck on the myth that boys tease the ones they love. Never mind that he'd been far away from the "boy" designation.

But he didn't love her. When he'd had a chance, he'd run away—leaving her to do the walk of shame. If he didn't have deep-down longings of love, why the hell couldn't he just accept her as an honorary sister? He seemed to accept Brook. He managed to dote on her whenever she had time in her schedule to visit. The whole situation hurt then and still hurt now, but she refused to break down in front of him. She hadn't cried because of his cruelty in years. She wasn't about to let him see her cry today. Or ever.

"I'll see you tomorrow." She spun on her heel and ran to her rental car. Adam called after her, but she pretended she couldn't hear him.

As she pulled away, tears stung her eyes. Why did she let him get to her? She was a grown woman, for goodness' sake. She should not be susceptible to assholic men with large egos and little...cars.

Allison was so close to putting Adam's favorite body part in that sentence, but she knew it was a lie. And the last thing she needed was to start thinking about all the things he could do with that particular body part.

She sighed as she pulled up to a traffic light. She placed her head on her hands as they rested on the steering wheel. She was repulsed by him...repulsed. She repeated the mantra over and over. Maybe if she said it enough, she'd start to believe it.

Allison banged her head on the seatback, knocking the images of his body from her mind. She swore she would do better the next time she saw him. No more dwelling on the past. This was a new and improved Allison Southby.

She drove through the intersection, the green light a beacon to her new mission. Determination turned her spine to steel. This was good. She could do this.

Doubt fluttered through her mind. She hoped she could do this, because otherwise, tomorrow would be another long day with Adam Byrnes. Either way, she'd rather have a root canal than deal with him again.

CHAPTER FOUR

ADAM STARED at the dark walls of his childhood home. No matter how hard he tried, sleep eluded him. He groaned, disgusted that the stillness didn't lull him to sleep. Tossing the covers to the hardwood floor, he admitted defeat and plodded down the creaky stairs.

He rubbed his sleep-deprived eyes as he flipped the kitchen switch. Stars danced across his vision from the blinding light glaring from the island chandelier. He grabbed the side of the red marble countertops for balance, waiting for the spots to disappear. Shuffling across the blurry mosaic tile floor, he located the remote for the flat-screen television.

The local news harped on about the Mörder case, and a low sigh resonated in his chest as he changed the channel. As far as he was concerned, it was just another mobster skirting the law. The screens flashed before his eyes, the light flickering between channel changes. Why were all the TV shows crap at six a.m.? Infomercials and reality TV. Ugh. He couldn't be the only person up at the crack of dawn.

He watched the antics of one of the many dysfunctional reality families play across the screen, but even their ridiculousness couldn't get the injured look he'd placed on Allison's face out of his head. He was such an ass. He was generally cognizant of people's feelings. However, when Allison was around, he became socially inept.

He pressed the button to start the coffee maker. For some reason, the world was much more manageable with a pint of caffeine coursing through his veins. He reached into the glossy, black cabinets and pulled out a frying pan.

"Why did I have to make that family comment?" he reprimanded himself audibly. The soft hiss and gurgle indicated his tonic was almost ready. After a quick pour, he brought the hot, dark liquid to his lips. His eyes closed and his head fell back in ecstasy as the caffeine slowly found its way into his bloodstream.

He glowered at the empty pan on the stove. Since the skillet didn't magically materialize a gourmet breakfast, he opened the refrigerator. The cold air washed over him, sending a chill down his spine.

Now he remembered why he'd been staying at the hotel the past few days. There was something to be said for room service. Although, being here with his mom was what kept him coming back. He pulled out a couple eggs and the butter, twisted on the burner, and broke the eggs into the pan once it heated up and the butter melted.

He stared at the sizzling egg whites, regret coloring his mood. It would probably be best for him leave Chicago as soon as possible. Once the reins were handed over, he was hitting the road. There was no point hanging around.

Sweat beaded down his neck, chest tightening. He dragged in a large gulp of air. "What the hell is wrong with me?" he asked the unresponsive skillet.

Was that fear? Why? What did he have to be afraid of? Leaving? He'd been gone for years. Why all of a sudden did it bother him? Allison's crystal-blue eyes flashed before him. He always had a hard time leaving her. The last time he'd left, he'd pathetically skulked away like a thief in the night.

He remembered that night so vividly. He'd been back home in Chicago, visiting his family. But the family wasn't what he'd enjoyed the most. It was a game of pool. It had been the best damn game of pool he'd ever played. He hadn't seen Allison in over a year, and she looked amazing. Her dark-blonde hair hung down in soft curls around her shoulders, and every time she'd bent down to take a shot—damn—there she was, her body smoking, cleavage heaving, eyes smoldering. He'd been unable to stop himself.

He'd wrapped her in his arms and finally tasted her lips. Heaven. He'd known he was a goner, but he didn't care. All his cares had disappeared the moment his lips met hers—his new promotion hadn't mattered. His partner's injury hadn't mattered. The guilt hadn't mattered. Nothing had mattered but her.

She'd consumed him. The wild, heart-stopping sex only made him want her more, but in the light of day...

He'd known he made a mistake. He couldn't stay. If she'd woken up with him still around, he would have never left Chicago—never left her. But he'd had to leave. His partner had been battling a gunshot wound, and every day Adam was away, he wasn't finding the sonofabitch responsible for the shooting. He'd owed his partner his life for stepping in front of the bullet.

He'd regretted hurting her, but he didn't regret leaving. Three days later, he caught the perp and locked up his sorry ass.

It had been one helluva Christmas present, locking up that jag-off.

The smell of cinders wafted to his nose, pulling him from the past. He looked down and flipped the eggs over. He snarled as he poked at the black, crunchy crust on the egg.

"I personally don't like my eggs blackened, but that's just me." Dale laughed.

Adam's heart leaped into his throat, and he glared at his brother. "Don't sneak up on a cop, unless you'd like to get hurt." Revulsion pierced Adam's stomach. No breakfast, and his brother was up. What a crappy way to start the day. Adam dumped the eggs in the garbage and tossed the pan into the sink.

Dale opened the refrigerator and took out the creamer. As if in perfect rhythm, Adam grabbed a mug and poured his brother a cup of coffee.

"Thanks." Dale took the cup from Adam.

"No problem." Adam tilted his cup back. "Where's Bambi?"

Dale huffed in exasperation. "I dropped Nadia at the gym. The woman loves her Pilates. That is one form of exercise I cannot get into." Dale giggled like a nervous schoolgirl and added, "I didn't feel like working out this morning. I'm worried about Mom. I want to make sure she's okay."

"You know she was heartbroken," Adam said flatly as Dale frowned. Adam reveled in his brother's discomfort. Dale had a lot of nerve pretending to care about his mother's feelings when he so willingly crushed them over and over again. "What do you expect? She lost her husband, and her youngest son is ranting like a lunatic with some woman on his arm."

"Can you just leave Nadia out of it? I'll apologize to Mom this morning. I haven't seen her yet. Have you?"

"I haven't seen her. Is she normally up this early?"

"Yeah, she likes to take care of her foster animals before breakfast. Without those animals, I think she'd go crazy."

Adam nodded his head and arched an eyebrow at Dale. "Why are you up this early? Doesn't your skin burn in the sunlight?"

"Nice." Dale rolled his eyes. "Actually, I wasn't able to sleep. My mind was racing. When Nadia asked for a ride, I figured, why not. I'm not sleeping."

"I know the feeling."

Adam stared as Dale looked furtively at his coffee cup sitting on the counter. He could almost see the wheels in Dale's mind spinning as his brother slowly lifted the cup to his mouth and sighed.

The beginning of a knot pulled on Adam's neck. The suspense was killing him. His brother was obviously struggling to share something, but he wasn't sure what it could possibly be. Not anything good. No one hemmed and hawed when they had good news to share.

More than likely, he just wanted money. The only time Dale ever talked to Adam was when he needed a loan or a handout. Damn. The last thing he wanted to do was fight with his brother. Adam had to admit, however, if his brother asked for money, control over his punching arm would be limited.

"So, Dale, what's on your mind? You obviously have something you want to talk about. Spill it."

"I want to run Dad's company." The words practically fell from Dale's lips.

"What?" What the hell was he talking about? For five years, the old man had asked Dale to come home and run the company. Now that their dad was gone, Dale suddenly had an urge to be a respected businessman? What would happen in three months when he decided he wanted to be a rodeo clown, or some other phase overtook his life? What would happen to the company then?

"Are you kidding?"

"No. I think it's important for us to keep it in the family." Dale looked so earnest, Adam almost believed him.

"When did you decide this?"

"Last night."

"What do you know about running a company?" Adam argued, realizing the effect this would have on Allison and all of the other employees. "Anyway, Dad was handing control over to Allison in six months. He trusted her to take the company into the future. I think we should adhere to his wishes."

"His wishes included handing the company over to his sons. Why else would he have willed it to us? It was a last-ditch effort to get us involved. Having Allison run the company was the last resort because we failed." Dale's face grew red with conviction. "Well, no more. I am fulfilling his dreams."

"Again, Dale, what do you know about running a multi-million-dollar company? There are people relying on this company's success, people with families and mortgages. They need a true leader."

"It would be nice if, just once, you had a bit of faith in me. I know I'm not the perfect son that you are, but that doesn't mean I need to be written off. I have a lot of skills that have gone to waste because I just haven't been given the chance. It's bad enough Dad never trusted me. Why don't you trust me?" Dale's voice rose.

"I just want what's best for Byrnes and Company. And you haven't been around. Trust is earned." Guilt crept down Adam's spine. He might have been a little hard on his brother, but there was only so much disappointment a man could take. And Dale seemed to have used up his allotment. "Anyway, I thought you wanted to sell."

"You haven't been around either, brother. And I

still think selling might be the best course of action, but I thought I'd man the helm until we decide what we should do. You don't have to go back to Phoenix right away. You can help me for a while, and then I'll take over."

"I have to go back..." Adam started to say.

"I thought you wanted what's best. You know this is what Dad would have wanted."

Arguments hung from Adam's tongue, but everything Dale said was true. Their father would have loved to hand the reins to one of his sons. It just should have happened when he was alive. Now, it seemed like a futile gesture. On top of that, Herb spent the past ten years training and molding Allison so she would take over. It wasn't fair to her.

"What about Allison? She's worked hard to get where she is."

"We won't take anything away from her. She can help me when you finally head back to Phoenix. She'll still be the vice president."

"I don't think this is right. If we wanted a part in Dad's business, we should have taken the chance while he was alive."

"I have 50 percent interest in this company. I am doing this with or without your help."

"Not if I don't approve it. I'm the other 50 percent."

"So, we're going to war over this?" Dale sighed. "Look, this is what Dad would have wanted. Give me a chance."

"Okay." Adam's heart ached. If Allison hated him

now, just wait till she found out that Dale was swooping in and taking over the company. Only a miracle would stop her from walking out the door, never to return.

His stomach wrenched in knots as he slumped into the chair at the kitchen table and placed his throbbing head in his hands. Grief constricted his skull, making it impossible to form consistent thoughts. He hadn't seen the woman in years, yet the thought of never seeing her again left a hole where his heart normally beat.

CHAPTER FIVE

ALLISON WOKE ON FRIDAY MORNING, limbs heavy with dread. She thought that getting some sleep would alleviate the pain of the past few days, but apparently, nightmare-infused dreams interspersed with bouts of insomnia didn't quite have the same effect as a full night of rest.

The office just wouldn't be the same without Herb and his sage advice. She slowly followed her morning rituals, wearing her favorite black silk skirt-suit. It was one of the first suits she bought after becoming Byrnes and Company management, and it fit her like a glove. With one last glance, she headed to the Chicago skyscraper where she worked day in and day out and parked in the underground garage.

She managed to enter the glass doors that led into the building before eight. She walked through the expansive glass atrium, filled with various plants, from a Madagascar dragon tree to spider plants and peace lilies. It was a tropical intermediary between the bustling Chicago streets and the high-powered offices upstairs.

She rode the elevator to the twenty-seventh floor, one of the four floors occupied by Byrnes and Company. The office was decorated with traditional woods and warm, welcoming colors.

Her vanilla chai sloshed in her hand as she walked past Julie's empty desk. Julie tended to be late on Fridays. Normally, the fact that Julie had to drop her son off at preschool before work wouldn't bother her. But today, Allison had so much she wanted to tell her coworker and friend. She was practically jumping out of her skin.

Even though Allison was a big proponent of keeping her work and private life separate, Julie had become a good friend over the years. She shared all of her highs and lows with the supportive woman. She even shared her fateful indiscretion with the boss's son.

As Allison made her way toward Herb's office, the realization hit her upside her head. He wouldn't be there. He wouldn't be there to talk about today's agenda or client issues. He wouldn't be there when the Dietrich Company asked for twenty redesigns before they ended up choosing the first design, as they had done for the last four jewelry purchases. He wouldn't be there just to talk.

She glanced into her late mentor's office, her voice box seizing as she gasped noiselessly. Her wide eyes took in the soft light streaming from the large office windows and a younger Herb hovering over a stack of paperwork. She reached for the doorjamb, catching herself as her legs buckled beneath her.

She gaped at the apparition sitting at the desk, seemingly lost in thought as he mused over the documents before him. Hot, wet tears rolled down her cheeks as she thought about all the times she'd walked into this office and found Herb sitting in just that position. She remembered the way his head would bob slightly as he worked, and his light-blond hair, which had turned gray over the years, would bounce right along with the motion as he focused on the bottom line.

Her eyes fluttered in disbelief. Oh, shit. It had finally happened. After all the crap she had dealt with in her life, this loss sent her over the edge. She figured someday it would happen. But she never thought when she lost her mind she would see ghosts.

She continued to stare. Frozen. Afraid if she closed her eyes, Herb would disappear again. Her illusion looked up, a bright smile overtaking his lips. With a wave, he said her name. Her heart stopped as she jumped, her feet momentarily airborne.

"Good morning, Allison. We need to talk. Why don't you put your things down and meet me back here," Dale said, turning his attention back to the file folder on Herb's desk.

She stared at him, stunned. That her mind had automatically thought Dale was a ghost hadn't been lost on her. Logically, she should have known it was Dale. He was the spitting image of his father when he was younger. Unfortunately, logic didn't appear to be her strong suit these days.

Allison headed down the hall to her office, closing the door behind her and placing her purse and bags on her desk. She stretched her neck back and forth, trying to stave off the headache creeping up the back of her head.

She clicked on her PC and then checked her phone messages. She tried to keep her mind on the mundane tasks of the day, but the alleged ghost-sighting and all the emotions of the morning crept past the everyday routine.

It didn't help that she had no clue why Dale was sitting in Herb's office, requesting a meeting. She figured Adam would be here to hand over the reins, not Dale.

The brothers couldn't have been more different. Adam was a responsible, anal-retentive, law-enforcing adult, while Dale was a pampered adolescent in a man's body. Both men had one thing in common—an inability to visit the parents who loved them.

Adam had established a life in Phoenix and hadn't been back to see his parents in almost two years. Dale wasn't much better. He hadn't been home for a visit in about fifteen months. He liked to spend his time finding himself. He spent six years finding himself in college and five years finding himself while traveling the globe. Herb and Loraine had shared the numerous postcards they received from him while he traveled from Russia to Singapore and everywhere in between.

Although she understood the allure of visiting different countries and locales, she never understood how the Byrne brothers left their parents or such a great company behind. Her thoughts shifted to her childhood. Her father had been an engineer with the army, which led to her family being stationed all over the world. Although the constant moving had forced her family to be very close, there weren't a lot of opportunities to put down roots.

She'd hated having to make new friends over and over again. Each new school had been a veritable unknown. She loved the roots she'd planted, this city, her family. Why would anyone want to live anywhere but Chicago?

This was her home. Her life. A sip of chai managed to warm her insides, calming her clattering nerves. Quiet strength flowed through her. This was her realm. She might not have control over any other aspect of her life, but work was always her rock—her port in life's storm.

Calm swept her body, knowing that once they announced her promotion, they would go back to their lives, leaving her to build Byrnes and Company into a success. Exactly where she wanted to be.

She shifted her attention to the cup in her hand. "I got this," she told the liquid and took another sip. After a deep breath, she picked up her leather file folder. She walked toward Herb's office, doubt shortening her normally long strides.

What was her problem? Why was she so nervous? Adam had said they'd be here today to hand over the reins. Maybe the jerk decided to sneak away in the dead of evening, so Dale was filling in for him. A smile curved her lips as she contemplated a day without Adam.

Unfortunately, an absent Adam only made her feel slightly better. He wasn't the only thing weighing on her overwhelmed mind. It was hard to believe that fifteen years of work had led to this. She was taking over the helm.

It was bittersweet. She had dreamed about this for years, but now that it was here, she was scared. The problem was the dream. In every dream of the future, Herb had been there handing over his company. He was standing over her shoulder, micromanaging her decisions as he'd done the past few months. She thought she'd have his knowledge and leadership to rely on for the first year... Heck, for the first few years. She figured she'd have to send him away kicking and screaming.

Even though she had been groomed to take over, fear bit at her heels. Knots twisted in her stomach. Was she ready? Could she make Herb proud and be the daughter she always wanted to be?

She walked toward Herb's office, delicately smiling at her well-wishing staff as they headed to their offices. These people, her people, had faith in her. They had been through a lot together, and she refused to let them down.

She shook all the negative thoughts from her mind. She'd worked too hard to wimp out now. She not only knew what this company needed today, but she knew she could take them into the next decade.

Herb and Allison had spent the past six months

designing a five-year plan to keep Byrnes and Company at the forefront of the jewelry market. They had successfully anticipated the market trends thus far. She had been taught by the best, and she'd be dammed if she was going to lure herself into self-deprecating thoughts.

She smiled when she saw Julie Connolly sitting at her desk behind the reception counter. Julie was not only responsible for keeping Herb on track, she was also the face of the company when people came into the office. With a desk right outside Herb's office, she was the pulse and nerve center of the organization.

Julie's ear was pressed up against the phone, while her hands clickity-clacked away on the computer keyboard. She turned her head and gave Allison a pained smile. She spun back toward her computer screen, continuing to talk with the client on the phone.

Alarm bells clanged a symphony in her brain, her head pounding in reverberating sympathy. Julie offering a pained smile? Not even making eye contact?

Allison's smile faded. Over the past few months, the women had become even closer as they had discussed the transition that would take place over the next couple of months. Julie would've slowly moved from being solely Herb's assistant to working with Allison as well.

She knocked on the doorframe to Herb's office, trying to get Dale's attention.

He raised his head and waved her in. "Is it that time already? I've been so busy going over Dad's notes."

He smiled and motioned to one of the leather chairs in front of the large flame-maple desk.

The office had been Herb's sanctuary. The portraits on the walls showing past hockey greats skating their way to Chicago hockey immortality offset the professional atmosphere of maple and leather.

Allison smiled. She only knew about their skating prowess from her years with the Byrnes family. It was difficult not to, especially when the Chicago Flurries hockey games were the norm from October to April. That didn't include the two months of playoffs that could potentially be tacked on to the end of the season. She didn't complain, but the insanity the season wrought on the office was sometimes overwhelming.

Allison glanced over at Dale and watched him smile warmly. "I just want to wait for my brother. We should both be here for this."

Allison smiled and relaxed into the black leather chair. His demeanor reminded her that nothing had changed. Dale was her age and had been the one who always welcomed her into their family home with open arms. While Adam tolerated her in their family outings, Dale had always been enthusiastic about her tagging along. She appreciated him for that.

Adam entered the office and closed the door. With one look at his expressionless face, Allison's shoulders tightened, sending another wave of gongs through her mind. Her eyes closed as she wrapped her fingers around the chain at her throat.

Inhale. Exhale. Inhale. Exhale.

The calming breaths and her good luck charm didn't seem to soothe her nerves.

How could she relax when Adam wouldn't even meet her stare?

"I'm glad we're meeting this morning. I wanted to make sure we were all on the same page before we make any announcements to the staff." Dale beamed and rose to his feet. He reached for a hockey puck sitting on the corner of the desk and tossed it from one hand to the other, softly tapping the edge to the desk in between each toss.

"We have the opportunity to make something extraordinary here, and I'm thrilled to be a part of it. Dad always wanted his sons to be a part of this company. It might be a bit late, but I guess it's true what they say, 'better late than never.'

"Allison, you've done such a great job over the years. We know how much Dad loved you. He had...we all have the utmost respect for what you've accomplished. Given that, we want you to stay on as vice president. I will take over the helm for the time being. It's what Dad would have wanted."

Allison forced herself to keep a nondescript expression on her face while anger seethed within her. Dale continued to yammer about the company's new direction as she fought the queasiness building in her stomach. All that work? Gone. All the late nights, analyzing and interpreting the market...for what? So the prodigal son could walk in and undo all of their progress.

"I'm so excited about the new ideas I can bring to

the company. I learned so much from my time in Singapore. It's really a wonderful place."

"Weren't you a bartender in Singapore?" Adam asked.

"I was, until I moved into the monastery," Dale snipped back. "The Taoists are wise people. There are many lessons we can learn from them."

"Taoism?" Adam sighed.

"I truly understand my place now. I think you should both spend some time with your spirituality. It was enlightening."

Allison wanted to scream. She wanted to throw a fit. Instead, she asked, "Don't Taoist's focus on moderation, compassion, and humility?"

"The three jewels. You've heard of it?" He smiled as she shook her head.

She held back a laugh. Only Dale discussed moderation, compassion, and humility while the lights glinted off of the platinum cufflinks on his tailor-made suit. It would seem a monastery could put the fifteen thousand dollars he was wearing to good use, feeding the hungry or spreading world peace.

Allison painted a smile on her face and somehow managed to make it through the rest of the meeting without killing Dale. It took every ounce of restraint, but she was proud of her self-control. Every time he opened his mouth, she just wanted to stuff the tap-tap-tapping hockey puck into it. She left Herb's office. Or, actually, it was now Dale's office. Ugh. What a nightmare.

That was five hours of her life she'd never get back.

Five hours of his nonsense, and it was only the beginning. Her head dropped in defeat. He was now her boss. Not just a boss in ownership, now he would be here every day. Every damn day. Day in, day out of listening to more variations of that rambling mess of a meeting.

Julie's forlorn look spoke volumes. "I'm so sorry, Allison. If there's anything I can do to help. I'm available for wine therapy anytime."

"Thanks, Julie. I'm fine." She forced a smile and walked a few feet. "Although, I might actually take you up on that later."

Julie smiled. "I thought you would. We can commiserate."

Allison practically ran to her office, and once inside her own sanctuary, she slumped in her chair. She slipped her shoes to the floor and rested her elbows on the bean-shaped desk. Black filing cabinets on one side and a three-foot-long mahogany cabinet on the other supported the desktop, and a black metal panel hid her legs, so she could remove her heels with visitors being none the wiser.

She loved the furniture. The contemporary design didn't match the other offices, but it was in line with her taste. She loved that Herb allowed her to pick her own furnishings, and with the black leather couches in her office seating area and contemporary art on the wall, she felt at home in the space.

Home. This had been like a home to her. Now what? It felt like everything had been flipped on its axis. One day she had control over her career, her life, and then, boom, it all went away. She got up and shuffled around her desk to the mini-fridge hiding in the corner. She stared inside, hoping a bottle of wine would suddenly materialize. She contemplated grabbing Julie and hitting the bar on the main level. A nice pinot sounded good right about now. Hmmm...

But no. It was commonly frowned upon to ditch work and hit the sauce before two in the afternoon.

She settled for a soda, neat, and stared out the back windows of her office. From the twenty-seventh floor, she watched the people scurrying around the city streets, everyone desperate to get somewhere.

At one time, she had been desperate to get somewhere too. Now it was lost time. She had nothing to show for dedicating her life to Byrnes and Company. Although she didn't regret all the time she spent with Herb, she regretted all the hours she didn't spend having a normal life.

All those hours devoted to work, with the position of CEO the proverbial brass ring. Now what? Her brass ring was just pilfered by Junior, and here she stood, alone, with nothing. Nothing to show for all of those years of working late, sacrificing a social life, declining dates.

She'd turned down a few good offers over the years, handsome men with great jobs. She'd also turned down a few questionable proposals as well, but those were easy. She'd thought of making a sign: "Grown Men Who Consider Delivery Pizza and Cartoons an Appropriate First Date Need Not Apply."

She always figured she had time to meet Mr. Right.

She thought back and cringed. The last time she had a date, George W.—crap, maybe it was Clinton—was in office.

From her high perch, she could barely make out women pushing baby carriages and men and women holding hands, laughing as they walked along the city streets. Her heart ached with longing. She had put this part of herself on hold for so long. After all, who had time for men when there was a teenager to raise and a company to run?

Who am I kidding? She sighed. Brook was an adult —with a law degree. Raising her wasn't a valid excuse any longer. Granted, working had stifled her social life over the past fifteen years, but Herb had spent many futile breaths trying to convince her that her job wasn't everything. He'd said she should let go. She would have loved to do so, but she really didn't know how.

CHAPTER SIX

ADAM WALKED UP to Allison's open office door and found her playing with the chain at her neck, gazing out the window. He was stunned how much she'd changed over the years. Gone was the cute, determined girl. She'd become a beautiful, resolute woman.

"Penny for your thoughts, Ally-gator."

Allison jumped and spun toward the door. A slow smile spread over her lips, and what nice lips they were.

"Your father always said that to me."

"He did. He always worried about you." He entered the office and sank into a guest chair.

"There's nothing to worry about." She sat on the edge of her desk, crossing her legs and swinging her stockinged foot back and forth. The hem of her skirt snuck up her leg, giving him a generous glimpse of her sugar-white thigh. From his recollection, those thighs tasted as good as they looked, and damn, they looked good enough to devour.

He averted his eyes from temptation and played

with the Newton's Cradle sitting on the edge of her desk. It was nowhere near as fun to play with the cold, hard metal toy, but he figured it was the only way to control the thoughts blazing through his mind, pulsing through his body.

"To what do I owe this visit?" Her question brought his mind back from gutter.

Damn. He needed a cold shower.

"I know this has been a rough day. I wanted to see how you're holding up." Part of him was also wondering if she was speaking to him after the day's events. He wouldn't blame her. He wasn't all that thrilled with the path the day had taken. It killed him that she was hurt by Dale's ridiculous decision.

"I'm fine. You Byrnes men need to stop concerning yourself over nothing."

"You're not nothing," he whispered to himself and shook his head. Thinking about how much she meant to him didn't help his situation. He had to remember that he was leaving in a few days.

"Excuse me?"

"Just mumbling." A long breath crawled through his lungs and escaped his lips. He ran a hand down the knot forming at the back of his neck. His nerves rattled and popped. Why did this woman make him so nervous? He inhaled and babbled on. "Would you like to grab some dinner tonight? I figure we both need to eat, and I haven't had a chance to go to Chicago's Kitchen and Wine Bar since I've been back. It was always one of my favorites. Yours too, right?"

"Rain check? I was hoping to head over to the

condo tonight. The lease on my apartment ends next month, so I need to start moving my stuff out."

"Rain check." He hoped he was able to keep the disappointment out of his voice.

"Sure."

Julie knocked, peeking her head around the door-frame. "Adam, I was able to get you a table for two at Chicago's Kitchen for seven tonight."

"Thank you, but Allison is heading over to the condo tonight. I think I'll just order room service. But if you'd like to take the reservation, I'd be happy to pay for your dinner."

Adam watched as the color drained from Julie's face. He forgot Julie hated handouts. He didn't think paying for dinner was considered a handout, but it must have upset her. "I'm sorry. You don't have to take the reservation."

"Um, no, thank you. That's very generous," she stuttered. "But I, ah, need to head out. Cody's daycare called, and I need to pick him up right away. He's sick. There's this stomach flu going around. I know his friend Dillon had it last week. He must have caught it."

"All right, take the rest of the day. Hopefully, it's nothing serious."

"Is there anything else I can do for either of you before I go?"

"No. I'm heading out early myself. I want to get a start on the condo." Allison smiled warmly.

"Allison, don't forget to call Doug Kaminski about your meeting next week. He likes to talk to you in person."

"Of course. Thank you, Julie."

"I hope Cody feels better. If there's anything I can do to help, please call. My mom worked with the Children's Hospital last year and knows a few of the pediatricians," Adam added.

"Thanks." Julie attempted a smile and left the office.

He twisted his neck to relieve the lump of concern growing and tugging on his upper spine. He'd never seen Julie act so strangely. There wasn't much he could do to help until she asked for it. And if she needed help, she'd ask. When it came to her son, Julie would make sure that Cody got the best care.

Adam shoved the worry from his mind and focused on Allison. A dinner with her would've been nice. It would've been nice to have a little company as he ate some gourmet Chicago cuisine.

A sigh escaped his lips. Instead, he'd spend another quiet night alone. Now he remembered why he couldn't wait to go back to Phoenix. Loneliness was never a problem when you worked every night.

━

ALLISON TRUDGED through the abandoned office. She had called Doug Kaminski and set up a meeting for first thing Monday morning. He'd always been a steady customer and a great friend to Herb. She figured meeting with him was a great way to start her week.

The conversation only lasted a few minutes, but apparently, it was long enough for the employees to stampede from the office and take advantage of a beautiful Friday afternoon. She was glad Adam sent out an email for everyone to leave a little early today. That they took the opportunity spoke volumes about the depth of their sadness—or it could have been the appeal of an early start to their weekends.

The brightly lit elevator barreled its way to the parking garage. Allison blinked as she slowly exited the car and entered the ominous expanse. A cacophony of street noises wafted through the exhaust-tinged air of the complex, and her heels clicked on the concrete as she walked up behind her car. She pressed the remote, and the car chirped to life.

She made her way to the driver's side door, but her eyes were drawn to the left rear tire. The familiar half-moon shape sagged into the concrete. Another flat? She shook her head as she leaned down and assessed the damage.

"Damn it." She rose and looked around the garage. With all of her experience in tire deflation, she should have triple A on speed dial. Or better yet, she should know how to fix the darn thing.

Why hadn't she taken a general car care course in college? Surely, that would have been more useful than that ceramics class. After all, how often had she called on her ability to carve and texture clay? She could have used Tire Changing 101 twice this week alone.

She pulled out her cell phone and sifted through the list of contacts. She smiled when she found the number of the motor club. She'd have to make sure she thanked Julie for setting her up. After the tire incident last week, Julie insisted she get some sort of service for the future. After all, Brook's boyfriends wouldn't always be around to perform basic car maintenance.

Allison clicked the contact and brought the phone to her ear. She listened to the silent hum of disconnectivity. Damn cell phone. Damn garage. Damn tire.

She stared at the desolate parking garage. There was no point staying here when there was a perfectly good phone at her desk. She made her way back to the elevator and waited for the doors to open. She tapped her foot and caught sight of the sparkly shoes on her feet.

She had never been interested in designer clothing or footwear until Loraine took her shopping a few years ago. Loraine felt that a vice president should have a few classic staples in her closet and was appalled when Allison had none of them. Allison hated the clothes at first. She felt like a fake. The clothes looked so sophisticated, and she was a woman who...who only used words like "sophisticated."

But, to the detriment of her wallet, she'd grown to love them, the clothes and the shoes. And the shopping trips with Loraine were just the icing on the blinged-out cake.

A ding sounded as the elevator opened its doors. She walked into the car, only to hit a brick wall. Well, it felt like a brick wall. Upon closer inspection, she'd run into a broad chest with thick shoulders. The force of the impact threw her equilibrium off. She started to stagger backward, and large hands wrapped around her arms.

The strong grip kept her body grounded as her mind spun like a Tilt-A-Whirl.

What did she hit? A semi-truck? She refocused her eyes and looked into the smiling face of the barrier.

"Are you okay?" Adam asked as he continued to hold her.

Shock from impact, or from the musky scent he wore, scattered her thoughts. She stared blankly as Adam's face furrowed in concern. He waved a hand in front of her eyes.

"Are you okay?" The distress in his voice managed to snap her out of her stupefaction.

"Yes," she whispered, inches from his face. His warm breath slid along her cheek. Her heartbeat accelerated as her sight moved from his eyes to his lips. No matter how hard she tried to fight the urge, she couldn't help but think about kissing those lips.

Adam's luscious, full lips... Gaaa! She snapped her head away and pulled out of Adam's grasp. Her feet staggered at the force of her retreat. She reached her arms out for balance and dug her heel into the ground. When the wobbling stopped, she steeled her spine and glared at the arrogant grin spreading across his face.

"What are you doing here?" She switched her voice to cold and unfeeling, to match his soul.

"I'm just leaving. Why are you going back?"

"My tire is flat. I'm calling the motor club."

"Do you have a spare?"

She was pretty sure she did. "Yes."

"Well." He took off his suit jacket and handed it to

her. "I'll take care of it. Where'd you park?" He held out his upturned hand.

Golden boy was going to change a tire, and he wanted to hold her hand? Maybe he'd dipped into his father's hidden liquor stash. Although the urge to grab his hand was overwhelming, she abstained. Willpower for the win.

His fingers wiggled.

Her hand itched, but she kept it by her side. "What?"

"Keys? So I can get your spare tire, unless you'd like to get it yourself."

Allison sighed. He didn't want to hold her hand. And she just knew her face had turned an embarrassing shade of red. Thank God the parking garage was dark. "No. Here." She handed him the jingling set of metal as he walked toward her car.

Adam leaned down, assessing the damage to the tire. "This tire's flat."

"I'm—wearing shoes."

"What?" His eyebrows curled in confusion as he walked to the trunk and inserted the key.

"I'm sorry. I thought we were playing Let's-State-the-Obvious."

A smile replaced the confusion. Heat spread over her body at the humor in his eyes. He lifted the trunk lid, and after a brief minute of tossing and flailing, he looked at Allison. "Where is your spare tire?"

"Isn't it in there? I think I only used it once."

"Did they return the spare when they put on the new tire?" He glanced at the right-hand side of her car.

Oops. She knew there was something she'd meant to do today.

His question was answered when he realized the front tire was currently the spare. "Allison," he huffed. "Why didn't you have your spare taken off and a permanent tire placed on the car?"

"I forgot," she said. "But in my defense, the car was running fine on the spare." Adam pinched the bridge of his nose. "You do understand the concept of the spare tire, correct? The spare allows you to take a car to the mechanic without having it towed."

"I'm well aware," she snapped. "However, some of us have been too busy running a company to have time for luxuries like car maintenance."

"It's not a luxury, it's a requirement."

"Bite me," she hissed and walked away. She should have called the motor club. They would have helped without all of the blasted commentary.

"Where are you going?"

"To call the motor club." She stomped toward the elevator.

Adam leaned against the car. "Look. By the time the motor club gets here, it's going to be dark. Why don't we just deal with this tomorrow? I can give you a ride to the condo, and I'll pick you up tomorrow morning. I can bring a spare from one of Dad's cars."

"Thank you. But the condo's only a few blocks away. I can walk."

"Actually, I'd love to see the old place again, if you don't mind. It beats heading to the hotel alone or going home and listening to my mom and Dale talk about the bliss that is 'action through inaction.'"

She turned at the sound of his voice. It almost sounded like begging. That might have been wishful thinking on her part. How she'd love to hear the man beg. Her posture softened as she realized she was going to take him up on his offer. Damn, she was a sucker when it came to Adam Byrnes. Looking into those eyes, any remaining annoyance slipped away. Her lips warmed into a smile as she said, "What does that mean? How do you act through inaction?"

Adam ran a hand through his deliciously rumpled hair, his mouth turning up into a devilish grin. The gleam in his eyes just melted her insides. "I have no clue, but apparently it has led to numerous philosophical debates in the Byrnes household."

"Sounds fascinating." She faced her now-defunct auto. "I suppose I'll take you up on that ride. Where's your car?"

"It's the blue thing over there." He pointed as they walked to the other side of the garage, toward a small compact car.

Her lips curved as she took in the vehicle. To call it a car was a stretch.

"Seriously? Were they out of, like, every other car known to man?" she joked as they walked up to the toy-like automobile. "Wow. Is this battery operated, or are there pedals? I think your father bought this same car for Julie's son for Christmas."

"Are you done mocking the rental?" He gently tapped the hood. "You might hurt her feelings, and then she might run you down like some 80s horror movie."

Allison's smile grew as she pictured the little car coming at her, and there she was, her right arm outstretched, holding it back by the hood, the car grunting and flashing its lights while she casually glanced at the nails of her left hand. *Are you done with your hissy fit?* Allison would ask it. It would honk in response.

She was still smiling as she squeezed her five-ten frame into the miniature car.

CHAPTER SEVEN

THEY CREPT through the seven blocks of Chicago traffic. Pedestrians lined the sidewalks and waited at crosswalks, headphones hanging from their ears. Rows and rows of red lights stood between them and their destination. Adam deftly navigated the overcrowded one-way streets of downtown to find the condo's parking garage. He stopped to pay the garage fee.

"Is that twenty dollars per day? I always figured they got a free parking spot just by living here." Allison's eyes bulged, and Adam laughed as her bottom lip plumped into a childlike pout. She was adorable when she sulked.

She must have noticed his attention, because she bit her lip and looked down at the floor. His body rattled and hummed in response to those lips, and he shook his head. He needed to control his thoughts.

He started racking his brain, thinking of anything to curb his reaction before the tent in his lap became too obvious. He looked around the garage for help. Large cars. Nope. Sports cars. Sexy curves. Nope. Damn. He looked over at Allison and ran a hand over his face. This wasn't working. Nothing was getting his mind off of Allison and those lips. *Ugh.*

Starting over, he remembered his mom slapping him upside his head for daydreaming. That was one way to ensure his body would calm down. Visions of parents tended to cool down the hottest of situations.

Satisfied with his impulse-suppression technique, he drove along the ramps of the parking structure, looking for an open spot.

"Twenty dollars a day. Wow." Allison said again.

"Yeah. They really like to rake you over the coals to own a car down here."

"I think I'll take my car to Brook's house in Oak Park. Now that I live so close to work, there's no point in paying what could be a mortgage payment for a parking spot."

He smiled as he pulled the clown car into the first available spot. He'd fought with the rental company to get something a little bigger—his legs bumped the dashboard every time he used the brakes. They'd explained that they had no other cars onsite but assured him they would call when the next mid-size or greater came available. That was three days ago, and he was still driving the matchbox.

As they walked to the elevator, Adam asked, "Have you been here before?"

"A few times. Your parents had their last company

Christmas party here. Since most of the employees are from the city, and the local news was calling for a huge snowstorm, they had decided to have the party downtown instead of the house in the 'burbs."

"So they scheduled their party according to television weather predictions?"

"Don't knock it. The weathermen in this town rock, and they're forecasts, not predictions. They're not fortune-tellers." She walked into the elevator. He pushed the button for the lobby as she stared at the twelve-inch television mounted to the elevator walls. Paul Mörder's face danced across the small screen while a woman's voice narrated the story.

"Mörder's lawyers have filed a motion to throw out the bribery charges. His defense team alleges that the State of Illinois has bullied these lawyers and judges into claiming Mörder bribed them. The state prosecutor on the case had this to say: 'This is just one more ploy from the Mörder camp. We need to stand strong against the real bullies who attempt to stifle the judicial process. He will be tried by a jury of his peers, and justice will prevail.' Strong words from a government that has had enough. Back to you, Robin..."

"I love this little TV. It's God's gift to those of us with ADD. We get to be bombarded with information while we wait in the elevator." Allison stared at the next news story in awe.

"I need to stop in the lobby to get my dad's mail."

"I'd love to see the lobby."

"Haven't you been in the lobby before?" he asked,

excitement building in his gut. He couldn't believe she hadn't seen it.

"No. I always went straight up from the parking garage."

The doors opened to the lobby, and Adam waited. He was not disappointed. Allison gasped as they ambled out into the large foyer. The fifty-foot-high enclosure sparkled as the light from the setting sun shone through the windows onto the white marble floors. They paused at the large porcelain water feature.

Poseidon sat with his arms spread, trident held high, hidden jets making water dance all around him.

His eyes roamed the bustling city within the four walls. To their left stood a lounge where inhabitants and visitors were enjoying an early evening aperitif. To their right was a full-service mailroom, grocery, and spa. In the center of the grandiose atrium were multiple banks of elevators.

They toured the floor, wandering past the selection of restaurants and bars until Adam found one of the doormen. Adam walked over to a young guy, probably no more than twenty-five, wearing a pressed gray tunic with silver buttons. His nondescript red tie, white gloves, and white shirt were spotless. His multiple ear piercings and subtle eyeliner conflicted with the slicked-back hair and immaculate uniform.

The doorman's attention seemed to be otherwise engaged. Adam followed the path of his gaze and landed on Allison. The young man's eyes shifted up and down her curves. Adam fought an urge to use his fist to divert the gawker's attention. After all, she was rather nice to look at, and technically, he had no claim on her.

"Hi." Adam moved to block his view and gain his attention. The guy turned, eyes wide. "Y-yes, sir."

Busted. He probably shouldn't be gawking at the building inhabitants. "I'm Herb Byrnes' son, Adam Byrnes, and the woman you were watching is Allison Southby. She's the new owner of the Byrnes' condo."

"Really." The man smiled and glanced back at Allison. Adam could relate. Having Allison at his place of employment had made work a lot more enjoyable, too. Of course, not counting the past week, she'd been just out of her teens when they'd worked together. Well, shit, this kid wasn't much older than a teenager. Adam knew what thoughts flew through the minds of hormone-driven practically teens.

A twinge of something mimicking jealousy shot through his gut at the child's obvious admiration of her. "Ahem. I'm here to pick up my father's mail. I spoke to someone a few days ago and asked to have it held at the front desk."

"Sure, Mr. Byrnes. It's being held in the mailroom. I'll go pick that up for you."

"Please, call me Adam. I don't want to take you away from your job. I'd be happy to get it..." He paused, not sure of the man's name. When he didn't offer it, Adam added, "And your name is?"

"Oh, my name is Matt." He pulled a name tag from

his pocket. Great place for it. "I can run to the post office. It's no problem. LaQuitha, I have to leave the desk for a minute. Can you hold down the fort?" A woman in a matching uniform nodded her head, and Matt went off to retrieve the mail. Within minutes, he was walking back, bag of mail in hand.

"Thanks." Adam smiled as he took the overstuffed plastic bag. He walked toward Allison as she entered the elevator car, standing outside the elevator and watching as she looked for the button for the fiftieth floor. Her eyebrows arched in confusion, and she raised her eyes to meet his.

He lifted an arm to hold the door open. "This bank of elevators doesn't go past the thirty-fifth floor. You have to go to the east bank," he said, pointing to a separate grouping across the way.

She exited the car, and he wrapped his arm around her shoulder. He glanced at Matt, whose pimply face fell as he watched them meander to the nearest penthouse-level elevator. Adam smiled in triumph. It wasn't his fault Matt misinterpreted his arm around her and thought they were a couple.

After all, he was just doing Allison a favor. She didn't need some hormonal child sniffing around her. Adam was helping to rid her of a future barely legal nuisance. They located the correct elevator, and Adam put the key into the slot to access the fiftieth floor.

"The elevator won't open unless you have the key. It keeps the common folk out," Adam joked.

Allison's eyes swept back and forth as they entered the elevator. She didn't speak, just seemed to take it all in as Adam used the key again to activate the button for the fiftieth floor.

The top ten floors of the building were all single occupancy, with each floor one condominium. Their destination was no different. The elegant elevator sped smoothly past all the other floors and gently glided to the penthouse level. The doors flew open, and they were greeted with the five-thousand-square-foot condo.

The entry was gold, from the walls to the glowing sconces to the wainscoting above the warm hardwood. Allison's heels clicked on the maple floor as they wandered into an oversized rotunda family room. Windows lined the circular back wall and led to the spectacular vista of the southern Chicago skyline. They walked over the shaggy, tan area rug, passing white couches and red marble coffee tables. Allison's eyes scanned the view outside the window, where the Hancock building soared in the backdrop.

He heard her breath hitch in her chest as she stared at the crisp blue stretch of sky. To the southeast, the visible horizon met the cool waves of Lake Michigan. This condo offered an unparalleled view of Chicago. It truly was amazing, but it didn't hold a candle to the woman standing next to him.

Adam's attention veered from the city in front of him and fell upon her. He had thought about that night with Allison so many times over the years. She had been wicked sexy back then, too, with sex appeal that could tempt the most virtuous saint. He was surprised he had waited as long as he did to make a move. Lord knew he had never been a virtuous saint.

He missed her soft, commanding hands and the gentle arch of her neck. He had dreamed about her small, perky breasts and the way she moaned for more. He fought the urge to wrap his arms around her waist, and his hand jerked back at the thought of running his hands up and down her body, pulling the pins from her hair and allowing it to tumble down her back.

Shit. He needed to get a grip.

Unfortunately, he knew how it felt to touch her, be touched by her, to be inside her, to be loved by her. He gulped, hoping to squash the overpowering need bubbling to the surface.

His eyes continued their visual caressing as he watched her lick the soft contours of her lips, those lips that had kissed him and cracked all of his inhibitions. He looked down at her hands hanging at her side. Those hands had brought him excessive pleasure as she stroked all apprehension from his body.

He shook his head in disgust. He knew it was wrong to start anything with her, even back then. After all, his parents considered her one of the family. However, every stroke, lick, and thrust shattered his defenses till he had to have her.

Adam forced his attention back to the cityscape. He watched the rise and swell of the lake, trying to control his racing heart rate and raging hard-on. The desire to touch her engulfed him. He slowly placed his hand on her back. He leaned in to breathe the floral scent of her perfume.

What the hell am I doing?

ALLISON STARED, mesmerized by the beauty before her. Cascading light fell over the city she so lovingly called home. Boats sparked and gleamed as they drifted over the glittering water. Brown and gold leaves hung from the tree-lined streets of the Streeterville neighborhood. There was something magical about weekends in the city of Chicago. Weekdays found people rushing about, but Friday, Saturday, and Sunday were for enjoying all this town had to offer.

Her mind wandered over the fall scenes. Soon the cold would take hold, covering the city in a blanket of white. For now, though, everyone lapped up the temperate climate. She was so engrossed in her love affair with the city that she almost didn't notice the warm hand resting on the small of her back. Adam leaned over, inches from her ear, and whispered, "Breathtaking."

Her skin quivered as his soft, warm breath tickled her neck. Her eyes closed as she inhaled. Shit, he smelled amazing. Her thoughts scattered.

His scent. The warmth of his hands. His arm moved to her waist, his fingers wrapping around her hip. She trembled, electricity zipping through her veins.

She needed to stop him. This feeling. Her reaction to him, but she couldn't remember why. Why? She exhaled, trying to release all lingering confusion. She stepped away, removing herself from his influence. Oh yeah. This was the arrogant, slime ball heartbreaker,

Adam Byrnes. Her mind went back to the empty bed so many years ago.

"Y-yes," she stuttered, glancing up at him as she moved closer to the window and further from him. "It's beautiful."

"I was talking about you," he murmured as he stepped closer, bridging the distance between them. His other hand reached out and trailed a finger down the side of her cheek, sending a shiver down her spine. He wrapped his fingers around her wrist and pulled her hand to his mouth.

Allison's eyes fluttered closed as her lungs gasped for air. Her heart sputtered. Silken, wet lips caressed her sensitive palm before moving to her fingers. His tongue stroked her fingertip. His teeth nibbled on the pad. Her thighs burned with desire.

Her mind told her to stop this idiocy, but every other part of her body was screaming, "Take me." Adam pulled her to him, pressing himself into her. Her hips hummed as she pushed forward into his growing interest. A small groan escaped through his clenched teeth. He wanted this. God knew she wanted this.

His green eyes burned, reflecting all the want and desire she felt. He angled his head toward her. His lips moved to her mouth. Soft. Hot. Demanding. Hunger seared her soul. Want drove her forward as she lost all sense of control and reason. She wanted him closer, inside of her. His kiss intensified, and her lips opened for him.

Her desperate hands ran through his hair and down

his strong back. She felt his taut muscles flex, sending pure heat radiating up and down her body. She was consumed with him. She gasped as his hands lifted her skirt, his thumbs trailing down her thighs. Throbbing need pulsed through her veins. She wanted him. Wanted him now. Her tongue moved over his, swirling with frenzied desire.

With his lips still on hers, he lifted her in his arms. She wrapped her legs around his waist as he pulled her tight against his erection. He stumbled down the hall, bumping into a table outside the master bedroom. A crystal vase wobbled as it spun on its rim. Somehow, though, it managed to teeter itself back into a standing position.

He opened the first bedroom door he came to and carried her in. He flicked on the light switch, and his gasp pierced her sexual haze, bringing her back to reality. Once Adam set her on her feet again, Allison turned and faced the room.

What might have been a gorgeous guest room was now more of a teenager's haven. Furniture was overturned, and drawers had been pulled onto the floor, their contents strewn about. The closet was emptied, and its holdings scattered.

She stared at the mess as Adam put a finger to his lips.

"Stay here," he whispered and walked out of the room. She slowly adjusted her clothes, trying to regulate her breathing. She tried to wrap her mind around what she almost did with Adam. But she didn't want to think about it. She also didn't want to think about the ramifications of what had happened here. How and why did someone destroy this room?

Adam walked back into the bedroom and pulled his cell phone from his pocket. "I need to report a break-in."

CHAPTER EIGHT

ALLISON'S HEAD WAS REELING. She mentally scrolled through the short list of suspects who might break into Herb's condo. No one came to mind. It seemed outrageous to think that someone would even consider invading another person's space like that.

Cops swarmed the rooms, looking for evidence and asking questions.

They'd spent the last hour reiterating the incidents that led up to their nine-one-one call, over and over again, ad nauseam. She could probably recite the events in her sleep at this point. Damn. She should have thought of that sooner and slept through the interrogation.

Her hand shot to her mouth as a yawn overwhelmed her. She'd had enough. Hunger gnawed at her stomach as she thought about the last time she ate. The apple, popcorn, and soda she'd downed throughout the day hadn't seemed to keep her stomach full enough to last through the evening. All she wanted was a good meal and a warm bed.

"Are we done here for tonight?" Adam asked Detective Washington as if reading Allison's mind.

"Sure. We'll be in touch." The detective nodded.

"Why don't I take you home tonight? You can stay here another night." Adam suggested and glanced down at Allison. Concern colored his eyes.

"I really don't want to go home." Her lips drooped down at the thought of being alone. "I'll call my sister." Allison took out her cell phone and dialed her sister's number, only to get her voicemail. "Brook, where are you tonight? Oh, yeah, it's Friday, you're probably out. Well, when you get back from whatever debauchery you've found, can you call me? Please. Bye."

She swiped the End icon and stared at the phone. "I left a message," she said out loud.

Despite her attempt at ESP, the phone did not ring. She sighed. The thought of staying anywhere alone frightened her more than she wanted to admit. After all, she was a strong independent woman, and this was just a simple robbery.

Simple robbery. What the hell was that? There was no such thing as a simple robbery. Even though she didn't live in the space and her stuff was miles away, locked in her own apartment, she felt violated. Devastated.

Adam stared at her, brows furrowed. "Are you hungry?"

She looked up, eyes glazed in confusion. Hungry? Yeah. She nodded.

"Let's go grab some dinner. I'm sure Brook will call while we're eating."

Allison got her purse, and within minutes they were heading down Michigan Avenue, the cool evening air whipping across their arms through the opened windows of his loaner. She leaned her head back against the headrest.

She hated the damsel in distress bit, but she sure felt the distress right now. She would like to think she would have been fine getting through it alone, but she was happy she didn't have to find out. And she hated to admit it but having Adam near made her feel better.

Even after all of the drama of the past few hours, she couldn't seem to forget how the evening began. She knew it was wrong, but she still wanted him. Those strong hands, those hot, wanting lips...

"Are you okay?" Adam asked before her imagination got too far away from her. "I'm fine."

"Are you sure? I've worked with a lot of people in your situation, and I know this isn't easy. This must be difficult, to have your new place broken into—"

"You know, I'd rather not talk about it," she interrupted and glanced out the passenger window. She braced for a fight. She was being ridiculous about this, and Adam never missed an opportunity to tell her when she was behaving like a child. After all, she barely owned the property. The fact that there had been a break-in shouldn't have bothered her as much as it did.

Surprisingly, though, silence came from the seat next to her until he asked, "Where do you want to eat?"

"How about Zydeco? I could use some comfort food." She ran her hands over her arms. She wasn't cold, but her nerves were leaving her chilled.

"I never thought of Cajun as comfort food."

"It was my dad's favorite." She watched her hands as her fingers intertwined and twisted. Just the mention of her father created a longing in her heart. Just one more dip in the roller-coaster of a day.

"Then Zydeco it is." He stared out the windshield as he maneuvered across the lanes of traffic. They sat in silence, until Adam smiled and turned to her. "You know, I never really understood how hard it must have been for you all those years ago. I just lost my dad, but you lost both your parents. And you had to raise your sister. I can't even imagine having to raise Dale. You are an amazing woman, Allison Southby."

The heat crawled up her neck. She never thought of herself as amazing. She'd made the best of a bad situation. Some would have done better, some worse, but she thought she did okay. It was nice to hear though. It was nice to hear she wasn't a complete screw-up.

"After all the years we've known each other, you don't talk about your parents much. Do you still miss them?"

"Yes." She hesitated. This was not a discussion she wanted to have—ever. She preferred to keep it locked in her heart. There was no point in reliving the loss by talking about it. It wouldn't bring them back. It would only prolong her suffering as she thought about loneliness and fear that tormented her that first year. Hell, her whole life.

It was one more way she and Brook were different. Brook talked about their parents, simple nostalgia creeping into her voice. Allison had never gotten to that point. She'd never had time to let them go.

"So, it's not going to get any better, huh?"

She looked into his eyes until his gaze returned to the road. Gazing at his profile, she let her thoughts fall from her mouth. "Yes, it gets better. One night you find that you haven't thought about them all day. Then you feel guilty because you think you're forgetting them. But eventually, you realize you're not. I guess it's worse when I think about things they would have loved to see.

"When Brook graduated college. They would have loved that, so I cried for hours. I'm dreading her wedding. I mean, I want her to get married, but my mother would have loved to plan a wedding. Look at me. I'm worried about something that hasn't even happened yet. I must sound like an idiot."

"Not at all. I'm sure your parents would have loved your graduation and wedding too."

She tried to smile. Talking about this was so hard. She would like to think her parents would have been proud of everything she had accomplished, but whenever she thought about it, her eyes watered. And after the waterworks following their death, she promised to keep her eye leakage to a minimum. Thinking about "what ifs" did not help in that goal.

"How's your mom doing?" She changed the focus. The best way to dodge unwanted questions was to divert attention.

"She's hanging in there. She spends a lot of time

with her animals. She's nursing a bird back to health that she found while horseback riding. That's keeping her busy. I don't know what she would do if she didn't have the animals.

"She tries to act strong, but she's miserable. She misses him. Not just him, but the little things. She misses pinochle. They would play pinochle at night. It was their way of winding down."

"That's so sad. Can you imagine being married for forty-four years and then one day the person's just gone?"

His eyes remained riveted to the road as he pulled into the parking garage a city block down from the restaurant. He parked and jumped out of the car. Allison unbuckled her seat belt and gathered her purse. She reached for the door handle, but Adam was already opening the door.

He held out his hand. "Shall we?"

With the heavy conversation behind them, she noticed the romance of the situation. Romance? Ugh. She didn't want to feel romance with Adam Byrnes. Of course, sex with Adam Byrnes wasn't the same as romance, but— No, just, no. Been there, done that. Burned the shirt. They'd dodged a bullet today. If a ransacked condo didn't prove their incompatibility, she didn't know what did.

Tonight was dinner with a friend. A friend who would leave. A friend who could break her heart if she let him. Thank goodness she was too smart to let him do that again.

They walked through the crisp fall night to the illuminated restaurant. Adam opened the door, and Allison walked in. The spicy aroma of New Orleans and the fast tempo of zydeco music made her feel at home. The smell of paprika and hot sauce filled the air, transporting diners to the bayou. Dark oak tables and chairs were dispersed throughout the rustically decorated establishment. Southern-inspired art adorned the golden walls. Beads and garlands in deep purple, green, and yellow hung from the intricate chandeliers.

Allison smiled. Her father had always said that Zydeco lived up to its name. He would adopt his best Southern drawl and tell her, "In one step, dahlin', you go from downtown Chicagee to N'awlins. 'Tis the best of both worlds, my little gris-gris." He had always been convinced she was his gris-gris—his good luck charm.

She had stopped feeling like a good luck charm the night he'd died. A true good luck charm wouldn't have let that happen. He hadn't lived long enough to find out she didn't bring him luck. Luck or no luck, her chest warmed at the thought that he believed she brought him some kind of good fortune.

"So, what's good here?" Adam asked as they were seated at a table.

"It's all good. You might want to avoid the burning-hot chicken if you're afraid of spice. They tend to lay it on a bit thick."

"Afraid? I have no fear," he scoffed as the waitress approached the table.

"Evening folks. Welcome. Can I get you something to drink?" The heavy-set waitress smiled, pulling a pen and paper from the pocket of her skirt.

"I'll have a Hurricane and the burning-hot chicken, extra hot." Allison smiled, and Adam playfully raised his eyebrows.

"Make that two burning-hot chickens, but I'll have a beer," Adam told the waitress without taking his eyes off Allison. The stare was fraught with challenge.

She teased, "You might want to bring him a pitcher of water."

His green eyes twinkled with defiance. He ran his hand through his sexily disheveled hair and picked up the glass of water sitting in front of him.

Her insides melted with every glimmer in his eye. She fought an urge to reach across the table and jump him in front of the restaurant full of patrons. She mentally slapped herself. Get a grip. This was a friendly dinner. Friends. Remember. Tonight would not end in an empty bed. Not again. She needed to get involved with him like she needed a noose of Mardi Gras beads.

Fortunately, if she remembered correctly, he was a wimp in the spice department. He had once cried while eating a taco with a few splashes of hot sauce. Granted, he had been a teenager at the time, so his manly taste buds might have developed over the years. Maybe spicy hot sauce no longer reduced the strong, virile man to whimpering like a child.

If everything worked according to plan, he would be too busy dealing with the heat from the burning-hot chicken for her to worry about anything sexual happening tonight. God bless capsaicin.

ADAM TRIED to smile while he fought back tears. A gallon of air slid past his lips as he tried to squelch the inferno blazing through his taste buds. He was convinced bursts of steam were shooting from his ears, like in the cartoons. The sweat trickled down the back of his shirt. Who would have thought chicken could be so damned hot? He glanced at Allison as he took another gulp of water.

She scooped another bite of fire-mix into her mouth. The Hurricane in front of her was untouched. However, her eyes were not watering, nor was sweat flowing down her brow. He wiped his lip. Dammit. Some big strong man he turned out to be.

The waitress stopped at their table, her eyes wide. "Are you okay? Can I get you some milk or more water?" She pointed at the empty pitcher sitting on the table.

Somehow, through the fire shooting up his nose and the numbness overwhelming his tongue, he managed to croak out, "I'm fine."

Allison laughed. "A glass of milk would help. Thanks."

As the waitress walked away, Adam gave in to the heat and guzzled the rest of the water. He took a few breaths through his mouth and ripped the glass of milk out of the returning waitress's hand. She managed to stifle a giggle as he drank down the tall glass.

He used his napkin to wipe the tears from his eyes.

Allison took another bite. "How can you possibly eat that without it affecting you?" He croaked.

"I love the heat. It feels good." She smiled. "Plus, I'm not such a lightweight."

"Apparently not." He grimaced and threw his napkin on the table. "I, unfortunately, am said lightweight."

"Do you want to order something else?" Allison asked.

"No. I think my mouth is scorched to oblivion. There's nothing going in my mouth but liquid." He pounded the remainder of the milk.

She took a sip of her Hurricane. A sip. He was so going to have to hand over his man card.

"That's unfortunate." She stared at him over the rim of the glass.

Adam's green eyes stared. Was she flirting? Please be flirting. What he wouldn't give to get her naked in his bed once again. Her soft skin and willing body —shit.

He poured another glass of water and drank. This time it wasn't to cool his charred tongue. This time it was to cool his firing libido from thinking about what he'd like to do to her with that tongue.

The waitress approached the table. "Can I get you anything else?"

"No, thanks. I am officially done." He laughed.

"I'll leave this with you then." She placed the bill on the table and whisked away the plates.

Allison reached into her purse and took out her wallet. She went to snatch the bill, but Adam got there first. There was no way he'd let her pay for dinner.

"So how much do I owe?" She played with the clasp on her wallet.

"I got this." He held the bill in one hand and reached across the table to steal her water with the other. After all, she wasn't using it, and his mouth was still blazing.

He could practically hear the war being waged in her mind as her narrow stare bored a hole in him. The argument over why she couldn't let him pay for dinner was obviously on the tip of her tongue. She obviously wanted to fight with him, but for some reason, she stopped and shrugged her shoulders before dumping her wallet back in her purse. "Okay. Thanks for dinner."

She took out her phone, and he saw Brook's name on the screen before she put the phone to her ear. After a few seconds, Allison sighed. Brook must not have answered.

"Are you ready to head out?" he asked as she tapped the end button on her phone. She stared at the dark screen, sighing again, and nodded.

They strolled out of the restaurant and made their way through the crowded streets. Allison periodically checked her phone, worry etched across her brow. They walked in silence—Adam's mind was miles away, as well. He couldn't stop thinking about the condo break-in.

Who broke in? Why? What if they were looking for Allison? What if they didn't stop at the condo? Her apartment wasn't safe. That would be the first place someone would look. He wasn't even sure she would be safe at her sister's, but he knew Brook's Oak Park home had a good alarm system. He'd given Brook the recommendation when she'd asked him.

Although, his father's condo had an alarm, and that didn't stop this guy. The only way he'd be sure she was safe was to watch her. He would never sleep worrying about her.

Leaving her alone tonight wasn't an option. If she went to her sister's, he would either stay in the house or sit outside the house in the car. He'd sat through his share of stakeouts, and this was no different. However, if her sister didn't answer, maybe she could stay with him at the hotel. No one would think to look there. Then again, talking Allison into going back to his hotel was going to take an act of God.

As they entered the parking garage, he pressed the button, and the rental car chirped to life. He opened the door and waited for Allison to slide into the passenger seat before he closed the door. He walked to his side and angled into the small car.

"Where are you taking me?" Allison asked, with another frown at the blank screen of her phone.

"To my place. Since you can't get ahold of Brook, you might as well stay at the hotel. The Mallord is closer to your car and the condo, anyway." He focused on driving and waited for the yelling to ensue. He knew a night with him wasn't on her top ten things to do. But hell, it was just one night.

"Okay," she said as they made their way to the hotel.

He had all the reasons why she needed to come with him lined up in his mind. He was ready to beg, borrow, or appeal for her to come with him to make sure she was safe tonight. Yet, he didn't have to say a word.

She must have been more scared then she let on, because somehow, he managed to dodge two arguments with her in one night.

CHAPTER NINE

ALLISON STOOD AGAINST THE WALL, nervously biting her lip as Adam slid the key card through the reader on the hotel room door. The lock clicked, and he pushed the door open allowing her to walk across the threshold first.

She didn't want to be here. There was way too much temptation standing next to her. At this point, though, she had little choice. She'd tried to reach her sister several times in the car, to no avail.

The only other option was to suck it up and go home to her empty apartment. Her quiet, solitary apartment. A sigh escaped her as she thought about her desolate home with all of its creaks, groans, and scrapes. It was an old building, and although she loved the charm, the noises caused by the historic structure expanding and contracting could be a little disheartening. Logic told her everything was fine. But once she was alone, she knew logic would not intervene, and her head would spin as she heard things go bump in the night. Each bump would inspire a vision of murderous muggers roaming through the apartment, stealing anything not nailed down.

Adam took off his shoes and placed his watch on the nightstand. One night with Adam was not going to be that big of a deal.

She focused her attention on the room before her and inwardly groaned at the lone king bed against one wall and the light-blue couch against the other. An evening of couching it. Ick.

She shook her head to ward off the self-pity. Her chin rose with conviction as she steeled her spine. She could do this. She could be in the same room with Adam and keep her hands to herself.

Pain stabbed through her as she remembered the deserted feeling from when he'd left the last time. She'd never felt so used and abused in her life. She'd loved him before their night together. That night, she honestly thought they were starting something good, something real. She'd been practically picking out their china pattern in her sleep. How stupid. Her chest ached, and tears threatened to fall down her cheeks.

She had to stop. This had to stop.

Fire brewed in her stomach as rage slithered down her spine. How could she have let this jackass of a man have this much control? She swore she'd never let him have this much power over her again.

Good. This was better. Anger felt like a good fit, considering the other option was fear or sadness.

She yanked the bedspread and a pillow from the bed and stomped over to the couch. She tossed the linens down.

"What are you doing?" He sounded confused.

"I'm getting my bed ready for the night."

"Allison," he sighed, "you can sleep in the bed."

"I'm not sleeping with you." Ever. She kept the last word to herself.

"I'm not asking you to have sex with me. I'm offering to share a bed with you." He pinched the bridge of his nose as his eyes closed. "I'll even sleep on the couch if it would make you more comfortable." Consideration and frustration oozed from every word.

She ignored the twinge in her heart at his thoughtfulness. Jackass. Remember he's a jackass.

"No, Adam. I'll sleep on the couch. This is your room."

"We're adults, Allison." His voice rose, anger swirling through his eyes. "We can share a bed without it leading to anything."

Of course, he could. Bastard. She beat the pillow and snapped the quilt across the cushions. The anger built as she thought about those words. Of course, he could keep his hands to himself. Heaven help her if she kept thinking—believing—they might have some sort of relationship. Her heart would split in two under the strain. She would crack from the pressure of just wanting one more night with him. And she knew he would take that night if she offered and abandon her in the morning.

"I'll sleep here"—she pointed to the couch and then jabbed her fists onto her hips— "or I'll get my own room."

The thought of her own room frightened her, but she would not budge on this. She glared, readying herself for the impending battle. Adam stared at her, making no move of opposition. He just watched, and stared, and gazed...

"What?" He seemed to stare right through to her soul. Like all her thoughts were there for him to see. She blew her bangs from her eyes, trying to block whatever he thought he saw.

"Fine." He grabbed a T-shirt and sleep pants from the dresser. He tossed them on the bed and nodded. "These have a drawstring, so they should fit if you want to get out of your work clothes. And there should be a spare travel toothbrush on the counter. I always pack two in case I drop one."

Allison reached for the garments as guilt overwhelmed her. "Thank you."

"You're welcome."

Allison nodded and made her way across the room, closing the bathroom door just as the valve burst. Tears pooled in her eyes and rolled down her cheeks. What had she gotten herself into?

—————

ADAM PULLED BACK his shirt and unzipped his pants. He rolled his shoulders, sucking a deep breath into his chest. The woman drove him nuts. He had to admit sharing a bed would have been difficult, but he would have dealt with it. They were adults.

Granted, they were adults with a sexual past, a very good, very hot, sexual past, but he was positive they could handle this. That was a long time ago. His thoughts drifted back to that night—the arch of her back, the pucker of her perfect breasts, the taste of her lips. It was the hottest night he'd had in a while. Hell, the memory still burned in his brain.

Damn, maybe they shouldn't share a bed.

So much had happened that night. He'd regretted walking out on her from the moment he snuck out the door, but he was... Shit. Being with her had stirred up something he had never experienced before. He'd known from the moment they started kissing he was in deep. He'd also known if he let himself stick around, he'd never leave.

But he had to.

The Phoenix Police Department had just made him detective. Even though he hadn't thought he'd deserved it, his partner, Tony, had. And Adam couldn't let Tony down, not after everything he'd sacrificed.

Adam's only option had been to get his butt back to his life in Phoenix. He never would have asked Allison to move to Phoenix. She loved Chicago. Her sister was here, his parents were here, and her life had always been here.

So, he'd done the most logical thing. He'd run like a coward. Looking back...

Damn. She deserved so much better than anything he had to offer.

He found a pair of black cotton lounge pants and slipped them on. He stared at the bed. She was right. Sharing a bed was a horrible idea. But he'd feel like such a heel if he let her sleep on the couch. He looked at the crude bed she created with the thick comforter and contemplated jumping under the covers.

Unfortunately, she would probably try to push him off the damn couch, he thought, sliding a T-shirt over his head. He laughed as he set his travel alarm clock. "I'd like to see her try."

Who was he kidding? He would let her push him to the floor. Why even bother starting the fight, when it could be worse? She might leave, and he liked having her around, even if she'd made it clear that sleeping with him was a fate worse than death.

He jerked back the remaining blankets and twisted into bed. He tried to make himself comfortable, pulling the blankets up over his chest. He stared at the wall while thoughts raced through his mind. What a day. Between Allison's car, the robbery, and ending up back here with her, today had been exhausting. He could only imagine how hard it was for her.

All he'd be able to do is imagine. She didn't want to talk to him. She didn't want his help. Hell, she wouldn't even take his bed. Allison fumbled with the knob on the bathroom door. He turned over as she hurried across the room.

Although the suit she'd worn this afternoon looked

amazing, something in line with a naughty librarian, he couldn't stop looking at her in his clothes. The rolled waistband hung seductively off her slim hips, barely keeping the pants from dragging on the floor.

She jerked back the quilt and jumped into the mock bed. Her hair hung loosely down her back, swaying as she wiggled beneath the covers. She pulled the blanket over her head, blocking his view of her. He turned toward the wall again and leaned his head on the soft pillow. He attempted to close his eyes, but his overactive mind avoided sleep. The tick-tock of the alarm clock dangled in the air.

Rustling blankets and pillows permeated the still room. Allison tossed and turned on the sofa, and guilt overtook Adam. He should have offered the bed again. He should have been more forceful.

He looked at the ceiling and sighed. She dominated his thoughts. He had just opened his mouth to offer the bed when a tiny stutter in Allison's breath caught his attention. Was she okay?

A small gasp floated over the tick-tock as she rose from the couch and walked back across the room, closing the bathroom door behind her. He shifted to face the bathroom as a light glowed from the gap beneath the door.

Tonight had been stressful for her. He should have known it affected her more than she'd shown. Hell, despite all the times he'd tried to get her to open up about her parents, she hadn't really talked about them until tonight. She'd always stuck to the safe subjects—

her job, her relationship with her sister, or growing up as an Army brat. She would talk about those, no problem. However, when it came to the hard conversations? She would avoid talking about anything personal when it came to her parents. She'd especially avoided their death. She had a habit of burying her feelings far beneath her hard exterior.

He walked to the door and knocked. After a minute of waiting, he opened the door.

▭

EXHAUSTION OVERTOOK Allison as she tiptoed to the bathroom, but even fatigue couldn't quiet the disturbing thoughts running through her mind. The past twenty-four hours had been pure disaster from start to finish, and she was so tired. Besides the emotional rollercoaster of having Adam back in her life, her job and her safety were now in jeopardy.

The walls of the hotel room closed around her until the breath was being pressed from her body. She pulled at the suddenly too-tight collar of the T-shirt—she needed to get out. But where on earth could she go? She couldn't imagine ever feeling safe again.

Pulling the door shut behind her, she threw on the bathroom light and leaned against the counter. Wet, salty tears rolled down her cheek, and she swiped at them with the back of her hand and tried to breathe. When had she become such a cry baby?

Her stomach dropped as she thought about living

in the condo. She felt so violated, so devastated by the break-in. She loved the condo, but what would happen when she moved her life there? The thought that someone could so easily scavenge through her things—through her home—scared the hell out of her.

At some level, she had always wanted a home and family, but she had never felt the full weight of that desire until today. Having Adam around was wonderful, but it wasn't the same as having a man who loved her wrapping his strong, protective arms around her. She wanted requited love. She wanted someone to love her back.

Loneliness stirred within her. A sob overwhelmed her. She was so tired of facing all of life's ups and downs on her own. She wanted a friend and partner to share her struggles with.

She pulled a tissue from the box on the counter and dabbed at her eyes. Her head whipped around at the turn of the doorknob. Anger built in her chest, but she was too tired to act on it.

She looked up at Adam's concerned face where he lurked in the doorway. "Hi," she said, tossing the tissue in the trash and getting another.

"Hey. Can I come in?"

"Sure. Why not." She waved him in with one large animated gesture, the tissue waving in the breeze.

He closed the door and reclined against the other side of the counter. His hand reached out and slid over her cheek. She closed her eyes, the warmth of his touch sending tingles down her spine. "Are you okay?"

"Yeah. It's been a rough day."

"I'm here if you need me," he offered while he continued to stroke her cheek.

"I know." She attempted a smile as a tear slid past her eyelashes. She looked into his deep green eyes. "I just feel..." She paused and leaned into his warm, strong hand. She should pull away, but it felt so nice. "I don't know how I feel. I just...don't want to feel anymore."

Her eyes closed as his thumb wiped away the last tear. She turned toward him and inched along the counter, resting her damp cheek on his chest. The scent of him tickled her senses, scrambling her thoughts. She loved his scent. She loved the subtle hint of spiced lavender from his cologne.

She was tired of struggling, tired of fighting him. He wrapped his muscular arms around her waist, stroking her back. Oh, my. She gasped as his lips pressed to her forehead, her head swimming with the soft, loving gesture.

She tipped her head back, drinking in his chiseled features. He moved toward her and brushed his lips over hers. She moaned as the soft, gentle caressing shot straight through her body. Her hips swayed restlessly as he trailed his hands toward her face.

All the uncertainty, fear, and isolation disappeared as his hand cupped her chin.

Her mouth opened for him as he ran his tongue along the inside of her lip.

She could live without the love. This, she couldn't live without.

Him. She needed him. She needed to be kissed and

loved into oblivion. She needed to forget. So what that he didn't feel the same? It was pretend. For tonight. She would deal with the repercussions tomorrow.

She stepped back and grabbed his hand. "Let's go to bed."

CHAPTER TEN

ADAM FOLLOWED behind Allison as she slid onto the bed and reclined on her back. God, she was beautiful with her flushed cheeks, pink lips, and sparkling blue eyes. And she was all his. She grasped his hand and tugged till he fell toward her. He lowered himself until he was leaning on his elbow, inches from her face.

His breath hitched as he hungrily sealed his lips to hers. Her eager gasp wrapped around his gut. She wanted him. He could feel it as she arched her back toward him, pushing her body against his. Hands stroking. Hips rocking. He grew harder with every pulsating thrust.

Threading her fingers in his hair, she pulled him closer. His lips grazed her skin, hungrily tracing the soft curve of her neck. Her body tensed as she threw her head back, giving him an all-access pass.

A low groan escaped her throat as his hand found its way to the soft skin beneath her T-shirt. He loved that sound. He loved that he brought that groan out of her. It shot straight to his hips.

His hands found her chest. The nipples tightened with every stroke. He longed to taste her, to feel her. He pulled back and lifted the bottom of her shirt over her head and flung it onto the floor. He leaned down, enveloping her breast with his wet mouth. The taut, hard pebble contracted beneath his tongue, rolling between his teeth. With each flick of his tongue, her hips writhed, demanding more attention.

He pulled his lips back and made quick work of removing her sweatpants. God, she was hot, her skin beckoning to be touched while her eyes flashed with desire. Desire for him.

She leaned into him, her breasts rubbing against his chest. His mouth encased hers, lips surging toward her until she opened for him. He consumed her, tasting the spiciness of her tongue, the sweetness of her lips.

Allison teased her fingers under the waistband of his pants, and he pulled back from the soft, tantalizing feel of her hand. If she kept that up, he might explode long before the actual performance. She trailed her fingers up his abdomen and rubbed her nails over his chest. Nerve endings blazed.

"You're overdressed."

He drew back and stood at the end of the bed. Allison crawled toward him and placed her hands on his hips. She leisurely ran her hands down his thighs, pulling his pants to the floor. Slow and seductive.

"Perfect," she whispered as she inched back and widened her silky legs, inviting him inside of her.

Her eyes caressed his growing member. He cupped her ankle and trailed his soft lips up her leg. He stopped at her thigh, and he pressed her legs to drop farther, wider, with his coaxing tongue. Salty. Sweet. Hot. The taste of her enveloped him as his tongue caressed up to the triangle of her soft curls.

Allison gasped as he nuzzled her, urging her thighs open with an ardent lick. Her hips rose to meet him as he flicked her over-sensitive nub with his tongue. He wrapped his arms around her, grabbing her ass, lifting her hips higher, and angling her toward him. He placed a finger inside her as he licked the length of her lower lips. A gasp escaped her lips. "Take me now."

"Not yet," he groaned as he inserted a second finger. He drove it into her as he kissed and teased her thighs.

"Please, Adam," she begged.

Pleasure kept him from giving in to her demands as his mouth traveled toward his hand. Her pleasure. His pleasure. Both intertwined. He sucked and titillated her sensitive opening as his fingers continued to thrust in hard, brutal strokes.

Her hands wrapped around the bedsheets as she screamed his name. Her body twitched, her inner walls pulsating around his digits. He watched her ride the wave of orgasm. He extracted the manual massagers and lifted his head to look into her eyes. He rubbed the wet opening and said, "Don't go anywhere."

He tried to pull away, but Allison reached down and lifted his face toward hers. "Where are you going?"

"Patience," he scolded as he took her mouth with

his. Her insolent hips rose again in desperation. She was already willing to go again. A groan escaped him as he gently pushed her down on the bed. His hands pressed her arms to the mattress as he kissed her forehead.

"One second."

"Better make it a quick second, Mr. Byrnes. I'm not done with you yet." Adam stood, admiring the view as a pout flitted across Allison's face. "Are you trying to torture me?"

He stared at her extended bottom lip—big, round, and ridiculously sexy. He would love to take that lip in his mouth, run his tongue along the edge. He smiled as he remembered that he could. He just had to hurry up and head over to the bed. Torture her? With his daydreaming? He appeared to be torturing himself.

"Maybe a little." He smirked and reached for his wallet, pulling out a condom.

She gazed at the hard length of him as he rolled it on. "It's working," she breathed.

He moved toward her and positioned himself between her spread thighs. His erection throbbed as he took her lower, pouty lip into his mouth and nibbled. His member, large and swollen, found its way inside of her. Filling her. She moaned in appreciation.

She reached up and put her hand on his cheek. He kissed the palm as his heart burst from the look in her eyes. With every thrust, it was so much more than just sex. His heart was tied to every surge of her body. Her moans elicited pure joy from him.

He rhythmically drew in and out, intensifying the

pleasure. She shifted her hips, allowing him to push deeper and deeper inside of her. Her muscles tightened around him as she continued to let him ride her at his determined pace, and he felt as if he would burst at any moment.

Adam rocked back and forth, his resolve waning. Her body shuddered in release as her contracting walls massaged his engorged member to a staggering climax. Allison screamed in pleasure, nails digging into his back, her body bucking in satisfaction.

Bodies entwined, they both fell asleep, smiling in gratification.

▭

ALLISON WOKE before the sun had a chance to peek through the curtains, her body pleasingly sore. She lifted her head and peered over the man next to her, but the clock face was as elusive as her freedom. Adam's arm was draped over her stomach, hindering her view and keeping her pinned to the bed. She thought about moving his arm, but the last thing she needed was Adam awake.

She rested her head against the soft hotel pillows and closed her eyes. Images of last night floated across her eyelids. She had such a good time—amazing, actually. It was unfortunate it wouldn't happen again. If she'd learned anything about Adam over the years, it was that he didn't stick around.

They'd both gotten what they'd wanted. Now they could go back to the relationship they'd had before he came home for the funeral. Where he ignored her existence. It had been hard to concentrate with him around, anyway.

Allison's stomach pinched, and her heart grew heavy. She glanced over at his sleeping face. He looked so innocent, so full of promise. Maybe this time would be different. Maybe this time, he'd want all of her, not just her body.

After all, the past twenty-four hours had been a nightmare, and Adam had been so good to her. She didn't want to be ignored. She liked having him in her life. She liked his humor and affection. The mind-blowing sex didn't seem to hurt things either.

And that, my friends, is why I need to get as far away from this man as possible. Thoughts like that always led to her heart being obliterated. She needed to rely on her instincts—they'd served her well over the past few years. She trusted them. Adam, on the other hand, had proven himself to be untrustworthy, and she would not make that mistake again. As the saying went, "Fool me once, shame on you; fool me twice, shame on me."

The hardest part was that she did trust Adam. She trusted him with her life, just not with her heart. He wasn't the type of man who would stick around to love her. And no matter how many times she tried to deny it; she had some embedded defect that couldn't stop loving him.

She needed to squelch those feelings. And quick. She couldn't enjoy the memory of last night if she were mooning over the man in her dreams. Those dreams would serve to keep her warm when he was gone. And he would go. The women of Phoenix probably missed their good-looking police officer.

Allison wrapped her fingers around his wrist and lifted his arm, inching toward the side of the bed. Her eyes widened, and she stopped all movement as he mumbled. She cringed when he swung onto his back, but his eyes never opened. His arm moved to his side, releasing her from its clutches.

She jumped from the bed and lunged for yesterday's suit on the floor. Her head swiveled around. *Where in the hell are the rest of my clothes?*

She grabbed her purse and palmed her underwear. She skulked toward the bathroom, gently shutting the door before she flicked on the bathroom vanity light. The mirror conveyed a frightening picture—mascara smudges and Medusa hair. Thank God Adam hadn't seen her like this.

She washed her face and dug through her purse for a brush. She needed to get out of the hotel before Adam woke, but that didn't mean she wanted to do the full-fledged walk of shame back to her apartment. Heaven forbid someone she knew—heck, one of her employees —saw her escaping this debasing booty call looking like she was...well, escaping a booty call.

She ran the brush through her snarled hair and dug through her purse for something to tie it away from her face. A ponytail clip held her shoulder-length, dark-blond hair in place as she quickly dressed in her clothes from the day before. She opened the bathroom door and peered through the darkness at Adam's sleeping form.

Relief colored her face as his chest moved up and down in a rhythmic pattern.

The last thing she wanted to do was deal with the "morning after." She made a beeline for the door to the hall and twisted the handle. She kept an eye on Adam as the handle opened under her hand.

His breathing remained constant as she whipped open the door and entered the hallway, the door closing behind her. Shoes in hand, she made her way to the elevator and pushed the down button, and then leaned against the decorative table in the center of the hallway, slipping the shoes on her feet. The elevator opened, and she darted into the car.

The breath she didn't know she was holding whooshed out of her lungs as she descended toward the liberty of Michigan Avenue. She slid her sunglasses from the side pocket of her purse.

Shit. She exhaled as she placed the sunglasses over her eyes. She thought of the pile of paperwork sitting on her desk at the office, and the possibility of running into Adam. She had no desire to see him, but she had to get work done this weekend. She had no choice but to stop at the office before she headed home. Hopefully, if she were quick enough, no one would see her making a pit stop in the suit she wore the day before.

The elevator doors opened to the crystal chandeliers and dark wood of the lobby. She whisked past the ornate dark-blue and gold carpeting and draperies lining the floors and walls. The fresh flower bouquet offered a subtle fragrance as she quickly made her way to the stairs leading to the street. She opened the door and was stopped by a man in a long black coat, a whistle hanging around his neck. She swore the doorman stared accusingly at her, however, that might have been her own guilt coloring her interpretation.

"May I get you a taxi, miss?" he asked.

"Yes, thank you," she responded and jumped into the cab he hailed. She leaned her head against the seat as the taxi pulled out into the serene daybreak of Chicago.

ADAM OPENED his eyes to an empty bed. Again. Normally, that wouldn't have fazed him, but he was still upset that Allison had left without a word. Just two days ago, he'd woken up hoping to spend the entire weekend tangled in the sheets with her. Instead, he'd woken up alone.

If that wasn't pathetic enough, he'd spent the weekend planning ways to bump into her. He'd managed to find busywork at Byrnes and Company and spent most of the daylight hours in the office. He'd even faked memory loss on some of the processes so he could call her cell phone. Then again, he hadn't worked in his dad's office for over ten years, so there might not have been as much faking as he'd have liked.

He hadn't "accidentally" bumped into her, and she wouldn't answer her phone.

He lifted himself from the bed and made his way to

the shower. He ran through the events of Friday. Nothing explained her bolting out the door.

At first, he thought she might have had a meeting, but how many meetings occurred on Saturday morning? Anyway, one meeting wouldn't have stopped her from calling him all weekend. She obviously didn't want to talk to him. People that wanted to talk managed to find thirty seconds in their day to say, "Hey, I'm swamped, but that was some exceptional sex we had. Let's do it again. I'll call you as soon as I'm done."

He finished his morning regimen and drove through the bumper-to-bumper traffic, vacillating between hurt and anger. He wasn't sure why this weekend bothered him. There was really no reason for him to be angry. It's not like they owed each other any explanations. Hell, they weren't even dating. It was just one of those things that happened.

Like it happened before. The déjà vu was weighing on his mind. Except it was different, because she always meant too much to him. He couldn't seem to shake the ache in his gut that Friday meant nothing to her.

He slammed his hand on the steering wheel and looked out the passenger window. A small gray-haired woman stared at him out the window of her large car, her eyes wide with alarm. He gave his best calming smile and waved when she turned off onto the next block. Great. Now, he was scaring the elderly.

He shook his head. Why did he care that Allison left? He didn't regret his actions. He only regretted that their time together had come to an end. Even though they were thrown together by difficult circumstances, he still had a good time with her. He loved her laugh. He loved how she challenged him. He loved...spending time with her.

Love. Huh. He felt the thump of his heartbeat in his ear as a lump lodged in his throat. Just because he loved being with her didn't mean he was in love with her. They were almost like relatives...relatives that slept together? Damn. They were nothing like relatives, and what he felt was way past friendship.

Damn...damn. He did not need this. He lived on the other side of the country. Love had nothing to do with this situation. He only cared that she ran out because it would make for a difficult working relationship. He owned the company she would undoubtedly run when Dale grew tired of the nine-to-five grind.

"This is strictly a professional concern," he said with determination to no one in particular. Since he would be returning to Phoenix soon, he just needed to know that she could contact him if the need ever arose.

Sitting down and talking after work would probably be best. After all, they needed to keep their situation quiet. They needed to maintain a businesslike appearance when he left. Having others question their ethical standards at this juncture would not be helpful.

He pulled into the Byrnes and Company parking garage and made his way up the elevator. He started down the hall to his office but couldn't seem to stop himself from passing by Allison's. His anger grew as he paused at her door, finding her office silent and untouched.

"Good morning, Adam," Julie announced, and Adam jumped like a child caught stealing the last cookie.

"Hi, Julie. Have you seen Allison this morning?" he asked, trying to control his annoyance.

"She had an early meeting with Doug Kaminski. I don't expect her till after lunch." Julie eyed him. He swore he had a sign on his forehead: I HAD SEX WITH ALLISON. Her gaze pierced through him, seeing all his secrets.

"Ah. Well, then I'll discuss this matter with her later," he said in his best corporate voice. He could, technically, have an important business matter to discuss.

He shook his head, disgust and embarrassment tweaking his nerves as he shuffled to his temporary office. Why was he letting this woman get to him? He had more pressing things to worry about than where Allison was. It hadn't been determined if his father's death was from natural causes, and he still needed to get things squared away so he could go back home to Phoenix.

He missed Phoenix. He missed the control he had over his life there. Allison had always messed with that sense of organization. It had been one of the reasons he left Chicago. He needed to get out of this city as soon as possible, before he made any more mistakes.

The realization hit him like a ton of bricks. It had been a mistake. The regret he thought wasn't there lodged in his throat. He never should have slept with her; this whole thing was a colossal mistake. He skulked to his desk and leaned his head back onto his brown leather chair. He closed his eyes. No more distractions. No more mistakes.

Well, no more mistakes after he talked to Allison and found out why she ran away like a pack of wild chickens. It wasn't like this situation made her sky fall. He was the one left alone.

CHAPTER ELEVEN

ALLISON ATTEMPTED to give Doug Kaminski her best smile. The meeting wasn't going as planned. This was supposed to be a simple meeting where they both discussed the upcoming fiftieth-anniversary gift for his staff. Instead, as she pulled out the replica of the jewelry, the conversation had taken a disturbing turn.

"I just don't want to give you my order and find myself scrambling when you shut your doors." He lifted a glass of water to his lips. "I pride myself on the personal gifts I give my staff. I don't want to be stuck buying off the rack."

She would've laughed as he pursed his lips at the thought of "buying off the rack," but she was too busy freaking out at the lost account. Where was he getting his information? "I assure you, Doug, you will not be buying off the rack. We have your order on file, we have given you the design, and we will be creating these pieces to your specifications."

"I just don't know..."

"Look, Doug, you and Herb go way back. Hell, we've worked together for years. Have I ever steered you wrong?" Allison looked into his eyes as she tried to exude confidence with her rigid back and no-nonsense attitude. This was always where she shone.

"No, but..."

"Then give me the benefit of the doubt. I don't know where you heard Byrnes and Company was closing their doors, but I guarantee that is a rumor. We're taking orders into the end of next year. That is not a company that plans on shutting their doors. You have my word."

"Okay, Allison. I'm with you. But I do want to talk about the design again. Ben had a few ideas that I liked."

"Ben?"

"Yeah. I'm sorry." Red crept up Doug's neck. "Ben Mooring was the one who told me about the closing. I guess I should have considered the source."

Anger clawed at Allison's throat. That sonofa... She should have known that weasel would strike. She just never thought he'd strike while Herb's body was still warm.

"No problem." She kept her voice light and professional. Just because Ben was an unprofessional douchebag didn't mean she had to be.

"Don't worry about it, Doug." She reached across the table and patted his hand. "Herb was very fond of you. He loved working with you. His favorite jewelry design was the opal stars you designed together ten years ago for your fortieth anniversary."

"Those were classic." Doug's chest puffed with pride as he spun the current replica brooch in his hand.

"So, this year, we're creating a tie clip for the men, and a brooch for the women. The brooch will be gold, with a round, brilliant-cut diamond at the center of a four-leaf clover. Pear-shaped emeralds will surround the diamond, giving it the clover look."

"That will be perfect. Now, I'd also like to have a string of diamonds covering the stem."

"Exquisite." Allison nodded and wrote the new requirement on the order form. "But that could get costly."

"I trust you can come up with a plan to make sure I don't have to pay more than three hundred dollars per brooch. That is what Ben quoted." Doug smiled as he took another drink.

The anger spun around Allison's throat again. The stem would take at least one carat of diamond chips. They were looking at five hundred and fifty, minimum, to add the diamonds. Where was Ben getting three hundred dollars? She took a deep, calming breath and said. "Did he know the number of diamonds it would take to cover the stem?"

"Sure. He had an exact replica like you have here." He placed the brooch on the table and picked up his drink.

How the hell had Ben gotten a hold of the design for her client? The design was on file with Byrnes, and very few people had access.

Pain shot down the side of her head as she looked at the specifications for the stem. This would never work.

She couldn't just give diamonds away for free; that would destroy Byrnes and Company. How was she going to salvage this?

"If you cover the stem, it will mask the gold. What if we incorporate diamonds along the stem? That way, you're not taking away from the gold."

"Oh, yeah, I didn't notice that. I want to show off the gold. That would be better."

"Great. I'll get the jewelry artists to work on the new design."

She continued writing as she started talking about the diamond quality, cost, and the generous discount. After all, the customer was staying with Byrnes. With Ben sniffing around, she was going to do everything in her power to make sure it stayed that way.

Allison headed back to the office after the most unusual meeting she'd ever attended with Kaminski. Heck, it was the most unusual meeting she'd ever sat through—period. Thankfully, she was able to convince him to stay with Byrnes and Company, but the fact that she had to convince him at all left her fuming.

Ben Mooring had not only tried to take Kaminski's business away, but somehow he'd gotten his grubby little hands on the actual prototype of the brooch.

The conniving jackass. He'd always been a grade "A" jerk.

Fresh out of college, Ben had worked for Byrnes and Company for two years. In that time, he'd learned everything he could about the jewelry business, making contacts and befriending the corporate customers. Herb had been ecstatic. Ben had schmoozed the customers and got them to spend big money on their jewelry purchases. A television hostess bought diamond rings for all of her staff that Christmas, and a large international company gave their district managers a personalized money clip. Byrnes and Company basked in their success. When Ben had decided he wanted to branch out on his own, Herb tried to get him to stay, but ultimately he knew Ben's heart was somewhere else.

That was why Herb had given Ben the loan, start-up money to finance his own company. It had been a win-win. Herb got to help a man he was impressed with, and he wouldn't have Ben as competition. Their agreement was that Herb would fulfill the bigger orders —his facility was larger—and Ben would take over the smaller orders.

Things had been going well until Herb's sales staff started being told by some of their clients that their companies would no longer be doing business with Byrnes and Company. They'd decided to move over to Mooring Industries. Ben had over half of the Byrnes customers before Herb even knew what was happening.

It had taken Byrnes and Company months to solidify their relationships with their customers and devise a strategy to attract some of the deserters back into the fold. Herb had been more hurt than angry. He'd looked at Ben as a son, and the stab to the back was intensified by his trust and affection for him.

To add insult to injury, Ben had been trying to buy Byrnes and Company for the last few years. Herb had politely declined over and over again, but that never deterred Ben from trying.

This new tactic of telling their customers that the Byrnes brothers were selling the company was just low. She didn't quite know how to handle it. Did Ben know something she didn't? After all the years of service, she couldn't see that happening. Even if the Byrnes men wanted to sell, their mother would have stopped them from doing anything that reckless. At least that was the reasoning she'd decided to hang her hat on.

Ben was in uber-jackass mode these days. That piranha had always been out for Byrnes's clients, but now he had Byrnes and Company's intellectual property—the jewelry designs. She'd received three concerned voicemails this morning from clients telling her that Ben was hounding them for their business. She'd also received two calls that clients were leaving Byrnes and Company altogether.

Something fishy was happening, and she needed to figure it out before Ben put them out of business. The idea of a leak passed through her mind. Who would do such a thing, though? Adam? Dale? No. No matter what her feelings were when it came to the brothers, she knew neither one would stab their father in the back by cavorting with the likes of Ben Mooring.

Calmer thoughts overtook her, and she shook her head in disbelief. There must be another answer. Even that goofball, Dale, wouldn't sell out the old man like that. It wasn't in his nature.

And Adam? Just thinking of Adam put her back in The Mallord hotel's bed with Adam's mouth, hands and...*oh, my*... The heat crawled up her spine. She was getting hot just thinking about that man.

Not good. Definitely not good at all.

She made her way down bustling Michigan Avenue. She had to admit, the meeting with Kaminski was convenient. She didn't want it to look like she was avoiding Adam. She couldn't decide which problem she wanted to tackle first—confronting Ben or talking to Adam. Neither sounded appealing.

She didn't know what to expect from Adam. He was royalty. He was heir to the Byrnes throne. While she was just common, Replaceable. At least that was what Dale was trying to do and Adam hadn't stopped him.

So seeing Adam again—he might stumble over his words, embarrassed that he'd slept with a commoner; or he might just ignore her and the fact that anything ever happened.

She wasn't sure which would hurt more—well, probably the commoner scenario, but the other one pretty much sucked too. Tears stung the back of her eyes as anger nipped at her heels. Either way, she was a mistake that would need to be dealt with. She hated being a mistake. She hated being *his* mistake.

She slowed, shuffling her feet. Confronting him while she was so volatile was never a good thing. She needed to get her head back on track before she tackled the emotional roller coaster that was Adam Byrnes.

As she approached the Byrnes and Company building, she remembered her ailing car. The flat tire had yet to be fixed. She'd thought about coming by and dealing with it over the weekend, but didn't want to chance a meeting with Adam. Pathetic. She could practically hear women's-libbers all over the world screaming in her ear, "What kind of woman backs down from a fight?"

Apparently, her kind. Whatever that was.

She might be a woman, but she sure wasn't roaring. Nope. A-roaring she was not.

She dialed the number for the motor club before she lost the cell phone signal and headed to the garage to wait for the technician. It might not have been her proudest moment, but hiding in the garage with theoretical ghosts beat confronting an actual Adam any day.

CHAPTER TWELVE

ADAM WALKED into the Byrnes and Company building. If Allison wasn't going to answer his calls, he'd go to her. He rode the elevator up to the corporate office. Julie sat behind the desk to his father's office—well, where his father used to call his office.

"Good morning, Adam," Julie said from her desk behind the counter.

"What a surprise. I wasn't expecting you today." She smiled.

"I THOUGHT I'd see how things are running." There was no way he'd admit to anyone he came to see Allison. They'd take his man-card and roll over it with a Zamboni, then back up and do it again.

Of course, the light in her office appeared to be off. Which meant she wasn't here anyway. Dammit.

The elevator dinged, and Adam turned, hoping to see Allison. But the heavy footfalls and the fat head didn't belong to the woman who'd left him in his bed. "Dale."

"Hey, brother. What are you doing here?"

"Just saying hello."

Dale looked at him sideways, like he wanted to say something. But he shook his head and smiled at Julie instead. "Good morning, Julie."

"Good morning, Mr. Byrnes."

"How many times do I have to tell you, after all that we've been through, I think it's appropriate for you to call me Dale."

She slid behind her desk, red creeping up the pale skin of her neck. "Sure, Dale." She said the words, but the way she said them told Adam there was a story there. Probably a story he didn't want to hear. It was no secret Julie had always had a crush on Dale.

No one could say she had good taste.

And Dale was too stupid to notice a nice woman that was interested in him. Now, if she had double-Ds and the IQ of a fruit fly, he'd be all over her. Julie picked up a stack of notes lying on her desk and walked them over to Dale. "I have a few messages for you. Ben Mooring called a few times. Is everything okay?"

"Yes. Everything is fine. You know how persistent he can be." Discomfort oozed from his tone. His brother was hiding something.

Ben was a lot of things, the least annoying was persistent. But for some reason, his father loved that guy. Probably because Ben wanted to learn the business, where his own sons didn't.

Dale flipped through the notes in his hand, either

ignoring or not noticing the rosy glow splattered across her face. She obviously still had that crush. And he obviously still didn't care. "Thanks. Did Accounting send down a file for me?"

"Yes, I put it on your desk." Her attention turned to the elevator as it dinged. The two detectives walked toward her desk.

"Good afternoon." Unease slid over Julie's features. She must have seen the badges hanging at their sides, so why discomfort?

"Ms. Connolly. I am Detective Washington, and this is Detective Perretti. We're with the Chicago Police Department. We need a few minutes of your time today." Detective Washington pulled her CPD star from her waistband.

Julie's smile wavered, and if these cops were any good, they'd noticed.

"What is this concerning?" Dale turned around, his voice stern, almost protective.

"Dale Byrnes, right?" Detective Washington nodded at Dale. She turned to Adam. "Lieutenant Byrnes, we meet again."

Adam nodded. He knew how this looked, he was everywhere the cops were. It would look suspicious. But he didn't care, he had nothing to hide.

"We're investigating the break-in at Allison South-by's condo." The detective stowed her star back on her belt.

"You can't possibly think that Julie had anything to do with that?" he snipped.

"We just have a few questions," Detective Washington assured him. "Speaking of which, we need to set up a time to talk with you as well."

"Call me anytime." Dale handed her a card. "However, I have to say I'm uncomfortable with you coming here, without warning, bothering my employees during the middle of the day. I would think she deserves the respect of an appointment."

Detective Perretti's posture stiffened, and Detective Washington glared through squinted eyes.

"Dale, it's okay. They're just doing their job." Julie's voice came out small.

"I don't want you in there alone with them."

"Why? Do you have something to hide?"

"No. I don't trust cops." His gaze moved to Adam.

Of course, he didn't trust him. But when it came to Julie, Adam didn't blame him. She was a family friend. He wasn't about to leave her alone in this. "I can sit in with you, if you'd feel more comfortable."

The hopeful look on Julie's face was almost too much. "Since I don't have a lawyer, can he?"

"Fine. Just you." Detective Washington pointed at Adam. She then pointed at Dale. "You wait out here."

"We can get a little privacy if we go into the south conference room." Julie led them down a hall and to the executive conference room.

Detective Washington took the seat at the head of the white and black marble-topped table. The other detective walked to the corner of the room, where a ficus tree basked in the sun streaming from the floor to ceiling windows. Adam shut the conference room door and leaned against the wall.

"May I get you both something to drink?" Julie asked.

"No, thank you," they said in unison.

"I'm just going to grab a glass of water, if that's okay?" She tried to smile.

"Sure," Detective Washington answered and pulled out a pen and notebook.

Julie walked to the other side of the room to the small kitchenette. She got herself a glass and stuck it under the faucet, twisting on the water. A steady stream filled her cup as she closed her eyes and inhaled.

Adam split his attention from her to the cops. She was trying to hide it, but she was nervous. What he didn't know was why.

She shut off the water and went back to sit across from the officers. "Are you aware there was a break-in at the Braelind Towers penthouse?" Julie nodded her head.

"There didn't appear to be a forced entry, so it had to be someone with the passcode and a key. Who would have that type of information for the condo?"

"Um, I'm assuming Allison, and we have a set of keys here at the office."

"Who has access to the set here?"

"Well, I lock it in a drawer for safekeeping, but anyone could get in there if they wanted to. It's an easy lock to pick."

Adam tried not to roll his eyes. His father was too damn trusting. The man had grown up in the sticks of Chicago—over fifty miles away, where cows roamed farms, and acres of land was plowed by the local farmers. Herb was never one to take security to heart, and it might have cost him.

"Why were you at Allison Southby's condo the night of the break-in? And before you deny anything, we saw the security tapes from that night."

Adam tried not to move, but he hadn't been aware Julie had been at the condo. He wanted to start asking his own questions. But this wasn't his ballgame. He had to sit quiet, or they'd kick him out. And he needed to know the answers.

"I just stopped by to pick up some of my clothes. I lived at the condo for about a year."

"When did you live in the condo?" The detective's pen flew over the page.

"Last year. I just recently moved out."

"That's rather unusual for a boss to allow an employee to live in their home. He was still using the condo, correct?"

"Sometimes. I'm sure you've seen the place. It's huge. Cody and I didn't take up much space. We had the room closest to the kitchen."

"Cody is your son?"

"Yes," she whispered.

"Both you and your son stayed at the condo?" Washington asked. Julie nodded. "What was the nature of your relationship with Herb Byrnes?"

"What do you mean?" Julie genuinely looked confused by the question. And although Adam knew why they were asking it, he wasn't all too thrilled with the implication.

"Well, he was in the city away from his wife..." the

detective started. "He was staying in the same home. You were there, alone. You're a woman. He was a man. Things happen."

Just the thought made Adam's stomach heave. It was one thing running these interrogations with strangers. It was a whole other thing when it was people you loved.

"What are you implying? I was his secretary, nothing more." Her tone hardened as tears streamed down her face. She didn't appear to like the direction this conversation was taking any more than he did. She pulled a tissue from the box on the center to the table.

"Why did you move into the condo? What happened to your previous residence?"

"I j-just..." she stuttered. "I just needed my own space."

"In Lincoln Park, right? That's a pretty upscale neighborhood. Why would you leave?" If Detective Washington knew anything about her father, she wouldn't have to ask the question. The guy was a nightmare to those he wasn't related to, he could only imagine how he treated his daughter. And from what Adam's mother had said, Adam's imagination couldn't do it justice.

"I was tired of living with my father and there was an excellent au pair who watched Cody. It was easier to get to her condo from the city."

"Yet you came back. Why?"

Julie shuffled the tissue between her fingers. Which was never good. Especially since up till now the answers had been flying fast and furious. Now, all of a sudden, she needed time to think. That was never a good sign.

As Adam waited for anything to spill from Julie's lips, the door whipped open, and Edward stormed into the room.

"What are you doing here?" Julie asked as she slumped in the chair. That her father had that effect on her was just sad. And the fact that Edward reveled in it was just evil.

"Dale had the good sense to call me." He spun toward Adam. "How could you let this happen?"

Adam's back straightened, and he thought of all the things he'd tell the arrogant Edward Connolly. But then Edward's attention was drawn to the police and Adam was forgotten.

"What is this about? Why didn't you contact me? My own daughter doesn't have the sense to wait for counsel."

"They just had a few questions..." She trembled.

"Are you arresting her?" Edward's face was turned away, but Adam heard the tone.

"Not yet. She's been very cooperative, Mr. Connolly."

"They have me on tape entering the condo the night of the reported break-in," Julie said.

"So, you entered the condo. That doesn't mean anything. It's circumstantial at best," he scoffed.

"We are just trying to establish a timeline to determine what happened," Shay assured him and attempted a different line of questioning. "Julie, you went to the condo to pick up your clothes. Was the home ransacked at that point?"

"I'm not sure. I went straight to my bedroom, grabbed the last of my items, and left." Julie couldn't seem to look Shay in the eyes.

"So when we get the fingerprint evidence back, we won't find your fingerprints anywhere else in the condo?" Joe asked.

"That's ridiculous. She lived there for about a year. Of course, she was in other rooms throughout the house. How do we know that it was ransacked after Mr. Byrnes' death? Perhaps he did it himself."

Shay nodded but didn't respond. Anything she'd say would be used against her. Smart. Which was probably why the tone of the interview changed with the addition of dear old Dad. "Julie, before the night of the break-in, when was the last time you were in the condo?"

"About two weeks ago."

"Was anything out of place at that time?"

"It might have been, I don't remember." Julie sniffled, and her father threw a glare her way. Not at the cops—although he'd thrown plenty their way too.

"Are we about done? My daughter is exhausted."

"Almost. Julie, where were you the day of Herb Byrnes's death?"

"I thought Herb's death was accidental? Are you saying my daughter caused a man to have a heart attack?"

"I'm not saying anything like that, Mr. Connolly.

This is standard procedure for a high-profile death where the family has requested an investigation."

"I don't mind answering," Julie put in, not looking at her father. "My son had a field trip to the Morton Arboretum. I was with the children until four o'clock. Then I brought Cody to the sitter and went out to dinner with a friend. I didn't get home until after eleven."

"Wow. That must be some friend to be out that late. What is the friend's name?" Shay asked.

"J-just a friend I know," she stammered.

"Well, I'll need to contact this friend to validate your alibi. So I will need their name."

Julie sighed and shifted a glance from Shay to her father.

"Oh, for God's sake, she was with Allison that night. They were shopping at the mall by our house," Edward growled.

A brief flinch glided across Julie's face when Edward spoke.

"So, Julie, when I call Allison, she'll corroborate your story? She'll tell me about the wonderful evening you two spent shopping in the suburbs the night of Herb's death."

"Well." Julie stared at her hands on the table. Her shoulders slumped further as she continued. "I wasn't out with Allison, it was a different friend. You don't know her."

"Who was it?" Edward had that glare down again.

"I'll give you the number." Julie's eyes pleaded with

Shay. Whoever the friend was, she didn't want her dad knowing who it was.

"How about you, Mr. Connolly? Where were you the day of Herb's death?"

"Who is this friend?" Like Edward would ever let it go.

"I'm sorry, but we've moved on." Shay smiled. "Where were you the day of Herb's death?"

"I was working all day, and then I was with my friend, Bettina Wilcox." He sighed. "This line of questioning is absurd. If you're looking for someone who had an ax to grind with Herb, try his son."

"Why do you say that?" Adam didn't realize he'd said the words until everyone was watching him. It was hard enough watching this devil of a man talk crap about his own daughter. But Adam couldn't stand anyone talking about his brother. That was his job.

Edward glared at Adam but then turned to the cops. His tone softened. "Herb was a good friend. He mentioned that Dale asked him for a hundred thousand dollars for gambling debts or some such nonsense. Herb told him no. He felt torn because he wanted to give him the money, but he was afraid Dale would never learn if he continually bailed him out. It was such a hard decision for Herb. I would hate to think that it might have cost him his life."

CHAPTER THIRTEEN

ADAM WALKED out of the conference room. They'd been in that room for thirty minutes, but it felt like thirty days. The anger pulsed down his neck. He knew Dale was trouble, but he asked their father for money. It probably wasn't the first time. And if their father were still alive, it wouldn't have been the last.

Edward's implication that Dale somehow had something to do with their father's death rubbed Adam's nerves raw.

He walked past Julie's desk, into his father's office. No Dale. He would ask Julie where he was, but she was in the conference room with him, she wouldn't know where his brother is.

"He's probably out to lunch." Julie stood in the doorway. Her normally pale skin was just a smidge paler. That thirty minutes had an effect on her as well.

"Where'd he go?"

"No clue." She shook her head, sadness ringed her eyes. "He never tells me where or with whom."

"You know you could do better." Adam hated watching the sadness grow deeper. "My brother isn't worth it."

"I know." She stepped out of the room and went to her desk. Apparently, she didn't want to talk about his brother any more than he did.

"Where's your dad?"

Julie dropped to her chair behind the desk. "Another man who I have no idea where he is."

Speaking of not knowing where someone was. "Any idea when Allison will be back?"

Julie attempted a smile, and it wasn't as fake as all the other ones she'd thrown today. "That is one person who actually shares her schedule with me." She clicked on her mouse and stared at the screen. "She had a meeting this morning and then a lunch with a client. She should be back here in a half-hour."

A half-hour. He could wait, or he could run and get lunch, hoping she didn't disappear when she found out he was looking for her. Hell, either way, she'd probably try to disappear.

At least if he stayed, she'd have a harder time dodging him. And honestly, he wasn't all that hungry. Not with the crap about his brother lingering in his head.

━━

ALLISON WALKED down the hall to her office, perplexed. Her car was fixed, but the mechanic concluded that her tire was punctured from unnatural causes. Unnatural causes? The slash was too large to be a simple nail and too perfect to be from roadside debris. The final conclusion was that it was an act of willful vandalism. If it wasn't for all the drama of late, she might not have believed that willful vandalism happened outside of the Hollywood silver screen. But now, nothing was outside the realm of possibility.

She sat in her office chair and leaned back, her eyes closing in defeat. What had become of her life? Things had gotten so crazy. Burglaries and car vandalism? These were not part of a normal person's daily life. When had her life veered so far off course?

She stood up and went to stare out the window. She normally loved the view from her office. Watching people from high atop her perch allowed her to step back and enjoy the hum of the city.

Today, however, she saw right through the city, not really seeing anything. Her mind was too cluttered with misdemeanors and corporate espionage to notice anything else. The only common denominator in all of this was her.

Were these things directed at her? Why?

She was a no one. And now that she wasn't taking over Byrnes and Company, there was no reason for someone to come after her at all. It just didn't make any sense.

Allison jumped when the phone on her desk sang its piercing jingle. She looked at the caller ID. Brook's number popped across the little screen.

She ignored the phone and returned to the view from the window, making a mental note to call her sister later. From the short conversation they'd had over the weekend, Brook had spent the entire two days in bed with some lawyer from her firm. And although Allison would love to hear about her sister's latest conquest, now was not the time. She needed to sort out everything that was happening around her.

Who would come after her? Why? Were they after her, or was this all a coincidence? What were they after, if not her? The questions came fast and furious, each one unanswerable on their own. She was missing some important piece of information. If she had any clue where to begin to find it, she would.

Her thoughts were interrupted by a loud, "Ahem."

She whipped around to find Adam leaning against the doorframe. Her breath faltered—in disappointment. Yeah, right. Disappointment. She couldn't even fool herself on that one.

Her eyes stared, unblinking, at Adam's crossed arms. The muscles bulged through his blue cotton dress shirt. She remembered those muscles, those arms that held her tight while he delighted all of her senses. Just the thought of that night made her mouth run drier than ice at a rock concert.

Adam smirked. "My eyes are up here."

Shit. He'd caught her gawking again. What was wrong with her eyes that they wouldn't stop caressing his body? Bad eyes. Obviously, they were insubordinate. She hadn't moved her eyes or her thoughts from his arms, chest, or thighs. She really liked looking him up and down and back again. Her cheeks blazed from embarrassment and need.

She yanked her lecherous gaze down to her desk. She'd had this meeting all planned out, all morning to prepare how this encounter would go. But now that they stood in the same room, she was lost. Lost in those nimble fingers—clever mouth— Enough!

Focus. She had a plan. Focus. How was she handling Adam? Oh, yeah. Deflect. If they had work to talk about, they couldn't talk about the other night. She knew it was a mistake, but she had no desire to hear how he thought it was a mistake.

"I actually wanted to talk to you. We have a problem. Ben Mooring has somehow gotten ahold of our customer's jewelry designs. He's going all over town attempting to steal our customers by underbidding us. Unfortunately, he's gotten to a few of them already. Beaker Industries and Statler have moved their business to Ben. These two were small accounts, but we need to make sure we don't lose any more."

"So there might be a leak?" Adam's eyes darkened in concern. He didn't seem to like what the situation implied, either. The Byrnes' employees were like a family. To think that any one of them would give information to Ben was heartbreaking.

"Yes." She sighed.

"Well, we should be on the lookout. No one is to be trusted until we figure out where this starts." His brows drew together. "Not even my brother."

"Okay." She didn't know where they brother thing came from, but she didn't trust him anyway, so that was never an issue. She sat in her chair, her feet sighing as her heels accidentally slid to the floor.

Adam stared at her, his eyes burrowing through to her soul. She focused on her desk and rearranged the papers and folders, anything to keep her eyes from dry humping him. Why couldn't she just look at him like a normal person? What was wrong with her?

"Nice job distracting me from the real problem."

"The real problem? I didn't know there was another problem." She leaned back. If he wasn't going to leave, she would play his game until he did.

"Yeah, you seemed to be enjoying the view." He smiled as he shut the office door. She couldn't decide if that was a good thing or a bad thing. Somehow, she felt like an innocent maiden, trapped in the room with the big bad wolf. The only difference, she wanted him to eat her—ugh.

"I didn't realize that was a problem." For him, anyway. For her, it was more a nightmare than a problem. "Did you actually want something, or did you just want to flaunt that body you like so much?"

"I came to see why my bed was empty Saturday morning. You wouldn't happen to know why, would you?"

"Look, Adam," she said and threw her shoulders back. "We seem to make this mistake every few years. I get it. I just figured I'd run out the door before you did. After all, it wouldn't be fair to make you run from your own room again."

"Who says I'm running? That was you sprinting out the door." He actually seemed angry. Angry. What did he have to be angry about? This was, after all, their way. One night of great sex and then abandonment in the morning. Hell, the only difference between this time and last was that he was a lot easier to track down.

But this time was different. She walked away, not him. That was probably killing him. It was some sort of macho-penis thing. Some ingrained Neanderthal belief that men left women, but women couldn't leave men. His poor, fragile male ego must have taken a hit when she didn't worship beside his post-coital bed.

Of course, she might be a bit bitter.

"Anyway, what exactly do you get?" he added.

"I get what this is," she spit out as she pointed between the two of them. Anger found its way beneath her skin as her voice raised an octave. Control. She needed to control the noise, the words, before they had witnesses to their ill-begotten love life.

"It's okay. Now we can go back to normal," she said in a quieter tone.

"Great. You can explain to me what this is and what exactly is back to normal." He sat on the couch across the room. He placed his ankle on his opposite knee and folded his hands in mock anticipation.

Arrogant ass.

What started as adulation for his body had morphed into contempt. She stared, the fury building within her veins. Her blood simmered. She didn't need his crap right now. She didn't necessarily want to fight; he was technically her boss. However, she was sick of... well...of him.

"Look, Adam. Let's just take this for what it is. We had fun. Now we can go back to being just coworkers."

"When have we ever been just coworkers?"

"Fine. We aren't really coworkers. We can go back to my being the employee and you being the big, bad company owner." Frustration tickled her temples. Adam seemed to incite headaches. Wherever he went, temple pain surely followed.

"That's not what I meant."

"Then what do you mean, Adam? Please, explain it to me." She slapped her hands against the desk. All that frustration bubbled to surface. She was so done with this... With him. "Please explain why you ignored me for all these years. Well, except for that one night. Another one of my proud moments, thank you very much, thinking you wanted more than a lay. But what happened the next day? You were gone. No phone call to say 'hi,' not even a 'screw you.' Nothing. So, what is it that you want from me now?"

The stricken look spreading across his face took her by surprise. Guilt almost crept through her. That may have been a bit harsh, but she'd earned the right to say it. It felt so good to say too. How long had she held that in?

She started to wonder if there was anything else she was holding in...the euphoria from letting it go might be worth the fight. Hell, she was even looking forward to fighting with him. It had been a long time coming.

"You're right."

"About what, pray tell, am I right?" She dropped her head back, energy spent.

Why were conversations with Adam so exhausting?

"Most of it. However, I did not ignore you. You were at the center of every thought." He rose to his feet.

"You have a funny way of showing that." She rested her elbows on the desk and raised her hands to her temples, trying to knead away the vise that was clamped around her head. She hated that she let him get to her like this. He just had a way of pressing the right buttons to drive her insane.

Her eyes slowly rose and caught Adam's stare. She waited for his argument. She waited for him to tell her she was wrong. But no words came. He just stared and stared.

"What?" she whispered.

"I'm sorry. I was young and incredibly stupid. And I knew that if I stayed with you that morning, I'd never leave." He inched his way toward her. "But do you really want to be just coworkers? I know I won't be here for much longer..."

He spun her chair so she was facing him. He boxed her in, his right hand resting on the chair and his left hand on the desk. She leaned back as he leaned forward. Distance. She needed distance. She twisted her head to the side and pushed farther into the chair. His breath brushed her cheek. Minty coolness mixed with spiced lavender overwhelmed her senses as he tilted closer.

Not far enough. Pain squeezed her heart. On one hand, she wanted him more than her next breath. On the other hand, he already said he wouldn't be here for much longer. Could she just let him walk away? Walk away without getting hurt?

His scent wrapped around her lungs as he skimmed her lips with his. The soft, gentle touch wound its way through her body. Dammit. She was already too invested. He had her heart in the palm of his hand. If she let herself hope, let herself care about him, he would undoubtedly hurt her again.

"But I don't want to stop what we have, no matter how temporary it may be."

Allison's body felt the gravitational pull of Adam deep in her hips. No matter what logic her mind threw out, her body had a very different idea. Heat pooled between her thighs as want coursed through her veins.

No, she didn't want this feeling to end.

"I don't either," she whispered and met his intense stare. He inclined toward her, and his tongue slowly traced the curve of her neck. Her heart pounded in her ears, drowning out her headache and any last remaining rational thought.

"Unfortunately, we do need to pause," he said as he nibbled her ear. "I have to be somewhere. Go with me to the Flurries game tonight."

He slowly pulled her to her feet and placed his lips on hers. A jolt passed through her as he drew her closer. Her body ached in need, every part screaming for more.

"Huh?" she murmured when his lips traveled to her ear.

He pulled his face away as his hand moved down the arc of her waist. "Are you going with me?"

"Yes." She threw her head back and sighed. She wasn't sure what she just agreed to, but she didn't care if it would keep his mouth and hands navigating her body.

"I'll pick you up at five thirty," he said and cupped her face, pressing his lips to hers. He groaned, pulling away, and took her arms. He moved her a foot away. "Now, you need to get home and get ready, or we'll be late."

She stared at him, lost. Late? Where were they going? What did she agree to?

She was finally able to formulate a lucid thought. "What just happened?" she asked.

"You just agreed to right an egregious wrong. You're going with me to the Flurries game tonight."

"I am? Why don't we just stay in?" She bit her bottom lip and reached for his shirt. He grabbed her arms again and placed them at her side. He pressed a soft kiss to the tip of her nose.

"Although I am totally on board with your plans for the evening, they're honoring my father tonight. I have to go to the game, and I thought you might want to come."

"I've never been," she said.

"I know. That's insane. You can't call yourself a Chicagoan if you've never been to a Flurries game." He smiled as her lip curled into a snarl. She didn't want to watch a bunch of barbarians skate across the ice. What was that saying? *I once went to a hockey game, and a boxing match broke out.* There were a million things she'd rather do than watch testosterone-driven thugs skate around the ice.

"I'd really like for you to be there, and I know it would have meant a lot to my father."

The candid look he gave her and the pleading in his

eyes broke down every defense and quieted every argument. She might regret this later, but for now, she hated disappointing that sweet face.

"Using your father to get to me, Lieutenant Byrnes?"

"Maybe. Did it work, Ms. Southby?"

"Maybe. What should I wear?"

"Jeans and a black T-shirt."

"Are you sure?" She knew this wasn't a fancy outing, but jeans and a tee? That seemed a bit understated for an outing with the public.

"And wear gym shoes."

"Really?"

"Trust me." He kissed her on the lips before disappearing from her office.

CHAPTER FOURTEEN

ALLISON SAT FORWARD in the bucket seats of the limo as she listened to Loraine talk about the animals currently under her ward. The devotion and love in her voice filled Allison with joy. She worried about Loraine, all alone after all these years. Although Dale and Nadia were living at the house, Allison knew they were no replacement for the love of her life. It was nice to see her still so passionate about something.

"My neighbor, John Schatz, stopped by a week ago with a stray dog he found on the side of the road. I decided to name him Schatzi. He had been well-fed, but he had a broken leg—his owners probably couldn't afford the vet costs associated with such a sick animal." A tear glistened in her eyes. "It must be hard to make that sort of decision, but I still don't understand how people can just drop them in the middle of the road. Herb would get so mad when he'd heard stories like that."

A sad smile crossed her lips. "That's probably why

I fell in love with him." Loraine dabbed her eyes with a tissue from her pocket.

"Are you okay?" Allison asked.

"Fine, dear. I just get a little weepy now and again, but I'm fine." Her eyes dried as she continued. "I just take it one day at a time. He would have wanted it that way."

Adam leaned over and placed his hand on hers. She drew the hand to her heart. "Mom, he would want you to be happy."

"I am happy, dear. I have my boys and girls to keep me on my toes. I also have the refuge. I am a very lucky woman." Loraine wrapped her other warm hand around Allison's and squeezed. "Speaking of girls, where is Brook tonight?"

"She has some big case she's been working on. They've been working nonstop for over a week. I can only imagine how exhausted she must be with all the hours she's put in."

"That girl needs to stop working so hard."

"I tried to tell her."

"Maybe I should talk to her. Then again, I try to tell you the same thing, and you don't listen to me either."

Guilt. The woman was a master of guilt.

"So, anyway, I can't stay tonight. Shortly after the ceremony, I'm heading back to care for Schatzi. He doesn't like being alone. I'll send the car back to pick you up."

"Mom, you didn't have to come tonight. We could have handled this," Adam said.

Allison's chest filled with emotion watching him

interact with his mother. He was so much like his parents, with his attentive nature and kind heart. That heart was the reason Allison found it impossible to stop the train wreck of feelings that always ran her down when he was around.

"I know you can, honey, but I'll mingle with the philanthropic crowd a bit, and then I'll head back to the barn. After all, if I want this refuge to grow, I'll need capital. It's important to keep these contacts."

Allison loved Loraine's large, giving heart. Despite the sadness darkening her eyes, her focus remained on the welfare of the orphaned animals. She always put others first, which was why it was so hard to watch her suffer through such loss.

The three sat in silence as they rode the last few blocks. Loraine opened her compact and fixed her makeup. Allison smiled at her basic outfit. They looked like twins in their black jeans and black T-shirts. It seemed a bit simple, but Adam swore that it would be perfect for a group outing watching hockey.

The limousine stopped at the large gray-brick coliseum. They pulled up to the private suite entrance and stepped out toward the Dietrich Arena.

They entered the exclusive entrance and rode the elevators to the penthouse suites. Allison wasn't sure what she expected, but the dapper hallways and sports memorabilia hanging along the walls were the perfect décor. The simple silver frames surrounding the iconic pictures enhanced the masculine vibe. The dark gray carpet and black leather chairs screamed ultimate man cave.

They made their way down the hall and located the Byrnes and Company suite. She entered the large room and walked across the light gray carpet, past the dark gray leather recliners facing a large flat-screen TV. A wet bar lined the back wall by the hallway door. She headed to the front of the room, where a huge opening led to fourteen plush stadium seats, overlooking the vast expanse of the Center.

She walked down the steps to the glass railing in front of the first row of stadium chairs. The cool, crisp air mixed with the smell of pizza and beer hit her as she leaned over the rail. The stands below were slowly filling with energized spectators.

Her family had never been into sports—playing or watching. Well, except for the ballet classes and gymnastics classes her mother forced her and Brook to take as children. Her parents never missed a chance to see their daughters twirl. But otherwise, sports weren't high on their list of priorities. It might have been due to their nomadic nature that they never had a team that was theirs, and therefore couldn't get into the competition. Who knew? All Allison knew was that she was a Chicagoan now, so this was her team. She was going to attempt to enjoy the game if it killed her. Or she had to be drunk to do it.

She jumped as small arms wrapped around her right leg. She looked down into two gorgeous green eyes. "Hey, small fry."

Julie's son, Cody, smiled a heartwarming grin up at her. "I not small, Auntie Al'son," Cody remarked. "I a growed up."

"That's too bad. I have a really cool toy in my purse for a three-year-old kid. Do you know any three-year-old kids that need a new toy, Mr. Grownup?" Allison pulled off his ball cap and tousled his blond hair.

"I need a new toy." Cody jumped up and down.

"Yeah, but this toy is for kids, not grownups."

"Oh." His face fell. Allison almost gave in, but instead, she held out while he tilted his head in thought.

"Well, I'n a kid. I only a growed up sontimes."

Allison smiled and reached in her purse for the action figure she'd picked up for Cody.

His eyes sparkled, and his mouth twisted into a grin as he took his new toy. "Tank you, Auntie Al'son. You is da best."

"I might have heard that somewhere. So, are you a kid again?" Allison smiled as Cody bobbed his head up and down.

"He's a kid, all right. I don't think grownups get in trouble for pouring glitter on Sandy Spencer." Julie lifted him in her arms and nuzzled his chin. "Now, go say hello to Aunt Loraine. She wants to see your cool new Flurries jersey."

"That is a nice jersey you got there." Allison grabbed the bottom of the tiny replica shirt.

"I got it from Mommy." His chest expanded as he ducked his chin to stare at the Flurries logo—a whirling tornado of snowflakes—on the front of his jersey.

Julie eased him down until his feet hit the floor, patting his butt as he ran back into the room, his new action figure's arm dragging along the floor. "No running, Cody! Please behave." She sighed as she straightened up.

"You okay?" Allison asked.

"Yeah. Sometimes it's hard being a single mom." Julie's eyes narrowed as she watched Cody run across the room again. "Cody."

The towheaded boy turned his chubby cheeks toward his mother. His little green eyes narrowed to match his mother's. "I'n being have, Mom."

Julie smiled and shook her head. "Please try to behave better. No running."

"Otay, Mommy." His little lips curled up into a heart-stopping smile.

"He's going to be breaking hearts and causing trouble before you know it." Allison nudged Julie.

"Don't remind me. I'm choosing to ignore that inevitable part of my future."

"I know this is a taboo subject, but does Cody's father live in the area? Maybe he could start helping out. If not willingly, you do have a lawyer for a father."

"Not necessary. I'll be fine," Julie said, and then changed the subject. "It looks like there's going to be a full house tonight."

Allison wasn't too surprised her friend dodged the question. The women had talked about love, fears, and sex. She knew everything about Julie, but Cody's father was forever and always off-limits.

She glanced back at the guests wandering into the suite. Apparently, the room had filled as she was gawking at the venue. Edward, Adam, and other guests were standing around talking business, and the odds of a Flurries Winner's Cup run.

"I'm actually surprised to see you here. How did they talk you into coming to the game?" Julie teased.

"They used guilt." She wasn't about to tell Julie who used said guilt. She knew she needed to tell Julie about Adam, but she wasn't ready yet. She didn't need another lecture about the idiocy of getting involved with him. Not yet. She was already getting that particular lecture series, hourly, from herself. "I'm here for Herb."

"You don't sound so thrilled."

"I just don't know anything about hockey. I mean, I've got a few things down, but not enough to sit through... How long are these things anyway?"

"There are three periods. Each one is twenty minutes."

"Oh, so a game only takes an hour?" Allison's mood was brightening. She thought for sure she would be here all night. An hour. What was one hour in the grand scheme of things? Nothing.

"Well, there are intermissions, and they stop the clock for penalties and time-outs. So it's more like two and a half to three hours."

"Oh," she snarled just as Adam walked over with drinks. He handed a glass of wine to Julie and a mug of tea to Allison. Allison stared at the drink, confused. Last time she checked, she was old enough to partake in a glass of wine. "Tea?"

Adam smiled. "Yes, since we'll be heading down to the ice shortly for the ceremony, I thought you'd like to be sober. You know, not trip and fall on the ice." Allison lifted the mug to her lips. She might find it amusing if Adam fell on the ice, but she probably shouldn't share that with him. She figured drinking would keep her snide comments at bay. After all, she didn't want anyone seeing him get to her. Fighting with Adam tended to be an aphrodisiac. Nobody needed to see that.

"Hey, I forgot to ask, how did the car trouble work out?" Julie took a sip from the glass in her hands.

"Good thanks to you. That motor club you set me up with was a lifesaver." Allison hadn't mentioned the technician's tire theory, but with Adam being a cop, it might not be a bad idea. "When the guy came by to fix it, he mentioned it looked like someone tampered with the tire."

"Tampered?" Adam's face hardened, and his spine stiffened.

"He called it 'willful vandalism.' He said it looked like the hole was made with a sharp instrument. Some sort of blade, knife, or screwdriver."

"Why didn't you tell me that?" He sounded a little angry, but it wasn't like she was hiding anything. Their last conversation didn't leave room for the required car-tampering discussion, what with all the flirting and relationship talk.

"I haven't really had an opportunity," Allison snapped back at him and then smiled at Julie. It was all good. Status quo. *See, I'm smiling—* And back to the whole fighting/aphrodisiac thing. What she didn't need was for Julie to figure out what was going on between her and Adam. Thankfully, Julie was staring at Cody, a look of concern and guilt on her face.

"Who could have done that?" Julie asked.

"I don't know." Allison shrugged.

"Disgruntled employee, dissatisfied customer, ex-boyfriend..." Adam almost seemed jealous when he gave the last suggestion. It might have been wishful thinking on her part. She tended to see things with "wishful" glasses when dealing with Adam Byrnes.

"No...I've thought about it, and I can't think of anyone."

Loraine walked down the steps, brow furrowed, concern clouding her face. "Have you seen your brother?"

"No," Adam said. "I'll call him. Excuse me."

Adam walked toward the door of the suite. He turned to Allison and mouthed the words, "We're not done here," as he yanked his phone from his jeans pocket. Adam calling his brother while mad, that was one more thing no one needed to see.

ADAM WALKED into a small seating area just off the hallway and dialed Dale's cell number. He'd tried calling him all day. He wanted to talk, which meant his brother was M.I.A. After three calls and a message, he gave up. Typical. Heaven forbid Dale was on time for anything. He sighed as the suite hostess walked up with a white plastic bag.

"You asked for two home jerseys, Mr. Byrnes."

"Thank you. Just put it on our account." He smiled and took the bag. He glanced at his phone. No one had called. Not that he thought Dale would call in the ten seconds since he last phoned, but he hoped. Dale's absence would upset his mom, and she was already emotionally high-strung.

He walked into the suite and found his mom and Allison standing where he left them. This shit with Allison's car had him thrown. When it was a simple break-in at the condo, he could chalk it up to his father's dealings. But now that someone took a shot at Allison—he didn't want to think about what might have happened. There was no way he was letting her out of his sight.

"Ladies, I have the shirts you need to wear during the ceremony." He handed one of the jerseys to his mom and the other to Allison.

"Um..." Allison stammered. "What is this for?"

"When we go on the ice and accept the award, we should be wearing blue and silver."

"I thought you were joking. I'm not going out there. That's a family moment," she argued.

"How silly," Loraine said, pulling the oversized jersey over her head. "You're family. We're all going together. It's a shame Brook couldn't make it."

She straightened the jersey. "What about your brother? Is he here yet?"

"No." Adam watched the Zamboni make short work of smoothing the ice. He made a conscious effort not to watch Allison as she put the jersey over her black T-shirt. There was nothing sexier than a woman in sports gear. Well, getting them out of said sports gear, maybe. Thinking about her seemed like a lot more fun than thinking about his deadbeat brother. Just when he thought his brother couldn't piss him off any more, he did.

"Well," Allison sighed. "Hopefully, he'll get here soon. The match should start soon, right?"

"The—" Julie shook her head at Allison, smirking. "The puck will drop in a half hour or so." She snorted when Allison frowned. "It's a hockey thing."

A woman in a navy dress suit knocked on the suite door. "Mr. Byrnes? I'm Megan South, the Event Coordinator." The woman walked over to Adam and shook his hand.

"Is it time to head downstairs?"

"In a few minutes, we'll escort you to the ice. Now, who will be going down with us?" Megan followed Adam's gestures as he introduced the group.

"My mother, Allison Southby, my brother, and myself were going to head down. So, we're looking at potentially four adults."

"I want to see da ice," Cody said, moving toward Julie. Adam smiled at the boy. He remembered the first time he was on the ice at a Flurries game. It was amazing. His father had designed the championship ring for the 1985 Flurries, and after that, he became a staple within the Flurries organization. Herb brought his sons to one of the division championship games when Adam was around five. After the game, Adam and Dale ran up and down the ice at the old Whiteout Arena, sliding back and forth, falling over and over again. Soon their father joined in, and the three of them laughed as they landed on top of each other in a pile.

Sports always produced some of the best stereotypical 1950s moments in his family's life. It was one thing they all had in common, the one topic on which they agreed.

"Cody will be coming with us, too, if that's okay?" Adam added.

"That's not a problem. I'll be back in a few minutes." Megan walked out of the suite.

Julie looked anxiously over at Adam. "That's very nice of you, but you don't have to take Cody on the ice."

"Don't be silly. You're practically family," Loraine said. "Besides, it's not like my boys are giving me grandchildren. I have to hijack what children come along." Loraine laughed, and Edward walked over.

"This side of the room appears to be having way too much fun," Edward said. "What's so funny?"

"I was just telling Julie that I'm borrowing your grandchild, since my boys refuse to give me one of my own. We're taking Cody on the ice when we accept Herb's award."

"I don't think that's such a great idea," Edward said through clenched teeth. All the eyes in the suite widened in surprise. He smiled and lightened his tone. "Julie, don't you think the ice is unsafe for a child? I just worry about him hurting himself."

"Yes, but—"

"I wanna go." Cody cried, tears streaming down his

face. He wrapped his arms around Julie's legs. "Please! Please! Please, Mommy."

"Fine," Julie said in defeat, staring at Edward. "Just be careful."

"We'll take good care of him," Adam assured them and swept Cody into his arms. Loraine and Allison followed Adam out the door. As they approached the elevator, the doors swung open. Adam's blood heated as Dale and Nadia waltzed out the doors.

"Hey, guys. Where are we heading?" Dale's laid-back tone grated on Adam's nerves, but he focused on the child in his arms and smiled.

"Oh, thank God, you made it," Loraine chirped and wrapped them in an embrace. "I was so worried."

"Why? The game doesn't start for another thirty minutes."

"Yes, but we have to be down by the ice early. The award presentation is before the game starts," Adam growled as anger swirled in his stomach. Damn. His brother pissed him off. But despite his desire to tell Dale just how disappointed he was, he pasted his mouth shut, lips probably turning white as he ground them closed. Dale should be thankful their mother was there. Without her, Adam's lips would be wagging, not molded shut.

The group made their way through the crowded halls of the Dietrich Arena.

Adam's annoyance subsided as he took the ice. His father deserved this award, and he wouldn't let him down.

CHAPTER FIFTEEN

THE GAME ENDED up being a lot more fun than anticipated. Allison found herself immersed in the competition. Adam and Julie took the time to explain some of the finer points of ice hockey, which helped her understand the player's movements and the spectators' interesting combinations of swear words throughout the game.

Between the rock music and the electric energy charging through the coliseum, she found it impossible to stay on the sidelines. She found herself singing and dancing every time the Flurries scored a goal. Which meant she found herself dancing a lot. The Flurries were on fire. They were up, five to two.

The four beers she had might have encouraged the singing and dancing and the occasional outburst of "Pull your dress up and score a goal!" Yeah, the beers definitely inspired that last one. They also made the third-period bathroom break necessary.

She stumbled down the hall until she found an

employee to direct her to the nearest restroom. She rushed to the penthouse washrooms, and once she felt gallons lighter, she tottered back. She rounded the corner just as an arm wrapped around her waist. She looked up and found Adam's green eyes staring at her.

He lifted a strand of hair out of her face and smiled. "If I didn't know any better, I'd say you were actually having a good time, Ms. Southby." He smirked. "At a hockey game."

"Maybe a little." She laughed. He pressed his lips to hers, her breath hitching with every intensifying kiss.

"Have I mentioned how hot you look in this jersey? I've wanted to rip it off you since you put it on." He grabbed the front of the jersey and pulled her closer to him. His lips glided along her jaw. "I want you."

He reached under her shirt, his gentle hands cupping her breast. She gasped in enjoyment. Pleasure snaked down her spine. It felt so good, but she knew they needed to stop this. She just couldn't seem to find the words. The hallway was not the place for sex with the boss, or anyone for that matter.

All the arguments seemed to lose their meaning as he nibbled on her ear. Her thighs burned as she tried to speak a coherent sentence.

Somehow, she managed to find her voice as she rasped, "We should probably find a more appropriate place for this."

He groaned as he pulled away. She stepped back, moving as far as possible. The greater the distance, she reasoned, the less likely she would fall under his spell again. "You seem to be right a lot today."

"I'm right all the time. It's about time you noticed," she teased.

Her heart kicked into overdrive as he gazed voraciously at her. He stepped toward her, and Allison's arm flew up to stop his pursuit. She rested her hand on his chest. She tried to ignore the strong muscles trembling beneath her hand. "Let's go to your place. The limo should be back by now."

They couldn't seem to move fast enough as they sprinted out of the building to the awaiting car.

———

A WEEK LATER, Adam lay in bed, staring at Allison's sleeping form. He hated to admit it, but he'd never been so happy. The past week with Allison had been amazing. They played virtuous coworkers during the day and then spent every night together being wicked to make up for their restraint.

Adam loved watching her talk business, her hair pulled back into a respectable twist. She'd led meetings and negotiated deals with impeccable ease. Those had been the times he had to fight the urge to tear her clothes off. She was sexy as hell. She hid it well beneath that prim-and-proper façade, but he knew better. It was almost like he knew a secret to which no one else was privy.

Her lips sighed as she dreamt. The full, voluptuous mouth called to him. He lowered his face to hers, to taste her soft, pliant lips. Her eyes fluttered open, and a grin spread over her face.

"Hi," she whispered as she stretched. "Morning."

"What time is it?"

"It's nine thirty. I figured we'd sleep in a little, but now it's time to join the living. What do you think about skipping room service and heading down to the restaurant today? You know, actually eat a meal out in the real world."

They'd spent most of the last week together. Adam and Allison had been standing by, helping Dale learn the ins-and-outs of the jewelry business. That had led to long days in the office. Fortunately, those long days had been offset by long nights of pleasure at the hotel. That hadn't left much time for formal meals, but that was why they invented room service. It was the best way to acquire food without the burden of clothes.

"Okay." She smiled and whipped the blankets from her body. "I just need to shower."

He smiled as she sashayed her naked behind to the bathroom. The hum of the water hitting the tiles drifted into the bedroom. He watched the steam inch its way through the cracked bathroom door. He closed his eyes and pictured the steam caressing her bare body. Before he knew what he was doing, he found himself wandering into the bathroom and sliding into the occupied shower.

"What are you doing?" Allison covered her sensitive areas, crimson crawling up her neck.

"You know, I've already seen all your parts. I happen to like them." He smiled as he pulled her arms down and drank in her glistening, naked form. She bit into her water-soaked lip, turning her head as her pale complexion was overtaken by embarrassment.

He leaned into her and whispered, "You are incredibly gorgeous."

She turned to him, her blue eyes glistening with hunger. It took all of his energy to keep the words he wanted to say trapped in his throat. Love would only mess this up, but damn, he felt it anyway.

He found the soap and lathered the bar between his hands before returning it to the soap dish. He ran his foamy hands down the soft curves of her body, kneeling as he slathered bubbles down her taut, welcoming thighs. He gently leaned her toward the spray of water and whisked the soap from her pink skin before he stood up, wrapping his arms around her waist. He kissed her neck, ignoring the water beating down as they embarked on yet another stormy sexual encounter.

When the wild squall ended, they finished getting ready and headed down to the hotel restaurant. Adam stared in the mirrors located at the restaurant entrance, a smile glued to his lips. Allison just seemed to have that effect on him.

The brightly lit establishment exuded elegance. The soft wooden walls with dark-red inlays and patterned carpet played off the dark wood of the furniture.

They were led to a table by an overly solicitous maître d'. Before they were able to decipher the menu, a flock of waitstaff mobbed the table. Men and women arrived, some bearing water or coffee, and one offering to take their order. The other staff waited around patiently to assist with any other mundane need Allison or Adam might express.

They ordered their breakfast and sipped their coffee. Allison placed her hand on the table, and Adam placed his hand on top of hers. An electric current shot down his arm as she wove her fingers through his and smiled. Adam leaned toward her, their eyes focused on one another.

All outside influences seemed to disappear as he stared into her eyes. Their attention otherwise engaged, they didn't notice a figure walking toward their table until a cold voice said, "Good morning. Imagine seeing you here."

Ben Mooring. A smirk crossed his face as he stared at their intertwined hands. Allison wrenched her hand away and placed it on her lap. The embarrassment crept up her neck to her face.

A fleeting pain flew across Adam's heart. Was it so awful for Ben to see them together? They were consenting adults.

"What would your staff think if they saw you here together?"

"Good morning, Ben. Did you need something?" Adam saw the questions in Ben's eyes. It was the last thing he felt like dealing with right now. Okay. Maybe Allison was right to pull away. The man wasn't exactly the picture of discretion. The rumor of Adam and Allison would be floating around Byrnes and Company, and who knew where else, in hours.

Adam's cell phone began to ring. There was no way

the rumor mill had moved that fast. He looked at the display, expecting to ignore his mother or brother. Unfortunately, caller ID came up unknown. Unknown. As a cop, unknown usually meant something was going down. It never meant anything good. And since the police station didn't come up on caller ID, he knew he had to take the call. He looked at Allison, her eyebrows furrowed in concern. "I need to take this. I'll be right back. Will you be okay?"

"Sure." She smiled. "I'll be here."

Adam placed his napkin on the table and walked toward the entrance. He hated leaving her alone with Ben, but if anyone could handle his crap, it was Allison. She had a gift for handling obnoxiously arrogant men... He was sure there was a lesson in that statement, but he refused to acknowledge it.

"Byrnes."

"Lieutenant Byrnes. This is Detective Perretti from the Chicago Police Department."

"Any new information?"

"Actually, yes. I really need to talk to you, but preferably not on the phone. It's about your brother."

Adam's head dropped as his heart clenched. "Is he okay? Is he hurt?" His voice rose on the last word.

"He's not hurt, but we need to talk. Let's call it professional courtesy. Do you have time today?"

"Sure. Give me an hour, and I'll meet you at my office downtown," Adam said. "Sounds good."

Adam headed back to the table, his mind reeling. What could his brother have gotten himself mixed up in now?

ALLISON WATCHED as Adam walked away. She'd love to tell him to stay, but the look on his face told her there was something wrong. She plastered a smile on her face and took a drink of her coffee. She attempted to ignore Ben, who still stood next to the table.

"May I sit down?" he asked.

"If you must." What a surprise. He actually asked, instead of just sitting his butt in the chair.

"Wow, you're cranky in the morning. So is your bitchiness a turn-on for the frat boy? I could see him enjoying a good tongue-lashing." He smiled as he sat in the chair across from Allison and shook his blond hair back. He was a good-looking guy, if only he weren't such an annoying ass.

A cocky grin lit up his stupid face. "What do you want, Ben?"

"Come on." He leaned back in the chair. "You know I'm just playing with you. I can't help it you get so riled up. You make it much too easy."

Her face softened as she played with the silverware on the table, never allowing her eyes to meet his. She really couldn't argue with that description, she did get worked up when he was around. However, it was never in a good way. He had always just made her angry.

"So, how long have you and the golden boy been doing the humpty-dance?"

Allison glared at him, contemplating the many ways to get rid of him. Murder was out of the question; she really didn't think she'd do well in prison. Black and white stripes were terrible for the figure, and she hated sharing a television with anyone.

Since Brook was the best defense lawyer in the business, Allison was sure her sister could work her magic, maybe get her off with an insanity plea. All the judge had to do was spend five minutes with this idiot, and they'd sympathize with her situation. Ahhh...the joy of fantasies.

"I'm just curious. I know how much it bothered you last time he skittered away. I just don't want to see you get hurt." He actually appeared to be sincere. But how did he know.

"Who told you about that?"

"Oh," he stumbled over his next breath, but then smiled. "It was written all over your moony face back in the day."

Moony face. *Dick.* "Thanks for caring, but I'm fine."

"Well, since you don't want to talk about this topic, we need to start discussing the future of Byrnes and Company."

Allison stared at him. She tried to open her mouth, but the shock of his words left her speechless. Did he honestly think there was something to discuss? Especially after he stole their design. She only knew about the Kaminski account, but Lord knew what else he'd managed to take.

She took a clarifying breath, and then spit out between clenched teeth, "What could we possibly have to discuss? Oh, wait, maybe you could tell me why you stole the design for the Kaminski project? That was our property. We designed it. We own it." She lowered her voice and took another breath. She knew this was neither the time nor the place to start a knockout brawl with Ben, but she really wanted to lay into the man.

Ben leaned in close as he slammed his fist into the table. "I didn't steal a damn thing, and I don't like what you're implying."

"I'm not implying. I'm declaring. You're a thief, and we have nothing further to discuss."

"You can't honestly think you'll be capable of running this company all on your own. I'm sure the golden boys will head back to whatever rocks they climbed out from under. Then what? You'll get stuck building the company for them, slaving away night and day, and all you'll end up doing is lining their overprivileged pockets. I'm giving you the chance to work for me. We can completely overtake the Midwest market..."

She couldn't believe she was allowing this conversation to continue. She saw his mouth moving, but she wasn't hearing anything he was spewing. Her stomach acid churned as disgust flooded her soul. It took every ounce of restraint to keep her voice low. She refused to make a scene.

"So, when can we sit down and discuss this?" Ben finally concluded.

"Are you kidding me?" Allison hissed. "Isn't it bad enough you've been trying to steal Byrnes' customers? Now you're beginning to poach our employees as well."

"Don't be so dramatic. Herb knew that business was business. He also knew that work wouldn't stop just because he's gone. I'm honoring his memory by upholding his work ethic."

Although she agreed that Herb had a fantastic work ethic, she didn't agree that he'd conduct business so rudely, or practice questionable recruitment practices. It just seemed too tacky to comprehend.

"Every day you procrastinate, the price I will pay goes down." He smirked and nodded toward the approaching Adam. "Try to talk the golden boys into selling."

With a grateful sigh, Allison watched Adam make his way back to the table. His eyebrows were furled tighter than when he left. Whatever the news, it did not seem to be good.

"Ben? You're still here," Adam said, perplexed.

"Just keeping this beautiful lady company for you."

"Oh. Thanks," he said distractedly. "Do you mind if we leave? I have something I need to do. I'll make it up to you."

"No problem." She got her purse while Adam spoke to one of the servers. He pulled out a few bills from his wallet and waited for Allison.

"Always a pleasure." She attempted to smile at Ben.

"I find that hard to believe." He grinned at her.

Allison pivoted on her heels and headed toward Adam, never looking back.

CHAPTER SIXTEEN

ADAM SAT at his father's desk—he couldn't quite call it Dale's desk yet—sifting through paperwork. His mind was running through the multiple scenarios that clouded his concentration. What did Joe Perretti want to tell him?

Shit. He stood up and walked over to the sideboard in the corner of his brother's office. He poured two fingers of cognac and looked over at the large, L-shaped, walnut desk facing away from the picture windows. He really had come to enjoy working with Allison at that desk. He never thought he would feel so at home at Byrnes, or here in Chicago.

Yet here he was, enjoying the city. He was enjoying the life he found in the city. For some reason, it just seemed to fit. Allison and the comfort of being home had made him happier than he'd been in a long time.

He looked around the office. It wasn't really that different from Allison's—a large room with low cabinets lining the bottom of the large windows. The windows spanned from one wall to the next, letting in an abundance of natural light. He had his desk on one side of the room, and on the other side was a seating area with a couch, chair, and coffee table on a Persian rug.

The office was nothing like his workspace back home. This desk alone would take up the entire shoebox the precinct called his office. His office in Phoenix had no windows, no privacy, but it was his all his. This wasn't. It was nice, but he couldn't see devoting himself to this job forever.

He wanted back on the streets. He missed the excitement and the challenge. He missed solving the mysteries and getting justice for the wronged of the world. This white-collar crap was a nice place to visit, but he sure as hell didn't want to hang his hat here.

He missed his real job—being a cop. Phoenix didn't have a corner on the crime market. Maybe it was just a reaction to the loss of his father, but for the first time in a long time, he felt like he could make a future here.

After all, it was great to be so close to his family. He missed his mom while he was away. He also missed... Well, Dale was a whole other story. Adam managed to get him off his mind for a few minutes, but if babysitting his younger brother would be a full-time stipulation of living in Chicago, he wasn't sure he wanted to stay.

Dale had spent the past twenty years getting into various levels of trouble. The cops had visited the Byrnes house many times over the years. They had brought him home after numerous benders and assorted bouts of illicit behavior. When a cop wanted to discuss his brother, Adam knew Dale had done something wrong. The only question was, how much trouble had Dale found this time?

Adam took another sip of cognac, hoping the spirit would stop his mind from going in that direction. For all he knew, Joe wanted to talk about one of Dale's charitable donations. Not that Adam ever knew Dale to be charitable, but he needed to keep his mind away from worrying.

He stood and stared out the window—the Chicago streets below a flurry of activity. He could see himself living here. He just wasn't sure he was ready to commit to uprooting his life. The only thing he did know was that he didn't want to think about it. Just one more thing he didn't want to think about. Damn. No topic seemed to be safe these days. Everything seemed to make him uncomfortable. He threw the rest of the cognac back, the liquor burning as it slowly slid down the back of his throat.

He glowered at the clock on the wall. Where the hell was Joe? They'd agreed to meet in one hour. Sitting here alone with his thoughts was dangerous. No one needed to think this much.

He was relieved that Joe and Shay had been put on this case. From all the research he'd done, they were good cops. Adam had called his precinct back home in Phoenix and got as much information as possible. He had to make sure the cops on his dad's case were the best, and so far, he was impressed.

He filled his glass again and glared at the seemingly unmoving clock. Out of the corner of his eye, he saw a figure hovering in the doorway. Joe sauntered into Adam's office and extended his hand.

"Perretti. Please, sit." Adam shook Joe's hand and motioned for him to sit on the unoccupied couch.

His guest complied and leaned back. "Nice office."

"Thanks. It serves its purpose," Adam offered as he sat in the chair next to the couch. He wasn't sure what Joe had come to say, but Adam had a feeling it was nothing good. He figured sitting in the lounge area would keep the conversation casual. He was hoping to avoid the need for a lawyer.

"How much longer are you planning on being in town?" Joe asked.

"Depends on what you've got to tell me. I was hoping to go back on Tuesday, but I'm not entirely sure I can leave yet. Can I get you a drink, or are you on duty?"

"I'm technically off duty now, but it's before noon, so I'll take water. You might want to switch to water as well."

"I know. It's just that the suspense is killing me," Adam said and walked over to his mini-fridge. "It's funny how I'm surrounded by death every day and I handle it, no problem. I walk people through this all the time. However, now... I don't know how to get through this."

Adam took out two bottles of water and set one before Joe and the other bottle next to his cognac. Why throw away a perfectly good drink? He would switch to a more respectable beverage later. If things kept going like this, he wouldn't have time to deal with his family's problems. He would be dealing with his own alcoholism.

"So, you wanted to talk to me about my brother. Is this about the condo?"

"Not the condo. We've set up a meeting with him in forty-five minutes and thought you might want to be there. You know, professional courtesy."

"So, it's about my father. Professional courtesy. Okay. I appreciate that." Since when was professional courtesy given in a murder investigation?

"First, I have some questions. While he was abroad, I heard your brother was in Russia."

"Among other places." Adam nodded as awareness crept in. Professional courtesy was another way of saying the interrogation wasn't over. If this were a simple heart attack, they wouldn't have any more questions. Shit.

"Do you know what he was doing over there?"

"I have no idea. I wouldn't be surprised if that's where he found his girlfriend, Nadia. Why?"

"We looked into what Edward said about Dale asking your father for money a few weeks before your father's death. It's true; your father denied him a loan or any type of handout."

Adam stood up and sighed. He stared out the window and considered the ramifications of what Joe had said. What if Dad had said no to a loan? Would Dale have hurt him? Tried to steal the money? Maybe tried to break into the condo to see what money was there?

He didn't want to believe that any of that would have

happened, but how would Dale have reacted? Who knew. Definitely not Adam. Even when he and Dale lived in the same house, they were miles apart in action and reaction.

"So, what does this mean?" Adam asked. Did he want the answer? Probably not.

"It means we're looking at him as a suspect for the condo break-in, and depending on the toxicology reports, we might be looking at him for your father's murder."

Adam moved back toward the windows. Murder? Sonofa... What the hell had Dale gotten into? What had he done?

"Look, Adam. I wanted to give you a heads-up. This could get ugly for him."

Adam took a drink from the glass and rubbed his hand over his face in frustration. Light filtered through the cognac as he spun the glass. The reddish-brown reminded him of the Maricopa Mountains in the faint light of sunrise. Longing filled his chest to see them again, but first, he had to fix this.

His heart broke at the thought that for the first time, his brother was in real trouble. "Is there anything I can do?"

"Just let us do our job."

The door to the office flew open. Dale's eyes took in the room, and he sucked in a deep breath before pasting a smile on his face. "Everything okay, bro?"

Adam spun the amber liquid in the glass. Anything to not look at his brother. If he'd betrayed their father, he would kill him.

"W-what's the matter?" Dale stammered.

"We need to talk. Remember Detective Perretti? He's looking into Dad's death."

"We have an appointment in a few minutes."

"Mr. Byrnes." Perretti stood, moving his jacket to give Dale a better look at his police star. "You sure are a difficult man to pin down. We've been trying to get an appointment for the past two weeks."

"I'm sorry about that. I never thought it would take this much work to run a company. I've been averaging ten-hour days." Dale sat on the couch and actually said that with a straight face.

Adam was staying at his mom's again, just like Dale. Although, if Dale kept annoying the crap out of him, Adam might start spending more time at the hotel. Adam watched the guy come and go. And there was no way he was working ten-hour days. But in the grand scheme, that didn't matter.

"Sounds challenging." Perretti raised a bottle of water to his lips.

"So, Detective, what did you need to talk about today?"

"My partner will be here shortly, and then we can begin."

"Great." Dale's sarcasm was astounding. The guy was in deep shit, and he still found it in him to be a dick.

An uncomfortable silence settled over the room. Dale looked from Joe to Adam, his knee bouncing up and down. Every action of his body screamed guilty.

This was not helping prove his innocence. And Adam needed him to be innocent.

A knock sounded on the door, a reprieve from the silence.

"Lieutenant Byrnes," Shay Washington said as she entered Adam's office.

She walked over to Adam and offered her hand for him to shake. "Detective," Adam replied as he shook.

"And Mr. Byrnes. It's nice to finally sit down and talk with you." She moved toward the sofa.

Dale stood up and shook her hand. "Please, call me Dale."

"I thought it was a good idea for Adam to sit in." Perretti nodded to a chair across the table.

"Then let's begin." Detective Washington ran a hand through her short bob as she sat in the chair. Joe stood and leaned against the wall, which meant Adam had to take a seat on the couch next to Dale.

She pulled out her notepad. "I'm actually glad you're both here. I'm afraid I don't have very good news. We received the autopsy results from your father's death. Adam, you mentioned your father had a heart arrhythmia, and he was on beta-blockers. Do either of you know if he was on any other medication?"

"Not that I'm aware of. My mother had a hell of a time getting him to even take those." The direction of this conversation was going nowhere good. "What was in the toxicology report?"

"I have a few questions first. Did he also suffer from depression? Was he seeing a doctor for any other health conditions?" Shay pressed.

"I don't think so," Dale said as Adam nodded in agreement.

"Are either of you on any type of medication?"

"No. What does this have to do with our father?" Dale asked.

"We found traces of another drug, an antipsychotic, in your father's blood. If it wasn't prescribed, he may not have been aware of any contraindications. Or—" Shay paused for one second. "Or perhaps he took them on purpose."

"Are you asking if he killed himself? My father was not depressed, and would not have killed himself." Adam couldn't believe that was even an option.

"We need to cover all the bases. We just want to make sure he didn't have an old prescription, maybe something his current doctor was unaware of. Some of these drug interactions are like a bomb waiting to happen. It might have been an accident. Do you know if your mother is on any medication?"

"No, she's not." Adam stood up and took the water bottle sitting next to the empty brandy glass on his desk. Probably a good idea to switch to water. This wasn't going to be an easy conversation for him.

"Dale, how about you or your wife? You did marry a Nadia Eltsina last year while in Russia. Correct?"

The color drain from Dale's face. Married?

"You're married?" Why was Adam even surprised?

"It was a last-minute thing." Dale looked at his brother. The tension hanging in the room was palpable. Adam huffed, dropped the water bottle to the table, and got to his feet. He walked to the sidebar.

"Anyone thirsty?" The other participants shook their heads.

"Are you sure you want another drink?" Joe asked him.

"Normally, I wouldn't." Adam filled another glass with two giant-fingers of cognac. "However, today I have decided to start drinking. Hopefully, tomorrow I'll go back to normal, but after all this, who the hell knows."

"Actually, Adam, I need to ask you a few questions. Could you wait to finish that till we're done?"

Adam stared at the glass and shook his head. "Yeah, sorry. It's been a long day. Hell, it's been a long few weeks." He dumped the contents of the glass, yanked the bottle of water off the table, and sat back down. He raised the bottle to his mouth. "What did you need to know?"

"First off, where were you the night of your father's death?"

"I was working a double. We had a triple homicide that night." Adam ran a hand through his hair. "I got the call about Dad while I was filling out the paperwork. Any number of officers can verify my whereabouts."

"Dale, where were you on the night of your father's death?"

"I was sleeping. Nadia went to help my mom with the animals, so I decided to take a nap. I took some cold medicine with a vodka chaser. I wasn't feeling well, between coughing and sneezing."

"Is there anyone who saw you there all night?"

"Nadia checked on me a few times. I'm assuming it was Nadia. I remember seeing the light from the hallway."

"I thought you were asleep?" Shay looked up from her notes and stared at Dale.

Stories that didn't add up were always a red flag. And this flag was waving right in Adam's face.

"I was, but the squeak of the hinge woke me up. I was so out of it."

"Do you or Nadia take any prescription medication?"

"Nadia does, but we kept them in her bathroom. I doubt my father would have gone in and taken them," Dale muttered. "Besides, there's a big difference between antidepressants and antipsychotics." His eyebrows furrowed.

"Could she have accidentally given him a pill or two?" Shay asked.

"What? No." Dale sat up straight. "And they're antidepressants. Mild stuff."

"Would she have access to your father's food or drink?"

"At home, yes, but not at work. Either way—she's my wife. Are you saying she gave him this medication on purpose? Where would she— Why?" His voice raised a few octaves. If Adam didn't know him any better, he'd be convinced the guy was guilty. As it stood, he was cautiously skeptical.

"Look, Dale, we know about the money and your debt to the Russian mob," Joe interjected from across the room.

"What?" Although Dale tried for a look of confusion, there was pure terror rippling through his features. His knuckles whitened as he gripped the leather armrests. His shoulders stiffened, and his eyes narrowed.

"We know you asked your father for money, and he turned you down. That is motive."

Dale sat in silence. He didn't move. It was like he just gave up. He looked at the detectives and sighed.

"I want my lawyer."

CHAPTER SEVENTEEN

ADAM ESCORTED the detectives to the door while Dale sat in the chair. How had the meeting gotten so out of hand? They'd decided that a formal meeting at the station might be best, including the family lawyer.

What was Dale hiding? Adam shook his head. After all, in his experience, people who were hiding things asked for lawyers, not innocent men. He stared after the detectives, keeping a stoic look on his face. The fire burned beneath the surface, but the authorities didn't need to see that. Dale was still his brother, and they needed to form a united front and get to the bottom of this. When they were safely out of earshot, Adam leaned into Dale.

"So, anything you'd like to tell me?" Adam said between clenched teeth. He didn't believe Dale murdered their father, but if he indirectly contributed, Adam would...would...shit. He didn't know what he'd do. What could he do?

"You don't really believe I had anything to do with

what happened to Dad? Do you?" Dale asked, and the pain in his younger brother's eyes cut through Adam's heart. The innocent, pleading look and doleful body language always got to him.

"Honestly? I don't know what to believe. I don't think you would hurt Dad or that you would willingly let anyone hurt him, if that's what you're asking."

"Thanks for believing in me." Dale breathed a sigh of relief.

Adam didn't necessarily believe in him, but the relief written across his brother's face forced him to keep his mouth shut. On that subject, at least. "So, you're married."

"Yeah, I met Nadia when I was in Russia. You know, Jacques, Kyle, and I left after college graduation to travel the world. Remember them from high school?"

Adam nodded but kept his thoughts to himself. Part of the reason Dale found trouble was Jacques and Kyle. The three tended to create mischief at every turn. Hell, they didn't just find trouble, they sought it out. Not that he blamed Jacques and Kyle for his brother's problems, it was just that the three of them were toxic together.

"We were all pretty messed up. We slept all day and then spent our nights with liquor, drugs, and various women. One morning, in Moscow, I woke up next to some woman, and I was sicker than a dog." Dale rose from the chair and walked to the sideboard. He whipped open the mini-fridge and pulled out a bottle of water. He opened the bottle and took a hard pull of the liquid.

"It scared the shit out of me. I realized then that I'd

hit bottom. I went to get some money out of my account, so I could fly home. The account was empty. I had the hotel covered for the rest of the month, but I stopped the booze and drugs. That wasn't a popular idea with my so-called friends. After all, I was the one paying for most of the parties. After a few days, they left. I don't know where they went. I was alone in a strange country with no money, no options." Dale's eyes welled with tears.

"I didn't know what to do. I finally decided to call Dad so he could send some money and I'd head back home. That morning, though, I met Nadia. She was beautiful and kind. The best part is that she didn't care about my money, or lack of it. I stayed with her for a while. We talked about marriage, but she was a working girl. Her boss, Maksim"—Dale used his hands to place boss in air quotes. Apparently, he didn't want to use the word pimp— "didn't like our relationship. He forbade her from seeing me. So, we left. She had some money set aside, and I sold everything I had. We headed for Kyle's place in Singapore and hid out there for a few months.

"Then Maksim found us and demanded a hundred thousand dollars for stealing his employee. We ran, and came home to ask Dad for the money. He said he wasn't that solvent, but that he'd look into it for us. But for now, we needed to figure it out on our own."

"Does Maksim know you're here? Could he have hurt Dad?" Adam felt the hair on his neck standing on end. This whole story was making Dale look more and more involved, even if it was on the outskirts.

"Yes. He knows we're here, but why would he hurt Dad? As far as he knows, that is where we were getting the money. If anything, I could see them holding him hostage or something, but that's all."

Adam's eyes bulged at the nonchalant mentioning of kidnapping. What was wrong with his brother that kidnapping didn't faze him? Especially when talking about his own father.

"Anyway, we paid him a good piece of what we owed him."

"How much?"

"Fifty thousand dollars."

"That's a large chunk of change. Where did you get that?" Adam choked. How does someone with an empty bank account find fifty grand?

"I sold some things." Dale's eyes shifted. "I was trying to take care of it on my own, and I was working on getting Dad to sell the company, or sell stock in the company. Anything would have worked. It's not like a hundred grand is that much to someone like him. His company is worth millions. I was going over the books, trying to find a way to spin the sale into something positive. I mean, c'mon, he didn't need the business anymore. He was halfway out the door and days away from retiring on a beach somewhere."

"Did you ever get a chance to talk to Dad about that?"

"No."

"Did you tell him you only needed another fifty thousand?"

"Yes. He kept saying that he was looking into some

things, but that I needed to take responsibility and find a way to make the money. I was trying to do just that, but I was running out of options."

"You know he never would have sold. What would you have done then?" Adam hated this whole conversation. If he were on this case, all signs would point to Dale. He couldn't see his brother as a murderer, but what the heck did he really know about him?

The truth was they never really had known each other. Or maybe they just never understood each other. Either way, he was way too close to this case to work it.

"I know that. I would have begged, and when that didn't work, I would have begged him to put a second mortgage on the house or sell the condo," Dale added and slowly took another drink.

"That might have worked." Adam sat in the chair across from his brother.

"I figured I had a better chance with that, than the company. If none of that worked, we would have left. We didn't want to get Dad involved."

"Does Nadia know about all of this? Does she know Dad wouldn't give you money?"

"Yes. But before you get all suspicious, she loves me, and she loved Dad. They got along great."

The pleading look Dale gave Adam was genuine. His brother's sincerity was reassuring, but he wasn't sure Dale's loyalty was based in fact. He'd like to believe every word Dale said, but he just couldn't muster the same faith that Dale had in his new bride and her ex-employer.

"Is there anything else?" Adam ran a hand through

his hair. He didn't want to ask that question. After all, you shouldn't ask the question if you really didn't want the answer. However, he figured he should get all the bad news out of the way. If there was any more, he wanted it now, as opposed to learning about it later from the Chicago PD.

"Well, I was hoping to do this under better circumstances. But I want to sell the company, at least my half. I want you to meet with Ben Mooring."

"You're joking, right? Ben?"

"Dad forgave him, why can't we? He wants the company. Do you know how many people are out there offering cash for jewelry businesses? None. I've looked. He could take Dad's dream further than you or I can. We'll both be leaving soon."

"I thought you wanted to run the company?"

"Come on, neither one of us wants to stay here and deal with this. I've checked the books..."

"So that's why you wanted to take over the company. You wanted access to the books." Adam didn't think he could be more disgusted with his brother. Then his brother did something like this. It had never been about their father and keeping the business in the family. He should have seen this coming.

"Don't get dramatic."

"That's not dramatic. It's fact."

Dale sighed. "We should give Ben a chance to make the company into something great."

"It's already great."

"Fine. He'll keep it great."

"Allison can keep it great," Adam asserted.

"She might, but there's no guarantee, and what if she needs help? We need to make a clean break and get back to our lives. Please, Adam. Go talk to him. For me," he begged. "Please do it for me. I don't ask you for much."

"Really?"

"Fine, I haven't asked for anything in a long time."

Skepticism and leeriness flooded Adam's mind. It must have shown on his face because Dale added, "Please. I need this."

After much pleading and against his better judgment, Adam agreed to meet with the notorious Ben Mooring.

▭

ALLISON SPENT Saturday packing up her life into boxes. The apartment was a nice place, but it just didn't fit any longer. It hadn't fit her in years, but now that she had the condo and only a week left on her current lease, it was time to move on. That left her with seven days to pack up almost half a lifetime's worth of stuff.

She managed to finish packing her living room and kitchen, unused pots and pans sticking out of the moving boxes lining her living room floor. It wasn't that she didn't know how to cook; she'd just rarely found the time. Putting her kitchen necessities in boxes wasn't all that upsetting in her restaurant-dependent lifestyle. With her dishes in exile, she avoided the guilt she felt for overusing her insider card at the local pizza joint.

She looked over the empty rooms and smiled. With each new area conquered, she got closer to residing in that gorgeous penthouse. Despite the break-in, she wanted to move in. She loved that condo. It was beautiful and reminded her of Herb. It might be a bit too much for one person, but she could see herself finding a husband and settling down there.

She never would have pictured herself in such a palace. After her last promotion, she had planned on buying a place of her own, but she just couldn't find the time to find the right neighborhood, let alone choose the appropriate house or condo.

Part of the problem was that she had been buying a home for the future she wanted, but she didn't know what that future entailed. She thought she would like to have children someday. Maybe. She'd thought about marriage, as well. Possibly. Both of those dreams seemed so far away, it was just easier to pretend she wasn't interested... And maybe she wasn't. She liked having her nights free to hang with the girls or try some new hotspot.

Oh, who am I kidding? She sighed as she made her way to her bedroom closet.

She wanted the husband, the children, and the white picket fence. She wanted it all. There just hadn't been anyone in her imminent future to share in those plans, so she was always waiting around for the man of her dreams to walk into her life.

She sighed as she looked at the two-by-twelve disaster that housed her clothing, shoes, and miscellaneous stuff. She started with the highest shelf. After all, if she kept it up high, she generally didn't need it. She pulled a few hatboxes, filled with stationery and other paperwork, and dumped them in an empty carton. She pulled down a few extra blankets and uncovered two large plastic boxes. Each container had a washed-out label with pieces of duct tape wrapped around the side, names written on the tape in black Sharpie. One was labeled Brooklyn, and the other was labeled Allison.

The marker had faded, but she could still see the words as she ran her hand over the faint gray loops of her mother's handwriting. Her fingers slid noiselessly over the soft, cracked grooves of the tape. She pictured her mother's hands securing the label on the boxes for her daughters. The love. The pride.

I miss her.

Loss stung the back of her sinuses, and a tear formed in her eye. A miserable dread kept her hands on the lid of the box. Once she opened the box, she knew the emotion from her childhood would suck her into sadness.

Somehow, she didn't care. She wanted to look inside, needed to look inside.

She unfastened the top of Brook's container and sifted through the Technicolor artwork from her sister's childhood. She smiled as she looked at the hand-drawn turkey from kindergarten. She rested her adult hand on the child's handprint that formed the outline of the turkey's body.

Staring at the small paper fowl, she started thinking about children. The tiny fingers of Brook's hand had made this simple art project. Yet Allison couldn't take her eyes off of the drawing as if it were a million-dollar painting. She remembered all the homework Brook had brought home over the years. They'd never been anything special to an outsider, but to Allison, they were brilliant.

The pride and accomplishment that had been written across Brook's cute little face made the whole world light up. Allison smiled as she saw her future roll out before her. She wanted a child, a child whose face lit up her world. She wanted the husband, house, and two-point-five kids. She wanted it all.

She sat on the floor thinking about her future, and Adam's face fluttered through the scene. The sad thing was, she saw the future, complete with Adam Byrnes, but that wasn't realistic. He was temporary. He'd always be temporary.

She placed the masterpiece back into the container and sighed. Her skin tingled as she remembered Adam's hands finding their way along her body. Her eyes closed, and her breath hitched at the way those hands had made her feel. Yeah. She could see herself with Adam. Her stomach flip-flopped as she thought about the way their hands had intertwined as they made love.

What the hell was wrong with her? She was daydreaming about a man who would be heading back to Phoenix as soon as his familial obligation was complete. Her heart squeezed as another wave of tears snuck past her eyelids. When he left, there would be no amount of shopping or wine therapy that would mend her heart this time.

Somehow, again she didn't care. Her wants and needs outweighed it all. She didn't care that he'd destroy her. She didn't care that her heart would go down in flames. She wanted him, needed him, if only for a short time.

She pushed a sigh through her lips, shut the container, and placed the boxes in the "keep" pile. She might be on her way to hoarding, but she couldn't get rid of her sister's innocent designs.

Her cell phone rang, music blaring from the phone's speaker. She skimmed the stacks of things strewn about the room. Where did she put that phone? She stopped and listened to hone in on its position. Allison jumped over boxes and scattered objects to get to the location of the song. She missed the organization of a semi-clean house—without a live-in obstacle course.

Profanity spilled from her lips as she stubbed her toe on the bed frame and hopped to the dresser. Clothes and books, piled high, covered the bellowing object. Allison randomly tossed the items aside as she searched. She finally grabbed the phone as the ringing stopped.

Damn phone.

She looked at the missed call log and saw Adam's number. Her lips curved into a smile. It must be a sign. He was thinking about her too. She hit redial.

"Hey, sexy," Allison chirped into the receiver.

"Hey, I need to take a rain check on dinner tonight, something came up."

"Oh," Allison's mood shifted. Maybe he wasn't

missing her as much as she missed him. She was such a fool. "Of course. Is everything okay?"

"It's nothing. Is your front door locked?"

"Yes."

"Please don't take any chances." He breathed in and out into the phone.

Allison swore she could hear the strain in his words. But at this juncture of their non-existent relationship, she was not in a position to judge his moods.

"Okay."

"Thanks. I'm so sorry."

"No problem. I'll see you at work." She tried to hide her disappointment as she touched the end button. She was looking forward to seeing him again. She sneered at the phone in her hand and tossed it on her cluttered bed.

Her heart rate accelerated as she rehashed last night: those gentle probing fingers that had touched her inside and out, those soft lips that had kissed and glided up and down her trembling body, his hard, throbbing...

"Enough!" she yelled at her empty room. She either needed to get out of the apartment or sift through these boxes and find her vibrator. Since she refused to stay home and wallow in her Adam-free evening, she jumped on her cluttered bed and scooped up her cell phone.

Ever since Adam mentioned the Chicago's Kitchen and Wine Bar, she'd wanted to stop in. She tapped the texting icon and sent Julie and her sister an invitation to dinner. When all else failed, calling for female reinforcement made everything better.

CHAPTER EIGHTEEN

ALLISON CROSSED her jean-clad legs as she sat across from Julie and Brook, sipping her red wine. The cacophony of noise wafted up to the second level of the elegant bar. The theatre-going, suit-and-tie set mingled during the Saturday happy-hour rush. Men and women laughed as they discussed the pretentious stage productions to which they would momentarily embark.

"So, Sponge Bob Smear-Pants started yelling about his latest court case." Brook leaned forward in her seat, and her black jean skirt rode up her skinny thighs. "Apparently, the judge was out to get him. The fact that he was too busy getting his rocks off in the coat closet with his secretary had nothing to do with the loss of the case."

"Smear-Pants? Are we five?" Allison laughed.

"Bite me. I call it like I see it," Brook sat back, her blue eyes even more vivid with the blue sweater she wore. She was model beautiful, plus she'd had enough brains to pass the bar.

Allison would be jealous, but Brook was her sister, and that would be wrong... No, she was still jealous. Even her sister's gnarled nails from constantly chewing on them didn't make the woman any less gorgeous.

Brook spun her blond hair around her finger as she continued, becoming more animated. "I mean, how does he expect to win when he forgets to cite federal law? You can't allow these companies to file injunctions in passive disputes. It's absolutely ridiculous. You know..."

Allison shook her head. No, she didn't know, but that didn't stop Brook from continuing. With a smirk, Julie lifted her vodka martini to her lips. Apparently, Julie had no clue what Brook was rambling on and on about either.

Allison watched her friend run a hand through her straight brown hair, a huge grin playing on her lips. Julie looked good tonight. There was just something different about her. Between the cute dark-blue sweater dress and the healthy glow in her cheeks, she seemed happy.

That was definitely a subject they needed to discuss. What, besides a man, put a smile like that on her face? Allison racked her brain, trying to remember if Julie had mentioned any new guy in her life. Nothing came to mind, and she was sure she'd remember something like that. A girl might forget some things a friend shares, but definitely not a new stud muffin.

Allison's attention moved back to her sister, who continued to rant about injunctions and disputes. Allison loved her sister's passion for all things, especially the law. It was fun to watch her arms wave and voice rise. However, there were more important topics to address.

"I know," Allison smiled and shook her head at the first pause in her sister's rampage. "Those damn passive disputes."

Brook downed the rest of her wine glass. "Okay, okay. No more work talk. You obviously don't have an appreciation for the finer nuances of passive disputes."

"No, please go on. This wine isn't quite putting me to sleep yet. Your story just might." Allison raised the glass to her lips as a cloth napkin flew at her head. She pulled the glass away; her red silk shirt would not survive being doused with wine. She stuck out her tongue as she launched the fabric back at her sister.

"You two are crazy." Julie smiled as the waiter stopped by the table, daggers flying from his eyes. Apparently, flying napkins were frowned upon in this eating establishment. Who knew?

The women ordered their dinner and another round of drinks, much to the server's chagrin. Fortunately, he kept his thoughts to himself. Unfortunately, his body language spoke volumes. Then again, Allison didn't care.

"Okay, Julie, let's get to the good stuff. What is with that grin you're wearing? Whoever put it there must be doing his job right," Allison fished, and then took a sip of wine.

"It's nothing." Julie ran her finger along the rim of her glass. "It's just Cody. He is the light of my life. When I left tonight, he was so sweet."

Allison swore a look of unease snuck across her friend's face, but it passed so quickly, she couldn't be sure.

"It's more interesting to talk about you. What is going on between you and Adam?" Julie asked as she stirred what was left of her vanilla vodka martini.

Allison froze as she contemplated the question. How did Julie know about her and Adam? They hadn't brought their relationship into the office. What had she seen? When? Who else knew? Shit.

What should she do? Should she just tell them the truth? *Ugh.* If she told them the truth, she would never hear the end of it. But she'd never lied to these two, and she didn't want to start now. She looked at Julie and said the first thing that came to mind.

"Huh?" she asked, already regretting her response.

"Please tell me you're not doing the hokey pokey with that asshole. The last time it happened, months of shopping therapy had to occur before you stopped mooning over him. Although I would love a wardrobe infusion, I'd rather have one happen naturally and not because he's messing with your emotions again," Brook said.

"The hokey pokey?" Allison's eyed her sister in disbelief. Sometimes talking to her was like talking to a teenager, all attitude and juvenile vocabulary.

"Would you rather I say coitus? Sexual intercourse? Does that please your delicate sensibilities?" Brook teased. "I mean, I've got a whole repertoire of words I can use. I mean, there's sex, boinking, fu—"

"All right. Please don't." Allison shook her head

and laughed. "So, we might be doing the hokey pokey, and we might be seeing each other, but that's all it is. Nothing more."

"So, it's just seeing and sex. When it comes to men, what else is there?" Julie asked, batting her lashes in innocence.

"Exactly." Allison smiled.

"Are you sure that's all it is?" Brook asked.

Allison sighed. She didn't know how to talk about this. How did you explain that you're having "I haven't had sex in so long, my vibrator proposed, so I'm desperate" sex with a man who would leave at any moment?

"Yes. I'm fine." Deep down, Allison knew that was a lie, but she hadn't admitted it to herself yet. She wasn't about to say it out loud. The extent to which she'd fallen for Adam was not up for discussion. She'd deal with the fallout later. Hopefully, much later. "Eventually, he will go back to Phoenix, and I'm okay with that. It's just nice to be enjoying the company of a man."

"Good, then it's about time." Brook sighed. "You two have been ogling each other for years."

"We have not..." Allison attempted to argue, but what was the point? She hadn't ogled him. She'd pined. Brook wouldn't appreciate a grammar lesson at this point, and ogling sounded a lot less pathetic than pining.

"I'm just saying. It's about time you enjoyed each other's company again." "How did you even know we were together?"

Julie's eyes returned to her glass. This time Allison

was sure she saw guilt pass through her friend's eyes. "I had breakfast with a friend the other day in the city and saw you." She took a long drink.

"So are we talking good sex? Is he still as fantastic as you remember? What about that little move you told me about? Details, please," Brook asked Allison.

"Brooklyn."

"What? I'm not getting any right now, so I have to live vicariously through you. Give me details." She leaned forward and wiggled her eyebrows.

"What about that defense lawyer, Bruce or whatever? Aren't you seeing him?" Julie asked as their food was delivered. Allison was grateful for the distraction. Maybe if they discussed Brook's love life, they'd forget about her.

"Bryce, actually, is a piece of work. He generously informed me that men aren't wired to be monogamous. I need to adjust my thinking to embrace the true nature of man. After all, it's okay that I walked into his office while some twenty-year-old intern slobbered his jimmy. It's natural, and if I don't like it, maybe I should look into becoming a nun because I'll never be happy with a man. After all, they have needs."

"Natural, my ass. Creep." Allison finished her wine.

"Where do you find these men? And I use the term 'men' loosely when I refer to these Neanderthals," Julie pointed out, air-quoting the word men. "I think we need another round."

Allison hailed the waiter, and they ordered more drinks. They sat and laughed as they discussed work, family, and the positive aspects of joining a nunnery. Two more rounds, dinner, and a delectable hazelnut praline ice cream later, Brook placed her napkin on her plate. "I'm sorry, ladies. I have to get to the airport." She slowly rose and gathered her purse. "I'll be back next week."

"Airport?" Julie asked. Brook placed cash in front of Allison.

"Yeah, the Central Bar Association meeting awaits."

"You're not driving to the airport by yourself, are you?" Julie's eyes widened in concern.

"Not a chance. Between traffic, parking, and wine consumption, it would take forever. I'm taking a taxi."

"A taxi? It may be quicker, but you'll have to mortgage your house just to pay for it. Why don't I go with you?" Julie offered.

"No way am I dragging you to the airport on a Saturday night. The firm pays my expenses, and that includes transportation. So it's all good." Brook embraced her sister.

Hot tears pooled in Allison's eyes. Whenever Brook headed out of town, Allison missed her the whole time. "Have fun in Dallas. Call me when you get back."

Brook walked away and down the stairs.

"Well, it's just you and me." Allison wiped the sadness from her eyes and lifted her glass to Julie.

Julie raised her glass and tapped Allison's with a clink. "To a girl's night out."

After a few more drinks, Allison stood and attempted to put on her cropped black leather jacket.

The jacket must be broken, she thought as she struggled with the unforgiving material, the sleeves twisting and making it impossible for her arms to get inside. Julie stepped behind her and offered a giggling assist.

The women staggered down the stairs toward the exit, walking past the few remaining patrons. Out of the corner of her eye, Allison noticed Ben Mooring sitting at a table.

She was just drunk enough to consider walking over to him and giving him a piece of her mind. Fortunately, she was also just sober enough to stop herself. After all, he wasn't alone. Even though she wasn't on the clock, she still represented Byrnes and Company and didn't want to embarrass them or herself.

The logical side won out in the tug-o-war until she took a second look at the man sitting across from Ben. Her stomach lurched with the sight of that familiar light brown hair sitting across his table. There must've been a mistake. What would Adam need to discuss with Ben?

Allison glanced at Julie, whose wide eyes, shifting from Allison to Adam, told her there was no mistake. Anger pulsed and throbbed, stealing the oxygen from Allison's lungs. How could he do this to her? To his father? Tears stung the back of her eyes, but she refused to cry. She dragged a long breath in through her nose and walked toward the two men. She felt Julie's hand on her arm, but she shook off the resistance. Nothing was stopping her from this confrontation.

What a jackass, she thought as the men noticed her approaching the table. Guilt lingered in Adam's eyes as he stared. She placed her hands on the table and leaned into Adam. His mouth opened, but she didn't want to hear whatever line of BS he was about to serve. "Don't. Say. A word."

"Allison..." he pleaded as he took his napkin from his lap and threw it on the table.

"Save it," she hissed and then continued, her voice growing louder with every sentence. "It's my own fault for believing your lies. I should have known you'd screw me and your father over. So how long have you been working on a deal to sell the company?"

"It's not like that," he asserted, and Allison grabbed his vodka tonic, lifted the glass, and dumped the contents over his head.

"Screw you. I'm sure the two of you will be very happy together." She slammed the glass on the table and rubbed her hands together in satisfaction. "Good-bye, Adam."

She turned toward the door and saw the reproving eyes of the few remaining diners and wait staff staring at her. The silence, mixed with the derisive snarls, almost triggered a whimper. Somehow, she managed to hold her head high as she walked out of the restaurant.

CHAPTER NINETEEN

AS ALLISON STOMPED down Michigan Avenue, the skies opened up. Nothing like kicking someone when they're down. Allison stopped in her tracks and glowered at the sky, sulking as the large drops pelted her in the face.

She used her hand to shield her eyes from the downpour, glancing around for a building awning where she could hide and wait out the storm. All she saw were huddled masses occupying the prime canopies up and down the avenue.

She laughed, but the humor was sucked out from the sound. "Well, at least no one will be able to tell when I break down and cry." Allison wrapped her leather jacket tighter around her shoulders and trudged the soggy few blocks to her new building.

A feeling of relief overwhelmed her as she plodded into the building entranceway, her drenched hair sticking to her face. She suppressed the urge to shake her head and dislodge the excess moisture. The lobby full of rain-dodgers and condo-dwellers might find that a bit too canine.

She shuffled through the frigid lobby, goose bumps crawling up her skin as the rain mixed with the building's air conditioning. Visions of a hot shower and mindless television dancing in her head, she noticed an orange sign draped from the half-open penthouse elevators. IN REPAIR.

"You've got to be kidding me." She'd accidentally said that out loud. She saw the doorman smile, and a technician popped his head out from behind the partially closed doors.

"No need to fret, little lady." The repairman grinned as he spoke to her chest. "I've got this all under control."

"Are all the penthouse elevators down?" she asked him as she looked at the open doors and out-of-order signs in front of all four elevators. Yes, stupid question. But there was a small glimmer of hope that maybe one of these damn things might work.

"Yeah, it's the damnedest thing." He shook his head and stared at the elevator bank. "Pardon my language, ma'am, but I've never seen four elevators go defunct at the same time. They should be up and running in twenty, thirty minutes, tops."

Allison felt the tears threatening her eyes as she worried the Celtic knot necklace at her throat. How could a day go so terribly wrong? It started out with promise, and yet deteriorated so quickly.

"Hi, Ms. Southby, I'm Matt. I work the door most evenings." Allison stared at the man who interrupted her pity-fest. Although his uniform screamed "doorman," his spiky black hair with red tips and ears with multiple piercings screamed something else.

"How do you know my name?" She eyed him as she tried to hide her skepticism. Random guys approaching a woman in the city of Chicago wasn't always a good thing. Even if he looked the doorman part.

"We try to know all the residents. It's our job. But Mr. Byrnes pointed you out the other day." He smiled and pulled on a red-tipped spike. "Don't mind the hair. I had a gig tonight and couldn't get home in time to de-punk myself."

"You're in a band." That explained the hair. "Please, call me Allison." She extended her hand and smiled. How could she not? His smile was both friendly and contagious. She smiled back. "Nice to meet you."

"Likewise." He reached for her hand, his chest puffed up with pride. "You should come see us play sometime. We're kind of like punk before punk music went all commercial."

"Sounds great. I would love to." She smiled, not really understanding what he was talking about. Her favorite radio station played some punk, but she couldn't honestly list any one of the bands, let alone tell the difference between music created before an exposure to commercialism versus after. She turned her attention to the elevators.

"If you're in a hurry, take one of the west elevators

up to the thirty-fifth floor and walk the rest of the way," Matt added.

"Thanks, I just might do that." She smiled, but the thought of climbing fifteen flights to her floor was as appealing as a root canal. However, with every passing second, the cold lobby was inviting chills—and imminent pneumonia.

She shuffled into one of the west elevators for her thirty-five-floor ride. The car was packed, but even with all the body heat, she was still cold. She blew into her cupped hands, trying to warm her frostbitten digits.

In the half-hour since she saw Adam, she hadn't thought about him once. Thank God for mechanical problems and Mother Nature. However, now that she was back on track, she couldn't seem to get him out of her mind. And he been with that piranha, Ben.

Knowing that Ben's only ambition was to take over the company, there was no reason why Adam should have met with him...unless, of course, he was considering selling. She expected this type of behavior from Dale, but she believed in Adam.

How could she have been so stupid and blind? She trusted him with the business, with her body, with her heart. The disappointment and embarrassment nipped at her eyes, and she rubbed her temples to try to control the waterworks. She would not let that cretin of a man get to her. With the cold elevator air bearing down on her soaked body, she didn't need to add tears.

Allison arrived on the thirty-fifth floor and headed for the stairwell. She opened the large metal door and pounded her way up the concrete stairs.

Her heels squished with every step, sending an unwelcome wave of water between her toes. She snarled as she passed a sign that read LEVEL 38. "Just twelve floors to go," she said out loud, just to fill the eerily barren stairwell with noise.

She continued climbing with only the squish of her shoes to keep her company. She started to wonder if she had made a mistake. Maybe she should have waited for an elevator. The stairwell was awfully dim, deserted, and lonely, not to mention a little creepy.

LEVEL 45

Crash!

She jumped at a loud clatter and the sound of voices. Her hand flew to her chest, heart reverberating in her chest. Cheerful tones floated upward as a door opened many floors below her, and then the sound disappeared. "Get a grip," she whispered, and persevered, knowing her imagination was getting the best of her.

LEVEL 49

She stopped and stared at the sign in front of her. One more floor. She smiled and leaned against the wall. The cool concrete was welcome on her flushed skin. The cold from the rain had been replaced with sweat. She was starting to remember why she went to the gym every day. With all of the drama of late, she'd neglected the elliptical machine, and it was showing. As she sucked in a ragged breath, she remembered why she used that awful torture device. Her labored breathing slowed, and she rejoined her upward ascent.

She rounded the corner on the intermediate

landing between level forty-nine and fifty, but a large-framed figure knocked her into the concrete wall. The room spun. Her head struck the cement, and bright colors danced before her eyes.

She moved to touch her head, but a heavy weight kept her arms bonded to the wall. She twisted to the left and right, but the figure had her easily pinned. With one arm pushing against her chest, they raised their other hand. She felt a buttery-leather glove cover her mouth. She forced open her lips and dug her teeth into the covered hand. Her mouth slid along the soft material. Her nose struggled for each desperate inhale.

Who are you? she wanted to ask, but she couldn't breathe, let alone ask a question. She shook her head, trying to dislodge the kaleidoscope embedded in her vision. She stared at the masked figure, his hazel eyes blazing with hate. From the stature and the size of the hands, she assumed it was a man. Not that she really cared at this point. She wanted out, wanted to break free.

Her eyes widened. Her heart raced. She squirmed in place. Escape. She must escape. Her legs flew forward, luckily making contact with her attacker's groin. He fell to the floor, letting go of her to protect himself. Still breathless, she took advantage of his momentary distraction and staggered up the stairs. A garbled sound escaped her throat as she attempted to scream.

"Help me. Please, help," she managed to croak as she teetered toward the exit on her floor. She jiggled the handle on the door, but it didn't move. Locked. She knelt down and turned over her bag, scattering the contents, tossing her checkbook and makeup to the side. Where were those damn keys?

She glanced over her shoulder. A low groan floated up from the man below. She turned back to the personal effects strewn about her. She clawed at the bottom of the bag, tears stinging the back of her eyes. A small clink echoed from the pocket. She breathed a sigh of relief and pulled the keys from her purse.

As she stood, she felt a hand reach up, grappling at her weakened legs. He struggled for purchase as she kicked his hands away. His long fingers encircled her ankle, and he yanked her off her feet and tried to drag her down the stairs. She thrashed her legs, but it only seemed to strengthen his hold. With one strong yank from him, she flew down the stairs and struck her temple on the metal handrail, slumping to the floor.

▭

ADAM COULDN'T BELIEVE the scene back at the restaurant. Allison blew everything out of proportion—it was just a meeting. It wasn't like he and Ben were going to do business.

Not that she knew that. And given the fact that Ben did nothing but give her grief and give his father grief—shit. He fucked up. Big time. Maybe not drink in his face big, but big enough to mean he needed to grovel. A lot.

Thank goodness for the rain. Although it was making it impossible to find Allison, it was Mother

Nature's natural washing machine for vodka-drenched hair and clothes. He raked his hand through his hair, trying to get rid of some of the sticky residue.

He just wished she had stuck around for an explanation. She would have understood if she had given him time. It was just like her, though, to shoot first and ask questions later.

This all started because of Dale. Damn him, Adam fumed. Dale had a gift for screwing up Adam's life... Not that this was all Dale's doing. It was his own fault for agreeing to the meeting in the first place. He knew it was a bad idea from the start.

Although he understood where Ben Mooring was coming from, he also knew when it came to business that Ben was a snake. Herb had mentioned that Ben worked his way up from nothing, and for some reason, Ben was petrified it would be taken away. Apparently, his parents weren't loving, nurturing people that instilled inspiration.

No childhood drama gave Ben the right to be an ass though. If that were the case, the jails would be empty. Everyone in a cell had some traumatic event that they swore made them the way they were.

Attending this meeting didn't change his perception, nor did he expect it to change his mind about selling. He would never sell his father's company to someone who so disrespected his father. Herb had long since forgiven the man. In fact, they had worked together recently on numerous occasions. Although Adam didn't hold any grudges, he was not about to let the snake into his father's office.

The rain began to pick up. Adam's pace quickened as he headed for the Braelind condo. He had to catch Allison and make her listen.

He walked into the refuge of the building and headed for the penthouse elevators. An orange sign warned of the downed elevators. Adam searched the crowd for Allison. She obviously couldn't get up to her condo.

As he contemplated where she might have gone, the doorman with the spiky hair and piercings walked up. "Good evening, Mr. Byrnes."

"Good afternoon, Matt," he said as he searched the sea of faces. "Is there something I can help you find?"

"Yeah, actually, I'm looking for Allison Southby." He looked at Matt, his red-tipped spiked hair a deep contrast to the slicked-back look.

"You just missed her. She rode the elevator to thirty-five and took the stairs the rest of the way." Matt pointed to the technician pulling down the orange sign. "But it looks like the penthouse elevators are fixed. You might just beat her up there."

"Thanks." Adam shook his head. Allison had no patience. Although that wasn't Adam's real problem— her stubborn streak was what he needed to overcome. She had to see reason. He ran a hand through his hair and fought his way through the packed lobby to the elevator bank.

▭

STARS PRANCED in Allison's eyes as she lay on the

ground, dumbfounded. A percussion solo thumped inside her head. She attempted to stand, but the fiend was on top of her, holding her arms with his muscular legs. Her lungs fought to draw in oxygen as two huge gloved hands wrapped around her throat. The necklace at her throat dug into her flesh as the hands squeezed tighter.

She reached for the hands, pulling ineffectively on the slick leather gloves. She didn't have the strength to remove the death grip. Panic shot down her spine as her lungs begged for air. She kicked her legs, but all she managed was to knee her captor in the back.

"Leave, bitch!" a deep voice hissed in her ear. "You don't belong here."

Allison gasped. Her lungs burned. Her eyes widened as her body begged for oxygen. She waved her arms toward the vise at her neck. The grip only got stronger. Black swirled in her open eyes, invading the edges of her vision.

Then the pressure was gone. Flurries of oxygen flooded her lungs as she gasped in sweet agony. She whirled onto her side, and hot, wet tears fell down her cheeks.

The beast said through a hazy fog, "I don't have time for your bullshit. Leave, or else."

As the venomous words spilled from his mouth, a welcome voice was heard.

Her eyes closed as everything faded to black.

CHAPTER TWENTY

"ALLISON? If you weren't mad at me, this would be a great time for an impatience joke. The elevator is fixed," Adam stood in the stairwell and yelled. Crunch. Adam lifted his foot. A crushed tube of lipstick lay on the concrete landing. He frowned at the other items strewn about. Allison's keyring? Her purse?

"Allison?"

Shuffling and the loud thump of feet echoed up the stairs. Confused, he walked a bit faster. He knew she was pissed, but running—really? His heart stopped in his chest when he found her lying on the next landing, motionless. He ran down the handful of stairs and knelt at her side. A stream of blood ran down the side of her face, pooling next to her head.

"Allison, can you hear me?" He reached for her wrist and placed his ear to her chest. He felt the faint beat of her pulse against his fingers.

He ripped off his soggy jacket and wadded it into a make-shift bandage, pressing it on the wound and reaching for his cell phone. The thick stairwell walls blocked any hope for a signal. He shook the phone in an attempt to magically produce some bars.

"Shit," he growled in frustration. He hated to leave her alone since he wasn't completely sure what happened, and he didn't want some creep coming back to finish what he started.

He stroked the side of her face. The ghastly pallor of her skin, the shallow breaths she fought to take... Shit. He might not be a doctor, but he knew that her pulse was weak. He needed to find help. Soon. He opened the heavy metal door to Allison's condo and looked at the useless handset. Damn it. Apparently, the signal needed more than just an open door.

He peered over the railing to check the stairwell for unwanted intruders. When it appeared to be empty, he ran back to Allison's cold, motionless body. He whispered, "I'll be right back, baby. You hang on."

He moved into the condo and toward the nearest window. He said a prayer that his cell phone would work, and stared as the bars wavered in and out. Once he had a signal, he dialed emergency services, and then the front desk of the building. He wanted to make sure Matt brought the EMTs to the correct area in the stairwell.

When all the bases were covered, he headed back to Allison's side and leaned against the wall. Misplaced adrenaline wrung his temples as his heartbeat pulsated in his ears. The fear in his heart was unbearable as he lowered himself to the floor. He lifted her hand, and a gold necklace fell onto the cement. He grabbed the intertwined ropes he was so used to seeing between her fingers and placed the chain in her palm, wrapping his hand around hers. "Hang on, sweetheart. You're going to be okay."

He wasn't sure if he was trying to convince her or if he was trying to convince himself. Either way, it was hard to watch her motionless body when there was nothing he could do. A tear threatened to fall down his cheek as he caressed her icy hand with his lips.

ALLISON STARED at the stark white walls of the hospital. She wasn't sure how she got there, but there was no mistaking where she was. She looked at the tubes attached to her arm and the TV playing reruns of sitcoms. That explained the dream she remembered about that hot young star.

Not that the dream had been unpleasant, quite the opposite, but halfway through the hottest part of the dream, the star morphed into Adam. She almost smiled as she tried to decide which part of the dream she liked best. Unfortunately, her grin was on hold, as she couldn't quite shake the distress over finding herself in the hospital.

What was she was doing here? She lifted her left arm, and pain radiated down her body as she noticed the sling wrapped around the limb. The throbbing doubled as she attempted to utilize that arm to sit up. She wanted to take in her surroundings, hoping to figure out what had happened, but her other arm didn't have the power needed to lift her torso.

In desolation, she slumped back on the bed, her head pounding from the exertion. She craned her neck and watched the rising sun spill red and gold into the room from the windows along the wall. The soft sunlight bounced off a slumbering Adam, breathing deeply on the bedside chair, his hair adorably disheveled.

Adorably disheveled? Ugh. She wasn't even going to go there. She had more important things to contemplate, like, how long had she been in the hospital? Even better, what had happened? She remembered packing up her apartment and the trip down memory lane as she'd looked through all of her belongings, but after that, nothing.

A nurse carrying a new IV bag walked into the room, interrupting Allison's thoughts on the day. He kneaded the bag and hung it on the stand next to the bed. Allison gazed at him with wide eyes.

"Good morning, sleepyhead. I'm Bill. How are you feeling?"

"I'm fine," she croaked through the sandpaper lodged in her throat. She ran her hand up and down her tender neck. The raw pain made it difficult to talk. "I think I'm fine. Where am I? What happened?"

"You're in the hospital. You had an accident. What is the last thing you remember?"

She gaped at Bill, racking her brain. What did she remember? Something must have happened. She looked at Adam, hoping to find the answer to the question in his face. He shuddered, and his eyes opened.

She shrugged. "I remember cleaning my house, um, and then I went to Chicago's Kitchen and Wine Bar for dinner. I remember walking home...and that terrible rain." Adam grabbed her hand, startling her. "Do you remember the elevators were broken? You rode up to the thirty-fifth floor and walked the rest of the way."

"I was cold. The air conditioning and the rain did not mix well."

"There was someone in the stairwell. You were attacked. Do you remember?" Bill asked as he checked her vitals and wrote them in her file.

Allison's eyes grew wider as the events unfolded in her mind. Her pulse quickened as her memory placed the attacker in her sights. Fear overwhelmed her senses as her hands began to shake.

"It's all right, sweetheart. You're safe." Adam caressed her fingers. "We'll find this bastard. Do you remember what happened?"

Allison recounted her trip up the stairs and the words that haunted her, "Leave, bitch. You don't belong here." As she described the events, her heart tripped, and her stomach clenched.

She stared at the sympathetic look on Adam's face. She started to remember other events of the evening. One by one. Adam and Ben sitting at a table flashed through her mind, and she pulled her hand away and glared at him. Fear morphed to anger as she pieced together the scene at Chicago's Kitchen.

"You couldn't have dinner with me, so what the

hell were you doing with Ben?" she grumbled, pain shooting through her throat. Talking had an adverse effect on her already weak voice. Yelling was ten times worse. She really needed to rethink doing that again anytime soon.

"That is my cue to leave." Bill placed her chart back in the holder at the foot of her bed. "Try not to use your voice too much. Let it rest."

"That was a misunderstanding," Adam started to explain once Bill walked out of the room.

"I don't want to fight," she cut in. She didn't have the energy to sort through his lies or listen to his excuses. She just wanted to move on. She was so tired of being hurt. All the anger and fight drained from her body. "And I don't want to talk about it."

Adam moved closer to her, grasping her hand. She pulled it from his grasp and attempted to cross her arms. The sling stopped any sideways motion.

"Then don't talk, just listen. I met with Ben due to some misguided advice. We were only talking. Nothing more. I am not selling the company."

Allison rolled to face the wall. She wanted to believe him, but she couldn't. He had a habit of breaking her heart. She knew he'd do it eventually, so maybe it was best if he just got it out of the way before she became more invested in the relationship.

Thankfully, Loraine's singsong voice broke through the tension. "How is the patient?"

Loraine and Dale wandered into the hospital room. Her gray hair was pulled back in a bun, allowing a better view of her rosy, plump cheeks. She removed her brown cashmere coat and gasped in horror. She threw the coat at Dale and hurried to Allison's side. Dale hung the jacket on a hook next to the bathroom and joined his mother.

A wince flittered across Loraine's face as she stared at Allison. Given the pain she felt in her jaw and neck, and the hideous bruising on her arms, Allison could only imagine how bad she looked. Loraine's horrified look spoke volumes, but just in case Allison wasn't sure how frightening she'd become, Loraine added, "You look horrible, dear."

"Mom." Adam and Dale called simultaneously, their eyes widening in shock.

"I didn't mean it like it sounded. I just don't understand who could do this to you." She frowned as she cradled Allison's face in her hands. Silence filled the room as concern colored Loraine's face. Only the sound of the morning news hung in the worry-riddled air.

"...Paul Mörder has made the news again, when he spoke out against the allegations of bribery and extortion..."

Loraine snatched the television remote and quieted the noise. "I'm sorry, but I'm so tired of hearing about that man. He's obviously a cheat. Do we really need to encourage him by plastering him all over the daily and nightly news?

"Now, more important things, how are you feeling?" Loraine asked as she bumped Adam to the side, making room next to the bed. Adam and Allison smiled at each other. Loraine had always been like a mother to her. The joke was that Allison was always her favorite child.

Allison didn't think she was necessarily the favorite. The women were close because Allison liked girl stuff. They loved shopping together and hitting the spa. They did things that boys wouldn't do. It didn't hurt that the men moved away, leaving Loraine without a child to pamper.

"I'm fine."

"Who would do this?" Loraine asked Adam, tears glistening in her eyes.

"I'm not sure, but I assure you I'm working on finding out," Adam said through clenched teeth.

"You're a good boy." She patted his cheek and turned back to Allison. She began to fluff the pillows and straighten the blankets. "So, when can you leave this place?"

"I'm not sure. I haven't seen the doctor yet." Allison looked to Adam for more details. It was disconcerting to be looking to everyone to give her information. She was normally in control, and she wasn't accustomed to relying on others for anything.

"The doctor was by earlier. She said we needed to wait for Allison to wake up, and then they'll run a few tests," he answered, his eyes fixed on the woman in the hospital bed. Allison turned to Loraine and forced a smile.

"I'm glad they're being thorough." The older woman looked suspiciously at her son and then at Allison. She reached out and patted her hand. "Well, whenever they decide to send you home, you're staying with me."

"I couldn't—" Allison tried to argue, but Loraine interrupted.

"You can, and you will. Don't argue with an old woman. It's not good for my heart. You will need someone to take care of you, and I need someone to take care of. It's a win-win," she said as she fussed with the pillow again.

"Thank you." Allison cleared her scratchy throat to stave off the incoming tears. She forgot how nice it was to have a mom, someone who doted and nurtured, someone who cared enough about you to use guilt to get their way. All these years of independence, she missed having the option to rely on someone. No matter how self-sufficient she might have become, she missed the support of family. A little bit, anyway.

"Do you need something to drink, dear?" Loraine asked as she placed a hand on Allison's forehead.

"Actually, that would be wonderful. Thank you."

Loraine patted her cheek and straightened the tray table over Allison's legs. "Dale, get her a drink."

Dale smiled as he got the plastic pitcher from the small cabinet against the wall. He poured a glass of water and handed it to Allison. "Well, Ally-gator. I should go pick up Nadia. I just wanted to make sure you were okay and drop off your new day nurse." Something between guilt and sadness was written all over his face. "I'm so sorry this happened to you."

"Thanks." Allison smiled as Dale wrapped his arms around her and kissed her cheek. "Be careful. Don't try to fight any more bad guys. If you are going to fight bad guys, make sure you can take 'em."

Allison barked out a small laugh and shook her head. She looked at Dale again. It wasn't guilt in his eyes. Sadness, yes. Fear, definitely. He was a good friend.

As Dale got himself ready to leave, a small woman wearing a white lab coat entered the room. With the diversion, Dale snuck out the door with one final wave.

"Good morning, Allison. I'm Doctor Marilu Castillo. It looks like you had an accident. How are you feeling?" she asked as she plucked the patient chart from the foot of the bed.

"My arm hurts a bit, and my throat, but other than that, I feel fine." The doctor glanced back and forth from the chart to the IV.

"On a scale from one to ten, one being the least, how would rate your pain?"

"About a five."

"We can increase your medication, but it might make you incoherent and groggy." She closed the file and placed it at the head of the bed.

"I'll suffer through." Allison cringed. The last thing she needed was to be more dependent. She enjoyed having Loraine help, but that didn't mean she wanted to be loopy.

"Tell us if your pain becomes unbearable," the doctor advised as she looked over the bruises.

"When can she leave?" Loraine asked her.

"We have a test to run before we can let her go."

"What kind of test?" Loraine asked.

"We need to perform a non-contrast CT to make sure she has no underlying injuries. The technician should be here to pick her up shortly." Dr. Castillo smiled and patted her foot. "Once we have those results, we'll have a better idea of her injuries."

CHAPTER TWENTY-ONE

ADAM WAITED for Allison to return from her testing. His mom left to harass the nurses and doctors. She wanted to make sure Allison would have a private room and the best possible care. Ensuring that level of care meant a million questions and obsessive micromanaging on her part.

He picked up his cell phone and stared at the screen. He had avoided this call, but he couldn't get around it any longer. He'd had every intention of heading back to Phoenix this week, but with Allison in danger, there was no way he'd leave her alone.

The ring back tone from the Phoenix police department chirped in his ear. "Captain Donnelley."

"Morning, Captain."

"Byrnes. I thought I'd hear from you. I'm sorry to hear about your father's murder."

"You heard?"

"Yeah. It's a small world."

"Let me guess, your college roommate in the mayor's office here in Chicago—"

"That would be wrong to resort to petty gossip. I only follow proper channels. How's the family handling the news?"

Adam smiled at the subject change. He might claim to follow proper channels, but Adam knew his boss would do whatever it took to make sure his officers were okay. Even if that meant checking with an old friend to make sure the investigation into the death of an officer's father was handled correctly.

"They're hanging in there. It's been a rough transition. In fact, that's what I wanted to talk to you about. I need to take a little more time—I still have a few more loose ends to tie up, so I might need to take a leave of absence."

"No problem. How much longer do you need?"

"A week. Two, tops."

"Two? You're not planning on sticking your nose into their investigation?"

"I'll stay out of their way, but this is personal."

"Let Chicago handle it. You of all people should know that things tend to get screwed up when they're personal."

"It's under control," Adam said between clenched teeth. He knew what he was doing. His captain should know him well enough to know he'd have complete command of the situation.

"All right. I guess I can transfer your cases to Jacobson and Schell while you're gone."

"Thanks, Captain."

Adam hit the end icon and stared out the window. What was he doing? He just signed up for a week—or two—more in Chicago. Why couldn't he just leave?

He didn't have to stay. Chicago PD could watch over Allison. She would probably prefer having them shadow her, anyway. From all indications, she didn't want anything to do with him. Even so, he stayed. He didn't trust the police to keep her safe. Only him.

He heard the pathetic excuses as he made them and shook his head. He could trust the cops, hell, he was the cops. It was hard to admit, but the main reason he couldn't go was because he was falling hard for Allison. Shit. That was the main reason he should be running back to Phoenix. He wasn't looking for this. But somehow, he couldn't imagine life without her. He couldn't imagine walking away. Somewhere in the midst of all this crap, he'd fallen in love with her.

His mother's voice brought his attention back to the hospital, her shrill demands torturing the poor staff. He wondered if she had been this demanding when he was in the hospital getting his tonsils out. He smiled. That explained why the nurses had avoided his room whenever his mom was around.

"So, we'll move her room before she gets back. I don't want her to be a part of it. I want it to appear seamless. She doesn't need the added stress." Loraine picked up Allison's personal items and began placing them into a plastic bag adorned with the hospital name. As she folded the clothes, Allison's broken necklace fell to the floor. A sad smile crossed her lips as she played with the broken clasp.

"I gave this to Allison for Christmas a few years ago. Your father let me design it for the girls." She massaged the mangled gold in her hand. "I gave one to Brook too. The Celtic knot design is said to protect the wearer. It must not have worked."

"Well, she's alive, and she's going to be okay. So maybe it did work, Mom." He watched as shadows crossed his mother's eyes. She put the broken chain in her pocket.

"Maybe. I suppose I should have it fixed and get it back to her, then. Anyway, they're preparing a private room for Allison. It's depressing enough around here. She should at least have her own room. We need to pack up all her personal items to take with us. Oh, and that reminds me— We need to hire a moving company to get Allison's apartment cleaned out. I just spoke with Brook, and her lease is up in a few days."

"You were able to reach her? I tried calling her, but she wouldn't answer the damn phone."

"Adam Montgomery Byrnes, don't swear in a hospital. I taught you better than that."

"So, I can swear outside of a hospital?"

"Don't get fresh. If you need something to occupy your time, go call the moving company," she scolded.

"I'll take care of it."

"I'm sure you will Later. Let's talk now." She sat down in a visitor's chair.

Whenever his mother wanted to talk, she was up to something. Or worse, she knew something. The question was, which was it? He had always been an expert at interrogation, and there was no doubt where he inherited that skill.

"So, what's going on with you and Allison?"

She knew. Although, knowing her, this was all some elaborate fishing trip, where she pretended to know things so Adam would stupidly give her the real details. Her skills were good, but his had gotten better over the years.

"What are you talking about?" A weasel tactic? Yes. He just asked a stupid question. But diversion was the best tactic. He powered on his phone and opened the Internet. "Did her sister tell you if Allison has a preference for moving companies?"

"No preference, and don't change the subject."

"Why do you think there's something going on with us?" He continued to stare at the small screen, scrolling through the search results. Not really seeing a darn thing, just hoping the action would stop the line of questioning.

"Oh, please, I'm not blind. I saw the way you were looking at each other. You two have been a relationship waiting to happen since she came into our life."

His eyes lifted from the screen, and he stared at his mother in disbelief. He didn't think he treated Allison any differently than he treated anyone else. In fact, he was, generally, more aloof with her.

"Don't try to tell me stories, young man. I can read you like a book."

"Fine. We were seeing each other."

"Were?"

"I fu— messed up. I don't know if she'll forgive me."
He hung his head and prayed she didn't ask why. He
didn't need his mom on the warpath. He was having
enough trouble dealing with one woman's disappointment. He didn't need another woman unhappy
with him.

"She'll forgive you," she said matter-of-factly.

"How can you be sure?" He loved the confidence
she had in Allison, in him.

"Anything you might have done was out of love.
You love her." She got up and walked over to him,
placing a hand on his arm. "And I can see it in her eyes.
She loves you."

He stared at his mom. He didn't know how Allison
felt about him, but he doubted love was involved. He
thought about the pain in her eyes as she walked up to
the table at the restaurant. It seemed like a lifetime ago.
He wished he felt that sure about impending forgive-
ness or love.

A nurse entered. "We have a private room available
if you'd like to follow me." She picked up Allison's
chart, and Loraine and Adam took her personal
belongings.

As they walked along the corridor, Loraine
bombarded the nurse with another round of a thousand
and one questions. Adam followed behind, praying the
staff didn't hold his mother's tormenting against Allison. Loraine had a kind heart, but sometimes she was
overwhelming.

Once they arrived at the new room, they didn't
have to wait long. A technician appeared, wheeling

Allison inside.

Adam couldn't fault his mom for her initial reaction to Allison. His heart broke at the bruising on her neck and face.

She rose from the wheelchair and then let the nurse help her into bed. She tried to hide the cringes when she bumped her arm or turned her neck too far, putting on a brave face as she climbed into the bed. She tried, but he could still see her pain, her fear.

No, he wasn't going anywhere. There was no way he'd leave her like this.

ALLISON'S TESTS had taken some of the fight out of her. She only had enough energy to complain about the room change and the extra cost associated with the private room for a few minutes, but eventually, she'd given up. She hated that the Byrnes were spending the extra money, but she knew it was futile. Loraine was a force of nature, and anyway, Allison was hoping this whole thing was temporary. She was banking on being sprung by tomorrow at the latest.

No matter how much she enjoyed the mom-helicopter hovering around, taking care of her, she was tired of spending time with the traitor. She was looking forward to moving into Loraine's house. Adam would go crawl under his rock at the hotel, and she could spend some time in peace.

Allison started to drift as Loraine and Adam watched the flat screen hanging on the wall, some show about a group of ghost hunters. Her eyelids popped open when Detectives Washington and Perretti walked in the door.

Shay inhaled and said, "I'm sick of seeing you both."

Allison smiled at the warmth in the woman's tone and muted the TV. "You're not exactly my favorite person these days either. You only come around when bad things happen."

"Sorry, we'll have to make a social call one of these days," Detective Perretti ribbed.

"Believe it or not, my life doesn't normally suck this bad."

"I would hope not. We need to talk to you both about the latest attack. Are you up to a few questions, Allison?"

"Sure." She had no desire to relive the events of the past twenty-four hours, but without the rehashing, they couldn't find the jerk and put him away, preferably for a long time.

"So, you walked up the stairs at the condo?"

"Yes. The penthouse elevators were being repaired, and I was freezing after being caught in the rain and coming into the air conditioning. I just wanted to get home." She sighed as she played with the IV line attached to her arm and looked around the room at the apprehensive faces. She must sound like an absolute lunatic. She felt the embarrassing redness creeping up her cheeks.

She recounted the events of the evening, with Adam adding his bits and pieces to round out the story.

After a grueling hour of redundancy, Allison's heavy eyes fought to close.

"Can we call it a night? She's exhausted," Loraine asked as Allison's eyes drooped. The detectives must have agreed, because the last thing Allison remembered was drifting off to the sound of Adam sinking into the chair beside the bed.

▭

THE NOISE of his cell phone woke him from his sound sleep. He rolled over and grabbed the chirping annoyance from his nightstand. Still half asleep, he flipped it open without checking caller ID.

"Hello."

"What the hell?" the familiar voice of Paul Mörder growled into the phone, making him regret even answering the damn thing. "Why am I still waiting? It's bad enough you let someone else figure out the specifics of our arrangement, but now I have to sit and wait for the evidence. If that information gets into the wrong hands... I have enough problems. I don't need to worry about your screw-ups."

"There's nothing to worry about, Paul," he assured the man on the other end as his eyes flew open. He tried to keep the annoyance out of his tone. He didn't need to coddle this psychopath on a regular basis. "I have everything under control. You just worry about staying out of trouble, and for God's sake, quit talking to the media. Even stupid politicians figure out when to shut the hell up."

"Are you telling me what to do, you sonofabitch?" Mörder screamed. He could almost hear the spit hitting the phone. "You forget who runs this operation. I own you! If you don't like the way I'm handling things, I'll send over my complaint department to hear your grievances. I guarantee you won't be complaining when they're done with you."

His annoyance morphed to anger. "Are you threatening me? I told you I didn't want to do this."

"You weren't so against it when you were cashing my checks. Don't forget. If I go down, I'm taking your ass with me."

"You know what, Paul? Don't call me anymore." He slammed the phone shut and threw it against the wall. Hanging up on a member of the Russian mob just put him in a whole new class of trouble. He needed to get that information to Mörder before he became just another casualty.

━━

ADAM SQUINTED as the sun's rays peeked out of the darkened sky. He had slept a few hours, but this video kept calling to him. He couldn't get his mind off Allison, guilt coursing through his veins when he thought about the other night. The television in his father's home office washed the room with blue as he scanned the security footage from Allison's building. So far, nothing stood out on the night she was attacked. No obvious crazies had wandered the halls or stairwells.

In fact, there wasn't a whole lot of action of any

kind. It was almost as bad as sitting through a stakeout, but at least a stakeout had the chance of excitement. He thought about pulling a few strings and getting the case file from the Chicago Police Department, but he'd promised his captain he'd stay out of it.

He'd tried to stay out of it. Well, he'd like to think he tried, but now Allison was involved. There was no way he was sitting on the sidelines. He would stay out of the way, but he had to make sure she was safe before he went back home.

Home.

Somehow, the word felt so hollow. A few days ago, he knew where he belonged. He had known home was in Phoenix. He craved the life he had back in Arizona. Now he didn't know what he wanted. So much had changed, and yet nothing had changed.

He still missed work. He still missed his friends. Yet, the empty house and the occasional attention of random police groupies had no draw for him any longer. He hated thinking about leaving his mom and Allison. The thought of walking away twisted him in knots.

Running a hand through his hair, he pushed the thoughts away. No matter what, he still wanted to follow protocol as closely as possible. He was not going to rock the boat and ask for the files from CPD. He needed his captain on his side, and with his ties to Chicago politics, any move Adam might make would get right back to him. He couldn't risk it. So instead, he sat through the video, hoping for any sort of clue on who would have attacked the woman he loved.

Loved? He loved her. Why did that phrase keep running through his mind? She hated him. He leaned his head against the office chair. What the hell was wrong with him? He must be hallucinating due to lack of sleep.

He lifted his head and stared through the empty halls flickering on the television screen. This was getting him nowhere. Whoever attacked her knew how to avoid the cameras. He clicked the TV off and threw the remote on the desk.

Shit.

So far, he hadn't come across anything that would help, and he was running out of time. Allison's doctor had advised her not to drive because of her pain meds, and Adam's mother was pushing that restriction. The few times Allison was let out of the house, family surrounded her, but he heard she was off the medication now and close to being released from house arrest. Once that happened, he would have a hell of a time making sure she was safe.

The whole thing was ludicrous. He'd talked with anyone who might be able to shed light on the situation —Brook, Julie, his mother—and they all said the same thing. "Allison has no enemies."

He was coming up blank at every turn and running out of time. He stared at the security discs on his desk, frustration oozing from every pore. Who was out to get Allison? And what did this whole thing have to do with his father?

First, the break-in, and then Allison was attacked at the condo. The common thread was the condo. He twirled a disc between his fingers. He needed to get back to that condo. He had a feeling all the answers were there.

CHAPTER TWENTY-TWO

ALLISON OPENED her eyes to darkness, and nostalgia overwhelmed her. She glanced around and saw the familiar fixtures of the Byrnes' guest room. She'd spent many nights in the warm comfort of this home. Herb and Loraine had been adamant about Brook and her staying the evening after late-night holidays and family gatherings. They had never liked the sisters driving the dark roads in the evening.

She glanced at the glaring numbers on the clock beside her overstuffed bed. Four a.m. She groaned and threw the down blanket over her head. It was so nice when she left the hospital. It had been heavenly recovering at the Byrnes's house, but she had a feeling that she needed to get back to work soon. Her mind and body yearned for more stimulation than soap operas and pinochle.

She supposed that her restlessness was a good thing. She must be getting better if sleep and rest had lost most of their appeal. Unfortunately, the doctor made it perfectly clear that she was not to return to work for two more weeks. At least she thought it was two more weeks. She stared at the ceiling. She couldn't remember what day it was.

Ugh. She knew Loraine wouldn't parole her until the doctor gave her a clean bill of health. Waiting for that clean bill of health might make her lose her sanity. She threw the blankets off and rose from the bed.

"No more sleep," she called to the shadows swirling around the empty room.

She walked to the window and looked over the silent gardens. The grounds that once ran flush with lilies and tulips were now barren, awaiting the impending winter snow. Soft moonlight bounced off the meticulously landscaped evergreens that encircled the area and led along the path to the private lake.

Green Acres, as it was lovingly called since they lived on ten acres of land with a horse barn and an eighty-five-hundred-square-foot manor, was located in a suburb forty miles outside of Chicago. It was never any wonder Herb hadn't wanted to commute here every day. A forty-mile trip took anywhere from an hour to three hours, depending on weather and traffic.

She turned away from the window and looked at her room. The antique-white wood posts of her king-size canopy bed welcomed guests with flowing purple silk fabric draped across the brass canopy. She walked to the dresser and picked out a pair of lacy pink panties and bra. She covered those with blue jeans and a mohair sweater and headed out the door to roam the silent house.

All was quiet. Apparently, everyone else was sleeping peacefully. She huffed and walked down the long west hall toward the kitchen. A nice cup of hot tea should help her get a jump start on her day, no matter how empty that day might be.

The soft pat of her feet hitting the carpeted floor was the only noise circulating about the house. She loved the Byrnes' home. The arched doorways and the stone and walnut finishes gave the large expanse of space a sense of intimacy. She walked through the ornate hallways and noticed a warm glow streaming from the kitchen. She stopped at the open doorway when she found Adam sitting at the breakfast bar reading the newspaper. Before she turned around, he glanced up and said, "Good morning."

"Morning. I thought I was the only one with sleep issues." She entered the room and walked over to the cupboards. She pulled a mug from the cabinet and searched for the box of teabags. The box was sitting in front of Adam. Great.

"Since when do you drink tea?"

"Ran out of coffee, and I always get up this early," he said easily as he folded the paper and then sifted through the box of teabags. He smiled, pulling a bag out, and walked over to Allison and her cup. "So, does this mean you're talking to me now?"

It was juvenile, but she ignored his question. The whole situation was juvenile. She hadn't talked to Adam since she left the hospital. She'd managed to avoid him, which took great talent since he'd also moved into the house. She made herself a cup of hot water, and Adam placed the teabag in the hot liquid for her. He went and got the honey from the pantry and squeezed some of the golden nectar into her steaming cup. She dunked the bag, ignoring the fact that he knew how she took her tea. It means nothing.

"So, I take it you haven't moved back to the hotel. You know, you don't have to stay here. I'm perfectly safe."

"Who says I'm staying here for you? Don't you think that's a bit arrogant, thinking that all my decisions are based on you?" he challenged and sat back down in his chair. He opened the paper and lifted his cup to his lips. "So, what type of sleep issues are you having?"

"Trouble staying asleep."

He nodded and put down his paper and coffee. "I can see that. It must be killing you to have to rely on someone besides yourself."

"What?"

He continued, smirking. "Or it could be that it's tough to sleep with me being in the next room. I radiate sexuality."

"Yeah." She rolled her eyes and removed the teabag, placing it on a saucer sitting on the counter. She took a sip and scowled. She really needed to get to civilization and grab a decent vanilla chai. It had gotten so bad, she would tear up every time she saw a Starbucks commercial. "That must be it. Your scorching sexual pull must be keeping me from a decent night's sleep. Maybe you should go back to the hotel to save me from your hotness."

"Nah." He smiled. "I have other ways to satiate that sexual pull."

Allison shook her head as she leaned against the counter. "Don't you need to get to work or something?"

"I'd much rather stay here and talk with you. I never thought you'd talk to me again." A somber tint glazed his eyes. "Anyway, it's the weekend. I have a meeting with Dale around nine, and then an excruciating luncheon with my mother, so I have a few hours yet. Since I sort of own the company, I can go in whenever I want." Adam walked over to the counter.

"Your arrogance is very unbecoming," she said, mentally beating her head against an imaginary wall. She'd thought it was Monday, but darn if it still wasn't the weekend. This hospice thing would never end at this rate.

Disappointment raced through her mind until she saw Adam edge closer to her. Her breath hitched as he moved within inches of her body. She felt his breath on her cheek as she tried to convince herself that his close proximity was doing nothing to her. Her dislike was causing her heart rate to skyrocket, not some loathsome infatuation with this jerk.

"I think you like it," he whispered, guiding a stray hair behind her ear. He leaned his head toward her. The scent of tea and mint wafted from him, her lips aching in desire.

Her mind was seconds away from mush. He should not have this effect on her, she reprimanded herself. He was a lying jerk. She started to remember why he infuriated her, and she pushed at his chest before his lips confused her further.

"Stop," she blurted, her fingers wrapping around his shirt.

"Why?" He leaned his forehead on hers, his breath enveloping her lips. God, she wanted to feel those lips on hers, but she knew that wasn't the answer.

"I don't trust you, Adam." She shook her head against his, wanting to pull away from the temptation. She couldn't, though. She wasn't moving. She was stuck. Her body stuck in front of him. Her mind stuck on him. Her heart stuck in love with him. Why did logic and common sense abandon her when she was around him?

"Allison, I swear I have no intention of selling to Mooring. I went there as a favor. I would never let that happen." He pulled his head away, his deep-green eyes penetrating her soul. Her heart thudded in her chest. "I need you to trust me."

"Why should I?" All of her defenses crumbled. Her hand still rested on his broad chest, the taut muscles crumbling all discipline.

"Because I love you, and I can't bear the thought of hurting you."

Her heart swelled in her chest. It warmed and pounded at the words. Did he really say that? Love? He'd spent so many years messing with her emotions, how dare he say the L-word to her?

"What?" She pulled away. He wrapped his muscled arms around her and held her against the counter. She stopped moving and stared at his beseeching eyes.

"Just listen, please. For the past few months, I've felt lost. I didn't know what it was until I thought I lost you. The thought of never seeing you again scared the hell out of me."

"Adam, we've gone down this road before," she argued.

"No, not like this. This is different, and you know it." He pulled his arms back and cupped her chin.

"You're right, this is worse."

"Worse?" His hand dropped to his side.

"Yes, don't you get it?" She pushed him away and stormed to the other side of the kitchen island. Nothing like three feet of granite to put a little distance between a girl and her problems. Although she only had one problem—one six-foot very sexy male problem. "Before, we were young and foolish, now—"

"Now we're old and foolish?" he finished for her, sarcasm and anger tingeing the words as he walked around the island.

"Yes." She sighed. "But we're not foolish. I'd like to think we've outgrown that. We had some fun together, but we have a good working relationship. Let's not ruin it."

The calm, logical side of her was teetering on the edge, but so far, she'd held it together. After all, he had no right to be mad. This was just like all the other times, but this time she was stronger and smarter. She would not let Adam Byrnes take advantage of her again, especially when he was throwing around words like love.

"I know you want me, and I've told you I love you. Why are you fighting it?"

"Why aren't you?" she said in frustration. "Is this some sort of game? Sweep into town and work gullible Allison into a frenzy and then leave? Because let me tell you, I don't want to play that game anymore."

"There's no sweeping. No leaving." He inched closer to her as tears bit at the back of her eyes. She blinked to keep them at bay. Adam's eyes lit up with awareness. "That's it, isn't it? You're scared."

Impulse and frustration bubbled to the surface as she belted out, "Damn right, I'm scared. Do you know how devastated I was the last time you left? I cried... Never mind. I'm sorry, I just don't have the strength to go through that again."

"I'm not leaving."

"What about Phoenix?" A traitorous tear trailed down her cheek.

"We'll figure out the logistics later. For now, just trust me."

She stared into his earnest eyes. Why couldn't she just trust him? What was holding her back? Yeah, he met with Ben, but deep down, she knew he wouldn't sell. This had nothing to do with the company.

Fear shivered down her spine as she stared at him. This had nothing to do with the company, and loving him wasn't the issue. Losing him was. She'd lost so much, and she couldn't bear to let him get close and lose him too.

"I love you," he said again.

"Stop saying that," she said, defeated. Her chest constricted as she forced the breath from her lungs. The thought of Adam going back to Phoenix and never seeing him again left a hole in the pit of her stomach. She sighed. She was already too invested in this relationship to back out now. There was no way to protect herself from getting hurt. Damn.

"Why?" He leaned over, cupping her chin in his hands.

Her gaze moved to his green eyes, brimming with concern. "I don't want to lose you." The floodgates opened as tears poured down her face. "No matter how you leave."

"Allison, I will never leave you willingly."

"What about unwillingly? I can't lose you." She lowered her eyes in humiliation.

"Then don't push me away. Give me—give us—a chance." He knuckled the tears from her cheek. "I don't know what our future holds, all I know is that I want to face it together. For fear of sounding like a fortune cookie, don't let your past dictate your happiness for the future."

She wanted to turn and run. She wanted to hide. But the look of unbridled love that shadowed his face mixed with her own overwhelming emotions and forced her to stand her ground. For years she thought was she was strong. She didn't need anyone, most of all a man. Yet, here she was in front of a wonderful man, and she was scared. All these years, it wasn't that she didn't need anyone. It was fear. She'd been afraid to let anyone get too close. She didn't want to be scared any longer.

"I want to face it with you too. Even if you do say corny things." She placed her hand on his cheek.

He kissed the palm of her hand. "So, where does that leave us now?"

"Make love to me."

He stared into her eyes and placed his soft lips on hers. An electric jolt shot straight to her belly and below. Her core blazed in delight as each touch fanned the flame. Wow, she wanted him. She craved all of him.

Her kisses intensified as his hands traveled up and down her overheated body. "Are you sure you want this? Because if we're going to stop, we should stop now." He pulled back, holding her good arm to her side.

"I want you. I love you."

Adam's face glowed with happiness as he covered her mouth with his. Her body responded to his probing tongue, every nerve ending igniting as she let herself feel loved. Had he really said that he loved her? Her body sure heard it, and her enraptured heart busted open. She had tried to control her feelings for Adam, but she never could remove them. She just managed to repress them now and again.

He took her hand and led her upstairs.

"We can't do this." She tried to pull away as he opened his bedroom door.

He drew in a large breath and pulled away. "I'm sorry. You're right. We'll wait until you're feeling better. Is your arm okay?"

"It's not that. My arm is fine."

"Then why can't we do this?"

"What about your mom and brother?"

He smiled and pushed her to the wall in the hall-way. Her heart raced as he pulled her leg up around his waist. He ran his tongue up her neck and stopped to hum in her ear. "It adds to the danger."

All logic dissipated as he licked and nibbled her ear. Her body throbbed in need. She managed to force out, "Bedroom. Now."

ADAM LIFTED her other leg and carried her to his bedroom. He tapped the door closed with his foot. His mouth tasted her as he strode across the room, pulling away after he laid her on the bed.

She raised an eyebrow and asked, "Where are you going?"

"You need to be patient." He kissed her forehead and stepped back. He smiled at the pleading in her eyes. It was nice to know he had the same effect on her as she had on him.

Adam unbuttoned his shirt. Allison's eyes grew dark as he unzipped his jeans. She sat up and inched her way down to the edge of the bed. She leaned toward him. She covered his hand with hers and slowly pushed his jeans down the length of his legs. Slow. Steady. Hot. She knelt on the floor in front of him, pulling down his boxer briefs and taking him in her hand. Up. Down.

He hissed and threw his head back. Damn. He had

to stop this, or he'd finish before they even started. He reached down and grabbed her hand. "Stop."

He helped her stand as he pulled off her sweater and opened her bra. He covered her mouth with his and angled her toward the bed. He bent down and peeled her jeans toward her bare toes. She lay before him, her hips swaying in the lacy pink underwear. She was sexy. Beautiful. Hot. He played with the pink lace and barely stopped himself from ripping the fabric from her body. He grabbed the edges and pulled them down slowly. Well, he meant to do it slowly, but something told him it was faster than he had wanted. The fabric trailed down her soft, creamy thighs. He leaned over her pliable body, a moan escaped her lips. Her eyes widened as she threw her hand over her mouth.

He reached for her uninjured hand and twined his fingers in hers as he pulled it to his lips. "I like when you're vocal."

"Yeah, but I bet no one else in the house does." She laughed.

Adam smiled wickedly and leaned into her. "But I like it," he whispered before melding his lips to hers. Yeah, he wanted to hear her moan in pleasure again. His goal was to hear that groan over and over again before they were through. He ran his hands over her body, laying the foundation for making that goal come true.

A few hours later, Adam lay in the darkness, watching Allison's chest rise and fall. The sun had finally risen, but the room-darkening shades managed to keep the bright light subdued. He twirled her dark-blond hair around his finger, careful to avoid waking her up. She might have had trouble sleeping before, but she seemed to be doing just fine now.

Even though it was the weekend, he really needed to continue investigating Allison's attack. The sooner she was safe, the sooner he figured out what he was going to do.

On top of that, his mother wanted him to go to some charitable luncheon, and he needed to help Dale with some paperwork at some point. Neither the lure of work nor the draw of mundane socializing left him with any desire to leave the warm shelter of the bed. Allison had gone through a rough couple of weeks, so he really couldn't leave. He might wake her up, and she needed her rest.

He rolled over and saw his cell phone on the night-stand. He swiped the text icon and sent Dale a message. As he hit send, Allison shuddered awake. Her glazed eyes stared at Adam.

"Morning, sunshine."

"Hi, what time is it?"

"A little before nine."

"Oh, shit." She bolted upright. "Didn't you have to work today?"

"I'm ditching. Don't tell the boss," he joked and pulled her down to kiss her neck.

"You are the boss." She smiled and nuzzled closer.

"Right. Don't tell me what I've done. I'd hate to have to write myself up for insubordination. So, what are we doing today?"

"Really? You're going to take me out of the house?"

She wrapped her arm around his neck as he nodded. "Thank you."

"You're easy to please." He smiled.

"I'm just so sick of being cooped up here. I miss driving, I miss civilization, I miss good tea."

"What?" He asked with mock horror. "Are you saying my tea's no good? I hope you know I got that from the best tea shop in Phoenix."

"No, I'm saying keep your day job. A barista, you are not."

"You're lucky I agree, or I'd be mildly offended." He brought his hands to his ironic, wounded heart.

"Sure, you would. Can we head over to the condo? I need to start making room for my stuff. It was nice of your mom to put all my stuff in storage, but it's silly when there is a perfectly good condo waiting to be filled."

"Are you sure you're ready to go back there?" He wasn't sure she was ready, but that did work nicely into his plans. He could keep an eye on her and search the condo.

"I'm not going to let someone scare me away from my home."

"All right. Let's go get your condo ready for habitation." He smiled and kissed her nose.

CHAPTER TWENTY-THREE

THE MUSICAL STYLINGS of the local easy listening station drifted from the speakers in the master bedroom as Allison looked at the extravagant king-size bed. The ornate carvings brought the bed to life, but she was really looking forward to sleeping in her own bed. The sooner she packed up Herb's possessions, the sooner she would get her own bed out of storage.

She wandered around her new bedroom. The differences between her new room and the old one were staggering. Her old bedroom had been small, cozy, and utilitarian, while the new bedroom was large and currently dressed for English monarchy. The large dark wood bed, draped in white and gold, stood against the far wall. She wrapped her good hand around the bulbous post, her broken arm still in a cast. It truly was a beautiful bed, and the matching period dresser, armoire, and leaded glass lamps added to the splendor of the set.

Hopefully, Loraine wanted it at the house.

Allison couldn't see keeping this furniture at the condo—it just wasn't her taste, even if it was truly a beautiful set. Her own king-size bed with its contemporary black frame was more her style. The sleek lines and simple design helped her relax after a stressful day.

She looked in the sitting room off the main bedroom. She just couldn't see herself relaxing in the hard, ornate Glastonbury chair. She had visions of hot chocolate, comfy slippers, and a small fire in the fireplace. She saw herself curling up in her bowl chair, reading a book by the warm glow of an overhead floor lamp.

Adam sauntered into the bedroom, carrying additional boxes. "I put the full boxes in the fourth bedroom. Are you sure you don't want to keep some of this stuff? It is yours, per the will."

"I'm sure. I want your mom to choose what she wants. After all, I wouldn't appreciate it the way she might."

"You could always sell it."

"I'd rather your mom have a chance to go through it first. If she wants to get rid of it, I can see if my sister wants it. She loves antique furniture. It's silly for this to go to waste."

"I also made room in there for the bed. Are you sure you want to get rid of it? It looks sturdy enough to survive a nuclear bomb." He smiled and walked over to Allison. He placed his hand on the post next to hers. She leaned in and rested her cheek above it.

"Luckily, we haven't had a whole lot of nuclear

attacks in Chicago. Otherwise, I might be tempted to keep this Victorian behemoth."

"Yeah." He scowled and inclined toward Allison. He stopped inches from Allison's lips. Her heart skipped as his breath tickled her cheek. Adam gradually pulled her hand around the post. "Keeping this would be rather tragic."

"I'm surprised you don't like it. I thought all golden boys loved expensive things."

He smiled a wicked grin and pushed her onto the bed. She playfully squirmed as he held her hips down. His intentions rose as he straddled her body, his hands pushing up her shirt, exposing her black lace bra. He leaned into her and whispered, "I'll admit it has its usefulness."

Her body burned, and her head spun as he kissed her neck. "We can't do this here," she whispered as his hands roamed her stiff nipples.

"Why? Do you have something against golden boys all of a sudden? Or are you against expensive things?"

"No, but it's your dad's bed."

He sighed and moved away, standing just in front of the bed. He reached for her hand and pulled her to her feet. "Let's get this thing out of here and get your bed in before I explode."

"Explode? Isn't that a little dramatic?" She laughed, but she understood the sentiment. The fireworks rumbled deep in her stomach, frustration taking over. She adjusted her T-shirt, re-covering her throbbing breasts.

"Haven't you heard men can die without it?"

"Honestly? Not since I was sixteen." She rolled her eyes and headed over to the closet, where she began filling boxes and placing them by the door. Adam helped, removing the boxes and putting them in a room down the hall.

When the closet was empty, she looked around the almost barren bedroom as her stomach growled. Her hand and eyes flew to her snarling belly. Her shirt was filthy. There was no way she could go out in public like this. She rummaged in the closet and found an old sweatshirt, pulling it over her head.

Adam cleared the last of the heavy bed frame from the room, leaving a big Turkish rug covering the floor. Although it tied the room together, Allison couldn't help but laugh at the delicate designs on the Turkish rug intermixed with the heavy Victorian fare.

Adam returned, and they began to roll the giant carpet. They carried the hundred-pound monstrosity to the spare bedroom, dropping the dust magnet onto the floor. Adam moved the furniture around, creating pathways, while Allison grabbed a broom and walked back to the empty master bedroom.

She swished the bristles back and forth, thinking of the pizza she planned on talking Adam into getting for lunch. Her mouth watered as she thought about Chicago deep-dish pizza.

She moved the broom, and one of the coarse fibers stuck to the floor. What the... She leaned down and followed a set of quarter-inch-wide lines in the floor with her finger. The lines outlined as square about the size of a large binder. She pushed the center of the square, but nothing happened. She bent over and pushed her narrow fingers in the line and tried to pull up on the floor. Nothing. Adam entered the room with his phone to his ear.

"Yes, Mom, the moving company will be there tomorrow afternoon to drop off the furniture and the rest of Dad's stuff. No, she doesn't want to keep anything... I asked her... Yes, I explained it's hers..." He smiled at Allison and lowered himself to Allison's level. "Okay. I have to go now... Yes... Okay... Bye".

"Good conversation?"

"She thinks I coerced you into giving her the furniture. For what purpose, I have no idea."

"Why would she think you coerced me?"

"Apparently, she's seen your furniture and can't believe you don't want to keep the stuff that's here."

Allison shook her head. She could just imagine how things would go from now on. Now that Loraine didn't have to save Allison from her awful apartment, she would try to save her from cheap furniture. Oh, the horror.

"What are you doing?" He knocked on the floor.

"I'm trying to figure out what this is. I've poked it, prodded it, and pulled it, and nothing happens."

Adam pushed on the center. He then attempted to put his fingers in the lines, same as she had, but his fingers were too large.

"I tried that already." She smiled the same grin she saved for people who insisted upon pushing the elevator button after it had already been pressed.

He took his hand away, and she tried pushing on

the right side of the bit of flooring, and then the left. Something clicked, and the piece of floor popped open, revealing a small steel door with a keypad.

"Okay, well, I guess it's something." She tapped the face of the safe. "What do you think the combination is?"

"I'm not sure. Maybe his birthday." He pressed the keys. He twisted the handle. Nothing.

"What about your mom's birthday?" she offered. He entered the digits, but again, nothing happened.

"How about your birthday, or Dale's? Parents' anniversary?"

She started throwing out important milestones, hoping one would stick. He entered another round of dates and stared at Allison. His eyes lit up, and he pushed in a set of numbers. He turned the handle, and the door opened, giving way as the interior shelves rose from the floor.

"That is one cool safe." She stared in awe as the final lighted shelf ascended, running parallel with the floor.

Adam nodded. "It's an auto-lift safe. The safe comes to you so you don't have to go digging around the floor."

"What was the combination?" she asked.

"Your birthday."

"My birthday?"

"You always were the favorite." He bumped her shoulder.

"You remember my birth date?"

"Yeah."

She smiled as a warm feeling flowed through to her toes. He remembered her birthday. She didn't think he even cared she had a birthday, let alone the actual date. She rolled her eyes. She was getting excited about a birthdate.

They sat on the floor, pulling paperwork from the safe. Adam snatched a large stack of papers but remained focused on the first item. Allison grabbed a box of chocolate and a manila envelope. Herb had told her to toss the box of mints before Loraine found it, but she hated to waste expensive chocolate. She put the box to the side and flipped the envelope over in her hand.

"It's sealed." She played with the flap of the envelope.

"So, open it." He stared at the contracts in his hand.

Allison opened the envelope. Her brows furrowed, first in concentration then in shock. "Do you know what this is?"

"There's a stack of stocks here." His eyes rounded.

"Can you please put that down and pay attention?" she said, a bit too harshly. "I need you to focus."

He looked at her with humor in his eyes. "You really don't care about how much money you have here? He left you the condo and all its contents. This is a content."

"No, I'm sure it's not mine, look at this." She handed over the envelope. He looked over the paperwork and began reading. His eyes slowly narrowed, and his grip tightened, probably as he read the words

"DNA Result Report." He looked over to Allison. "Did you know about this?"

"No. Julie always told us Cody's father was out of the picture. I take it you didn't know either."

"No. How did she keep something like this from all of us? We need to talk to her." He stood up and headed for the door. Allison chased after him.

"We? Are you sure this isn't a family matter?" She didn't want to impose. This was huge. And they wouldn't need some outsider.

"Allison, you've always been like family."

"That's not what you've said in the past." The words just fell out. And the hurt that echoed in those words was just hanging there. Shit.

Adam looked at her—not just looked—stared. "You know why that was, don't you?"

"No."

"I couldn't stand seeing you as my sister when I was thinking of all the things I wanted to do to you."

Allison's lips curled up. Even though it had killed her, she understood.

Adam slid his hand on her cheek. The warmth seeping into her pores and warming her whole body. "You are my family. Now, we should go." He pulled away.

She ran back to the floor and yanked the paperwork from the safe. She ran toward the front of the condo and followed Adam to the elevator. "Let's go."

EDWARD CONNOLLY STOOD in his study and reached for the pain reliever in the top drawer. Why were things always so damn complicated? It had all started out innocently enough. He'd started helping Paul Mörder with a few legal issues. A few legal issues that somehow transformed into bribery and extortion.

With all of the media attention these days, it was just a matter of time before he somehow got roped into the media shitstorm. He was hoping the journalists would drop the story, but apparently, there were multiple slow news days, so Paul had remained front and center.

He knew the Feds had been after Paul for years due to his organized crime connection—the crazy Kraut managed to weasel his way into the Kolosov crime family at an early age. Edward hadn't been doing all that much for the man in the beginning, but recently, however, his role had changed.

He had gone from pretending that he didn't know the judges, lawyers, and jurors were getting paid off to actually handing over the envelopes filled with cash. He'd had the political and legal connections to get close to the necessary people, and the pay was great.

Edward crossed the room and stared out the window. Why had Herb gotten involved? Edward warned him to stop looking into those damn books. If he just would have let it go—his friend would still be alive.

The doorbell broke him out of his stupor. He walked to the door and greeted his unexpected visitors.

"Adam, Allison, what a nice surprise." He motioned for them to enter. "To what do I owe this honor?"

Adam pulled out some paperwork and handed it to Edward. "Did you know about this?"

Edward read the document in disbelief. How had they found this paperwork? Herb had said it was in a safe place. They must have found his hiding spot. What else had they found in there?

"Unfortunately, I did, but I just found out recently. Where did you find this?"

"It was in my dad's safe at the condo. Does Dale know?"

"I don't think he knows yet. Julie was very adamant about him not finding out. She was afraid he'd try to take Cody away from her."

"That's absurd. Why didn't you tell us?"

"I discovered this recently," he lied, "and with your father's passing, I thought this was an inappropriate time to bring it up. Come, sit down."

"No. I want to talk to Julie." Adam ran a hand through his hair.

"She's at her boyfriend's house." He smiled. With them chasing Julie, he would have time to check the safe at the condo. "I can get you the address."

"Please do."

He spun the Rolodex on his desk. He located Ben's address and wrote it down on a small piece of paper. He escorted them out the door and watched as they left the driveway.

Then he wrenched his keys from the desk and headed for the condo.

CHAPTER TWENTY-FOUR

ADAM SPED down the Eisenhower Expressway toward the suburbs, while Allison sifted through the contracts and miscellaneous documents in front of her. She pulled out a dog-eared set of pages and sighed.

"What did you find? Please tell me there aren't any more secret babies in the family."

"No, nothing like that, it looks like a handful of bank statements. There are three deposits of half a million."

"Dollars?" He glanced at Allison for a second, eyes wide. He really should be focused on the road in front of him, but those documents in her hand—they could be the key to figuring out what happened to his father.

Unfortunately, he was having trouble focusing on anything other than that damn DNA report. Why hadn't his father told him? Why hadn't Dale? Heck, even his mother had said nothing. Had his father told them?

He'd never thought his family was the secretive

type. But between the murder and this little gem of information, it looked like there were hidden facts sprinkled throughout Chicago. He had no way of knowing who knew. That was why he wanted to talk to Julie.

She was another disappointment. Over the years, they'd become friends, or at least friendly. They had talked when given the opportunity. Why would she have kept this from him?

And as if this whole nightmare wasn't insane enough, now bank statements were roaming around. He couldn't wait to tie this up. The whole situation was exhausting.

"Yeah, a half-million dollars."

"Where were these deposits? Does it give a bank name?"

"It doesn't say. All the documents have are account numbers." She flipped another page. "Wait, Connolly is written in the corner. It looks like your father's handwriting. Could this be Julie's account? Why would he have given her money... Maybe for Cody?"

"I'm not sure, but that's one hell of a trust fund."

They pulled into the driveway of a well-maintained bungalow. A few orange and burgundy leaves twirled down from the mature trees, joining the others decorating the neat lawn. The white trim around the windows and door was offset by the dark bricks and the evergreen shrubs surrounding the property. The white flower boxes hanging below the windows were bare.

Adam walked up the steps to the landing and knocked on the navy-blue door. He walked down a few steps and looked around the quiet Oak Park neighborhood. Huge yards with mature trees lined the streets. Million-dollar Victorian and French Normandy homes rounded out the eclectic vibe of the area. A minor scuffling was heard from inside the residence. The lock tumbled, and the door opened wide.

Ben Mooring opened the door, his bare chest rising and falling as if he'd just run a race. Adam gave a small prayer of thanks that Ben took the time to put on a pair of jeans before he came to the door. Unfortunately, the jeans were bulging in unsettling places.

"Ben?"

"Hey, Byrnes. Allison. Did you finally get the balls to sell?"

"It has nothing to do with balls. Is Julie Connolly here?" Adam angled himself so Ben couldn't slam the door in his face.

"Why?" Ben asked.

"It's important. We need to talk to her," Adam growled.

"About what?" He crossed his arms, maintaining a defensive posture and looming over the pair.

Anger engulfed Adam as his hands clenched at his sides. He was pulling his right hand up to act when a soft hand touched his arm.

"Ben, must you be a jerk your whole life?" Allison slowly moved her fingers down his arm and massaged Adam's hand open. "We were looking for Julie, but Edward must have given us the wrong address. She isn't here, is she?"

Julie skulked out from behind the door wearing

sweatpants and what had to be Ben's oversized college T-shirt. Julie bit her bottom lip and ran a hand through her disheveled hair.

"Please tell me this isn't what it looks like." Allison's eyes narrowed as her hands flew to her hips.

"Allison, I'm sorry. I wanted to tell you, but I was afraid you wouldn't understand."

"You're right. I don't understand. Are you sleeping with this jackass?"

"Can we take this inside? I have neighbors that don't want to hear your tirade," Ben said.

They walked across the hardwood floors into the multi-windowed living room. Julie sighed and sat in exhaustion, her head hanging low. Ben walked to her side and placed a hand on her shoulder for support.

"I'm sorry I didn't tell you, but now you know. Ben and I have been seeing each other for a while, and I'm in love with him."

Adam stared incredulously at Ben and Julie. The whole thing was ludicrous.

Apparently, Allison felt the same way, and her anger radiated from every pore.

She hissed at Ben, "You are lower than even I can imagine." She rounded on Julie. "Don't you get it? He's using you. He's trying to get the Byrnes's company, and then he'll run for the hills."

Something triggered in Allison's eyes—a realization.

"You didn't?" Allison hit her forehead with the palm of her hand. "Oh, God, tell me you didn't give him the list of client specifications?"

"What?" Julie looked as if someone punched her in the stomach.

"I have been trying to figure out how Ben has known all of our clients' information—their names, their jewelry designs. I have been running all over the city of Chicago trying to get our clients back." She lunged for Ben, and her fist met his nose with a crunch. "You slimy sonofabitch. How dare you use her like that?"

She pulled back to hit him again, but Adam managed to catch her before she connected. Julie jumped up and stood in front of Ben.

"Enough. Allison, I don't know what you're talking about. Ben doesn't have any client information. Have you ever thought maybe he's just good at his job? If you spent half as much time worrying about your job as you worry about what Ben's doing, Byrnes might be doing better."

"Bite me." Anger seethed down Allison's spine as she stood behind Adam, his arms still holding her back.

"Well, it's nice to see we can be grown up about all of this." Ben wiped the blood from his nose.

"I'll get you a tissue," Julie said gently to Ben. She swirled around to glare at Allison and growled, "I think you should leave." She glared at her bosses and stomped out of the room.

Adam looked over at Ben. "Where did you get the list?"

Ben moved his eyes from Adam to Allison. "It's not important. Just know Julie had nothing to do with it."

Julie walked into the living room, tissue in hand.

Her eyes opened wide. "Ben, is there some sort of a list?"

Ben kept looking forward, not meeting Julie's stare. Adam was shocked by the pain reflected in his eyes. Julie's disappointment almost appeared to hurt him. If Ben was using her, he was one hell of an actor. Either way, Adam was sure Julie had nothing to do with providing him inside information.

Who else would have given it to him though?

The realization roiled through his stomach. Pain and frustration wrenched his heart. He was almost afraid to ask the question, but... "How much did you pay Dale for the information?"

"Fifty thousand." He sighed and stared at Julie. But she wasn't talking. He reached out to touch her, and a fist hit his nose with another crunch.

"Dammit." His hand flew back to his nose, liquid pouring down his face. "You're lucky that's all I did." Julie pulled away and paced a hole in his living room carpet. "Why would you buy their client information?"

"Why do you think?" His head tilted back, his bloody hand pressed to his nostrils. "You know we're in trouble. I needed some sort of edge, and Dale needed money. It seemed like a good idea at the time."

He fell into a chair and focused on Adam. "Why are you even here? Was it to bust my chops about some damn list?"

"Actually, no."

"Yeah, um, Julie, I'm really sorry for accusing you of stealing the client list. I'm a real shitty friend." Allison played with the collar of her sweatshirt.

"You are," Julie agreed and gave a small smile. "But I guess I understand."

"Well, hold that thought." Allison looked from Julie to Adam and then back to Julie. "Adam and I found the paternity test."

Julie's face crumbled in fear, and panic swam in her eyes as they darted from person to person. "Oh."

"What paternity test?" Ben asked. "What is she talking about? Cody?"

"Where did you find it?" Julie sat on the loveseat, ignoring him.

"It was in the condo." Allison sat next to Julie and wiped away a tear from her cheek. "Why didn't you tell me?"

"I couldn't tell anyone. My father said if the Byrnes family found out they had a grandson, they'd try to take him away. I had to protect him. I couldn't let them get my son."

"But Herb knew about it?"

"Yeah, but only recently. My father said he was trying to make sure Herb wouldn't take him away."

You cannot be serious!" Ben's jumped from the chair and moved within inches of Adam's face. "Adam is Cody's father?"

"No," Julie screeched out. "Dale is his father."

Ben stepped back as the realization of those words hit him. "You told me the father was out of Cody's life. What else have you lied about?"

"He is—was—out of Cody's life. He doesn't even know about him. I never lied to you. And anyway, what about you? You haven't been the picture of honesty lately." Tears flowed down Julie's cheeks.

"You're right." He shook his head in disgust.

"I'm sorry to interrupt, but what about the money?" Adam asked.

"What money?"

Adam pulled out the bank statement, and Julie grabbed it from him. "One-point-five million. I don't know anything about money. I swear."

"Is this why you broke into the condo a few weeks ago?" Adam asked.

"You broke into the condo?" Ben's voice was an octave higher than normal.

"That was you?" Allison asked.

"No. I mean, yes. I didn't break in. I had a key. I just went in to find the paternity test. My father wanted to make sure that no one tried to take Cody. He was protecting us."

"You keep saying you need protection. From what? Do you honestly think we'd take your child away from you?" Adam couldn't think of one reason for her to think they'd ever do anything so heartless.

"I don't know. I just know I love him and I would do anything for him. He's all I have," she sobbed, her breath catching as she tried to bring in air.

"Okay, sweetheart." Allison put her arm around her shoulder as she glared at Adam. "It'll be okay."

CHAPTER TWENTY-FIVE

"JULIE, your father asked you to find the paternity test?" Allison asked as she rubbed her friend's hand in support. The terror and pain in Julie's eyes were overwhelming. Allison always knew Edward instilled a sense of fear in Julie, but she never realized it was this bad. The Byrnes family would have never taken a child from his mother. The fear was baseless, and Edward would have known that.

"Yes, he told me to look for the paternity test and find out where it was hidden."

"Why does he care where it's hidden?" Adam asked.

"I don't know. Why don't you ask him? He's been worried since Cody was born that the Byrnes family would find out. He wouldn't even let me put Dale's name on the birth certificate." She sniffed and wiped her nose with the tissue in her hand.

"Wait, we saw him this morning, and he said he

just found out about Dale and Cody's connection a few months ago," Adam said.

"I don't know why he'd say that." Julie frowned at Adam. "He's known since I found out I was pregnant."

"Apparently, lying runs in the family," Ben hissed.

Anger swelled as she watched Julie's eyes water again. She understood Ben was angry, but that didn't give him the right to be a jerk. Then again, jerk was his natural demeanor.

"Well, this has been about as much fun as a prostate exam. I'm heading upstairs. I'm assuming you all can find your way out the door." Ben motioned to the door before stomping up the stairs. Julie stared at him in disbelief.

"Are you okay?" Allison pushed a strand of hair from her friend's eyes.

"No. I'm angry and confused." She jumped to her feet and ran a frenzied hand over her face. "What a mess."

"Will you and Ben be okay?" Allison asked the question as a loud thunk came from the entryway. They looked up to find Julie's purse lying at the foot of the stairs. Women's clothing came raining down onto the foyer floor.

"I'm thinking no." She sniffled. "I think I finally screwed up yet another relationship."

Julie scooped up her clothes and looked at Adam. "I'm sorry. I would have told Dale, but I didn't think it was best for Cody or for me."

He nodded. "Are you going to tell him?"

"I suppose I have to."

"Did you want us to tell him?" Allison asked.

"No. I'll do it. I got myself into this mess. I'll get myself out." She sighed, and a tear slid down her cheek.

"Do you need a ride home?" Adam asked.

"No. My car is in the garage. I'm going to head home and change, and then I'll call him. Should I come into work on Monday?"

"Why? Are you planning on being sick?" Allison joked. Maybe this wasn't the best time for a joke, but she wanted to break the tension hanging in the room. Okay, poor timing. "If you need a little time to get yourself together, we understand."

"No." Julie sighed. "I mean, do I still have a job?"

Silence wrapped its claws around the room, stealing the air from Allison's lungs. She didn't know how to respond. She hadn't even thought of that. Allison had no intention of letting Julie go, but what if Adam had other plans. Crap. If he let her go... Well, she'd just have to talk him out of it.

"Yeah. I mean, yeah, you've always been like family." Adam lowered his head and faced the window. He seemed conflicted, but Allison couldn't help but embrace the relief flowing through her. No matter what, Julie had always been a good friend, and Allison didn't see that changing anytime soon.

EDWARD STARED at the floor safe in front of him. He was pleased to find it open, but then the darn thing was empty. Empty. They must have moved the documentation. He roamed the house, ripping open doors, drawers, and cabinets. It must be here somewhere. If Allison and Adam had found the bank information, they would've asked him about it.

He should have taken care of Allison in the stairwell. He'd known they would find those bank statements if they kept snooping around. He'd thought giving her a little scare would postpone their scavenger hunt. He'd figured it would give him enough time to find the documents before they did.

However, he'd had two weeks and didn't find a thing. Allison and Adam managed to find it in one day. He must not have known Herb as well as he thought. He whipped through the condo again, pulling up his ill-fitting leather gloves.

He couldn't believe he hadn't thought to look for a floor safe. He should have known Herb would have documents hidden in an obscure location. Hindsight was always twenty/twenty after all.

He looked at the empty safe as he walked across the room. Dammit. He kicked the protruding metal. The safe rattled as pain shot down his foot. He sat down on the floor, twirling his ankle to remove the sting of stupidity.

He took in a cleansing breath. Focus. Adam and Allison had the bank statements showing that Mörder had bribed him and numerous judges to get his extortion charges and various racketeering charges dropped.

They'd been lucky over the years. Edward and the judges in Mörder's pocket had handed Mörder positive verdicts and mistrials as directed, and no one had been the wiser. No, luck had nothing to do with it. Over the years, Edward had simply made sure that the paper trail was so convoluted that if you looked close enough, it would lead to Siberia.

Unfortunately, Mörder had taken over and was doing things his way. A kindergartner hid money better than that idiot. It was a miracle the man tied his own shoes. Stupid people drove Edward crazy.

Unfortunately, Herb hadn't been stupid. That had ultimately led to his undoing. Edward had been funneling the money from his extracurricular activities into one of Herb's personal accounts. Herb had been so busy with Byrnes and Company that he hadn't known half the assets he owned.

Until, of course, that little ingrate came back to the States. If Dale had just stayed away, Edward wouldn't be in this mess. Herb never would have found that account, but then he started looking for money to give that beggar. If Herb had just stuck with his initial instinct and said, "No," then this wouldn't have happened. Dammit. The whole situation sucked.

He stared at the wall. If Adam and Allison got the information to the cops, he could be looking at a maximum of fifteen years in prison. He refused to go to jail with the common riffraff.

He needed to get that paperwork before they got to the police. He needed to keep them quiet. He placed his head in his hands. He didn't like where this was going. It was one thing to simply drop some medication in Herb's coffee and let it take effect naturally, quite another to commit cold-blooded murder. Unfortunately, he didn't think that slipping some drugs into their food would work to rid him of Allison and Adam. He was afraid that the only way to eliminate the problem was to eliminate them.

He left the condo and headed back home. He needed to find his forty-five before he lost his nerve.

CHAPTER TWENTY-SIX

TWO HOURS LATER, Allison and Adam stared at the disaster-area family room in her condo. They'd helped Julie pack up her stuff and stack it in her car. She'd been heartbroken, but Allison offered to stay with her, but she'd said she needed time. Adam understood. That scene had been horrible for her.

And he also now knew she couldn't have ransacked the condo.

"Well, we know it's not Julie or Ben. We were just with them." Adam attempted humor despite the anger simmering underneath his skin. He toured the condo, but whoever did this was long gone. "I think it's time to invest in a state-of-the-art security system, and we need to change the code for the floor."

"Do you think the building would consider changing the key for the elevator? That might not hurt either." Allison picked up a fallen vase, a tear glistening in her eye.

"I'm not planning on giving them a choice. Obviously, the whole world knows how to access this condo. I can't have you staying here like this." Anger engulfed him as a gasp tumbled from the front hall. He pulled his gun and stared at his brother, who was gawking at the mess.

"Geez, don't shoot. What the hell happened here?"

"Don't sneak up on a cop. We're not sure, but we were just about to call CPD. How did you get in?" Adam asked, his gun still drawn.

"I have a key, and I know the code." Dale shrugged as he took off his coat. "Put that thing down."

"What are you doing here, Dale?" Adam kept the gun leveled at his brother. He hated the thoughts swimming through his head, but what were the odds his brother would show up while all this was happening? He even had the damn key.

"Mom sent me." Dale picked up his jacket and reached a trembling hand into the inner pocket. He pulled out a jewelry box and waved it above his head. "For Allison."

Allison walked over to Dale and took the box. She opened the lid, and her eyes glowed as a smile crossed her lips. "My necklace. I thought I lost it."

"Nah, Mom rescued it."

"Can you put it on me?"

"Yep." He kept his arms bent above his head. "Truce, bro? I come in peace."

"Fine." Adam lowered his weapon. He watched his brother place the pendant around Allison's neck. Even he had to admit he was a bit jumpy these days. Dale was harmless. He looked back at the disaster in the family room. Shit. Maybe he hadn't been jumpy enough if someone had gotten into the condo again. He slipped his cell phone from his pocket.

"You must have the Chicago police on speed dial by now. They have got to be tired of hearing from you." Dale shook his head as Allison let down her hair around the golden chain.

Allison smiled. "Probably. By the way, have you heard from Julie today?"

"No. Should I have?"

"Just checking. I'll be right back." She jiggled the documents in her hands at Adam and headed to the bedroom.

"Adam, I hope you know I didn't do any of this. I've been with Mom all day long. Nadia and I went with her to the luncheon for the animal shelter. Remember, you were supposed to go after we put a few hours in at the office. Familial responsibilities. Ring a bell?"

"Yeah." Adam sighed as Perretti's voicemail clicked on. He hit End and scrolled through his cell phone contacts.

"Way to blow me off, brother." Dale grinned as he flipped over a coffee table and set it on its feet. "So, we okay?"

"Yeah. Sorry, this has been a shit day."

"I can see that. I just can't believe someone got in again."

"Well, it won't happen again. I'm going to find a company to install a security system before I let her come back here again."

"Let me?" Allison had returned to the living room

without the paperwork, her unbroken arm angled with her hand. Even though he meant every word he said, Adam probably should have found a better way of saying it. The best way to start a fight with Allison was to tell her what to do. Hell, it was one of his favorite pastimes.

"You could always stay at Mom's until it's operational. In fact, after this, you'll be lucky if she lets you out of the house at all. She might lock you in your bedroom," Dale joked.

"Adam'd break me out though, right?" She gave a small grin, and Adam nodded. He owed his brother for that little diversion.

"I might break in, but I probably wouldn't break you out. I have an overwhelming desire to keep you safe." He wrapped his arms around her and kissed her forehead. "I think I'm going to try Joe's cell again."

"Do we have to? I think Dale's right, they're probably sick of us."

"Probably, but every piece of the puzzle will help them find this bastard." Adam kissed her head and released her.

Adam had just located Joe's number when someone cleared their throat at the front of the room. The three turned to find Edward leaning against the doorframe.

"How convenient. You're just the people I need to talk to."

"You found us. What do you need, Edward?" Adam said as Edward pushed his way into the family room.

"I need the statements you found in your father's safe," he said calmly.

Adam stared warily at Edward. There was something off about his demeanor. He'd always been cold, but his eyes were frighteningly disassociated, and his movements were a little erratic.

"I can help you." Adam soothed, trying to hide the adrenaline coursing through his veins. Every instinct was tingling. He needed to get Allison far away from this man. "Dale, why don't you take Allison downstairs to get the mail. I'll take care of things up here."

"They stay. You all stay." Edward sidled closer.

Allison's eyes widened as she backed up toward the bedroom. She looked terrified. Adam felt the same way.

Edward pulled a gun from his pocket. "Don't move!"

Allison's movements stopped except for her unbroken arm, which instinctively shot out to her side.

"Edward, everything's going to be fine." Adam eased toward him, his arms forward in a reassuring manner. He wasn't sure who he was reassuring—Edward, Allison, Dale, or himself. "Think about what you're doing."

"Am I missing something?" Dale asked as Adam angled himself between Allison and the gun.

"You are always missing something, you stupid piece of shit. You knock up my daughter, ruin her life, and then you come back to town looking for handouts, forcing your father to look at accounts that he would have just left alone. Mörder would have gone away, and none of this would've happened. No one wants you here, that's what you're missing," Edward shouted and fired two rounds at Dale.

Dale fell to the ground.

Allison yelled, "Stop. Please. We'll give you what you want."

"I want those statements."

ALLISON RAN to Dale when he fell on the floor. Another discharge of the gun stopped her in her tracks. Her eyes, which must have been the size of cymbals, stared Adam up and down. No injuries. She looked to Dale again, who was lying still, blood seeping out onto the floor.

"Stop!" Edward yelled. "Where is the bank information?"

"I put the paperwork in the safe," she stammered past the piercing thump of her heart. The fear engulfed her lungs as she forced them to expand and contract.

Edward waved the gun toward the master bedroom, following a few feet behind Adam and Allison as they trekked through the living room. Nerves, fear, inability to concentrate with a gun pointed at her—whatever the reason, Allison found herself tripping over her feet as she walked down the hallway. Adam gripped her arm before she hit the floor. He leaned into her and whispered in a low, commanding voice, "Run into the bedroom and lock the door."

She looked into his eyes, the heat from his chest radiating down her arm. She wanted to shake her head, say no, do anything to stop this. If she ran into the bedroom, he would be alone with this psychopath.

"Do it. I'll be fine." He must have seen the indecision that haunted her. He pushed her forward and pled, "Please."

He slowed his pace, which also slowed Edward's progress toward the bedroom. Allison quickened her pace, putting her at the master bedroom two full strides ahead of the men. Allison stepped into the master bedroom just as Adam reached the table in the hall. She saw him stumble into the table and knock the crystal vase to the floor. The loud noise diverted Edward's attention long enough for Adam to throw his elbow back into the raised gun.

Allison screamed as a loud bang resonated through the hallway, the gun discharging into the ceiling. Plaster spilled from the dime-sized hole onto Adam's head as he pushed Edward to the wall. Edward's hands remained frozen in place as Adam tried to peel his fingers from the stock. Frustrated, Adam punched Edward in the face, and the gun wobbled in Edward's hand.

Adam tried to grab the weapon as the two men struggled, bouncing from wall to wall. Allison stared as Edward twisted the gun and fired. A bright explosion was propelled from the handgun, and then Adam slumped to the floor.

"No!" Allison screamed and ran toward Adam. "No," she sobbed. The tears blocked her view as she dove to his side. Not Adam. She got within inches when her head snapped back, her hair follicles screaming in protest. Edward's hand was still wound in her hair as he tossed her against the opposite wall.

She landed on her broken arm, tears falling from her eyes as the pain radiated up the busted appendage. She cradled her arm, pulling it into her chest as Edward moved toward her, anger apparent in his eyes.

"Enough of this. Open the safe." Spittle flew from his lips with the force of his demand.

Sobs hitched in her chest as she looked over at Adam. He lay there, unmoving, blood flowing down the front of his shirt.

Her body moved on autopilot, her broken arm hanging lifeless at her side. She stumbled to her feet and ungracefully skittered to the floor safe. She fell to her knees and entered her birthdate. Nothing. The safe wouldn't open.

She wiped the moisture from her eyes. With trembling hands, she pressed the numbers again. Nothing. Panic welled. Her focus moved to the gun. *He will kill me.* Terror pushed her attention back to the safe. She fumbled with the keypad. Nothing.

Her head bounced forward as a hard object hit the back of her skull. Stars danced in her vision as she grabbed her head. She felt warm, sticky liquid seep through her hair.

"Hurry up! I don't have all day."

Allison removed her blood-soaked hand from her

head and returned her shaking fingers to the keys of the keypad. Dark spots danced in front of her eyes. Pain flew down her neck. *What am I doing?* She looked at the floor safe through the hazy edges of her vision.

Safe. Lock. Password.

When the hell is my birthday?

Zero. Six. One. Zero. Her fingers trembled, but she still managed to punch in the next four numbers.

The safe finally popped open, and the shelves rose from the floor. Edward took her by the shoulders and pushed her out of the way. He yanked the papers from the safe and tore through the documents, mumbling.

Allison scooted backward toward the bathroom, getting as far away as possible. Now that Edward had what he wanted, there was no telling what he'd do to her. Her stomach lurched. She edged backward.

She slid over the threshold of the bathroom and kicked the door closed with her foot. She gripped the counter and trembled to her feet. Darkness pulsed before her eyes. Through the fog, she saw the door—the only way into the bathroom—the only barrier between her and Edward. Falling toward the door, she turned the feeble lock.

She leaned against the wall. Pain throbbed in her arm, her head... hell, everything hurt. The high-pitched whine that she'd heard since Edward hit her in the head crescendoed in her ears.

She needed to find a phone, and fast, or even better, an escape. A window hung over the hot tub along the west wall. She unlocked the latch and threw the window open as the door handle jingled outside the room.

"Allison," Edward said. "If I have to chase you, it will just make me angry. You don't want me to be angry. I don't want me to be angry. Come on out. I'm just interested in talking."

Allison ignored the words spoken in the creepy, melodious tone. She'd seen horror movies. She knew how sweet words from crazy people ended—usually with the non-virgin butchered. She looked out the window, but a heavy screen and fifty floors separated her from the ground below. She heaved the vanity drawers open, looking for something she could use as a weapon. Desperate, she grabbed the porcelain tank lid and pressed back into the space beside the door.

A series of loud cracks made her jump, and splinters flew from the wood around the door handle as bullets came through the door and lodged in the bathroom wall. Then the door shuddered under the force of a kick, and Allison jumped out of the way as the door flew open. She lifted her makeshift weapon over her head and slammed the tank lid into his temple.

The gun fell to the ground when Edward curled his arms around his head in self-defense. Allison lunged for the gun, but her dive was cut short by a hand grabbing the back of her jeans. She gasped, unforgiving denim digging into her stomach.

Edward climbed over her body, inching his way to the gun. Her elbow cracked into his bleeding head. He stilled as she reached for the gun and wrapped her fingers around the hard, cold handle. She pushed her body against the cabinets behind her. She had to get away. She had to stop him. The heavy firearm jiggled as she raised the muzzle and pointed it at Edward.

Tears streamed down her face as he got on his knees. He staggered to his feet, and with a shake of his head, he lunged toward her. Terror slithered down her spine as she pulled the trigger.

Crack!

Time stilled. Edward stumbled.

Horror, fear, and disbelief ghosted through his widening eyes. He looked down at the river of red spreading down the side of his body. He covered the gushing breach with his hand, falling to his knees again.

She watched, realization dawning. She'd shot him. Her eyes moved to the gun in her hand. Shit. She wanted to toss the smoking monstrosity away. She wanted to run, but a soft moan echoed from the hallway. She'd done the right thing. It was the only way to stop Edward.

Adam. She bobbled through the bedroom and found Adam lying against the hallway wall. She knelt on the shattered pieces of the vase and put the gun down beside him.

"Are you okay?" she asked and stared at the red pool soaking his shirt.

Adam gasped between sputtering breaths. "I love you," he whispered, closing his eyes.

"I love you too." She kissed his forehead. "Adam? Adam? You hold on." Tears ran down her cheek as his head fell forward.

His chest. She swore people on TV lived after a

bullet to the chest. Didn't they? There was so much blood.

She needed to control the bleeding. That much she knew. She pulled off her sweatshirt. She rolled the fabric into a ball and used her left hand to apply pressure to the wound. She arched her arm to feel his neck for a pulse, and a stabbing pain shot through the useless limb. A faint heartbeat thrummed through her fingertips.

The police. She had to call the police. She patted her jean pockets. No phone. Dammit. She must have left her lifeline in her purse. Where the heck was her purse? She couldn't remember.

She needed another phone. She reached in Adam's pocket and found his cell phone. She tried to extract it without significantly moving him around. If she'd learned anything from watching cop movies, it's that you don't want to cause additional damage by shifting the body. Thank God for cop shows, or she'd be clueless.

She managed to wiggle the phone from his pocket and dialed 911. "Please help me." She stayed on the line with the operator, pressing on Adam's shoulder.

The woman on the line calmly took her information. "Allison, you're doing great. I've called the Chicago police and the ambulance. They should be there shortly," she soothed. "Are you hanging in there? Your friends' names are Adam and Dale, right?"

"Yes."

"How is their breathing?" the operator asked.

Allison leaned in to feel his breath. A loud noise

sounded as something struck her shoulder blade. Darkness dashed across her eyes as she soared onto her stomach

Stars. Pain. Enough.

She lay dumbstruck as Edward spun her onto her back and jumped on top of her, wrapping his hands around her neck. She covered them with her own, grasping at his fingers. But even though this time there were no gloves, she still couldn't gain purchase.

Terror sizzled in her chest as hopelessness overwhelmed her. Not again. She kicked and squirmed, but his legs pressed her to the ground. Blood moistened her fingers. She grappled at his arms, but her hands were slippery with blood. She needed a weapon.

She pawed the ground until she found a large shard of glass. She aimed the serrated edge at Edward and lodged it in his arm.

Her airway opened. She turned on her side and gasped for air, while Edward removed the glass with a trembling hand.

"You bitch." He wobbled to his feet and reached for the gun on the floor. "Why. Couldn't. You. Just. Let. It. Go?"

Edward hovered over Allison. There was nothing for her to do. She was locked in a fetal position, her arms covering her head. Not that it would help once he fired that gun. She was so screwed.

"Stop, Connolly!" a man's voice screamed. "Drop the gun."

Allison uncovered her head. The detectives. Washington and Perretti. They stood on the other side of the room, their guns aimed at Edward. He looked at the officers with a mixture of astonishment and anger, but he kept the gun leveled at her.

"Don't do anything stupid, Connolly. We have you surrounded. Throw the gun down," Shay reiterated.

Edward's eyes flew back and forth between Allison and the detectives. And with each turn, Allison's life flashed before her eyes. Maybe not her whole life. Maybe it was just her mistakes. But either way, she wanted to live long enough to correct them.

"Last chance." Joe's voice told Allison he wasn't playing. Edward just stood there, not getting the message. Then Edward smirked, and Allison's heart stopped. He pulled the gun away from Allison and aimed it at Shay.

Her partner didn't hesitate. A loud bang echoed off the walls, hitting Edward in the chest—just shy of his heart. His gun flew across the room as the lawyer screamed in pain.

"Shit," Edward yelled as the hole gushed. He fell to his knees.

"You're under arrest." Shay pulled the cuffs from her belt. She pushed Edward into the wall and yanked his arms behind his back.

"Why didn't you shoot to kill." Joe helped Shay cuff the man.

"I didn't want the paperwork."

Joe dropped down and placed his fingers on Adam's neck. "I feel a heartbeat."

Allison rushed to Adam's side, picking up the cell phone. "Hello?" She wasn't sure if they stayed on the call after all that. They had to have heard the cops announce themselves.

"Allison, are you all right?" The operator sounded worried. Join the club. Allison was pretty damn freaked out about now. But she had to take care of Adam. Then she could have the breakdown she deserved.

"I'm all right. The police are here." She lifted herself from the ground, clutching the back of her head.

Joe stood up from checking Adam's vitals. "Is that 911?".

"Yes."

"Ask them what's the ETA on the ambulance? We have multiple injuries." Joe leaned in to check the back of her head.

"I heard that. Let me check." Clicking came through the line as the operator did her magic. "They're in the lobby. They should be up in a minute."

"Thanks," Allison said as Shay handed her a stack of towels.

"This should help stop the bleeding."

"Thanks."

Shay ran over to Edward and used another towel to wrap his shoulder.

"Focus on Adam. I'll check on Dale," Joe called over to Shay.

Shay shook her head. "I'll be there in a second. I'll be damned if this piece of shit is going to say we didn't take care of him. He's a slimy enough lawyer that he'll get the charges dropped over something stupid like that."

Adam's eyes fluttered open. And just like that, Allison's breathing seemed to start up again.

"Are you okay?"

He tried to get up, but Allison pushed on his shoulder. "No. Wait for the EMTs."

"Dale?" Adam mumbled.

"He's banged up but breathing," Shay called from the other side of the room. "We'll get him the help he needs."

She finished Edward's makeshift bandage and brought towels over to Adam. Allison reached for the stack and used one to apply pressure to Adam's oozing wound.

As if on cue, the security guard entered the condo, trailed by the EMTs and additional police officers. The officers helped Edward off the floor, while a medic verified that his injuries weren't life-threatening. When they established that he'd make it safely to the hospital, the cops turned to Joe.

"We're taking this one in. Do you need him for anything?"

"No, we're done with him." Joe smirked. "And if he accidentally walks into a few walls, I wouldn't be upset about it."

EPILOGUE

ALLISON SAT AT HER DESK, poring over the numbers before her. If they followed Herb's expansion plan, they just might come out ahead this year. The door to her office swung open, and Adam peered inside.

"Hey," he said and strolled over to the couch. He sat down and rested his ankle on his bent knee.

Allison continued to study the financials, ignoring the tap-tap-tap of the foot across the room. This was her company now. She was running the show. And she'd never been so happy. The guy across the room didn't hurt that feeling.

"Apparently, you are not taking the hint. I'm hungry. Feed me."

"It's not time to leave yet," she said reasonably. Well, she tried to reason with the man. They were flying out to Phoenix tomorrow to pack up his house, and he'd been impossible ever since they booked the flight.

Adam stood up and walked behind her to massage

her shoulders. Her eyes closed as his touch erased all the stresses of the day. She sighed as the tension gradually dissipated.

"I have some things to do before I can go for the weekend..." She moaned when he hit a good spot. How was it the man knew all the good spots?

"You know, we still have to pack, so we should probably head out early. If we don't leave soon, we won't have time to eat, pack, and have mind-blowing sex," he whispered as he continued to work on her neck muscles.

"Heaven forbid we not have time for sex." Allison laughed.

"Who said there wasn't time for sex? There's always time for sex. I just figured you'd want mind-blowing sex over the quickie kind. I'm thinking of you."

"How generous of you."

"That's how I roll, always giving. So let's get out of here. You know, I'm still healing. I almost died. You don't want me to starve." He clutched his arm in mock terror.

Allison rolled her eyes. "It's been over a month. Last time I checked, your shoulder had healed just fine. Besides, I don't think the CPD would have taken you if you were still injured. Anyway, you know, the owner and boss might not like you fondling the staff."

"I have a feeling you'd enjoy my fondling of you. Of course, I hear the woman running this place is a hard-ass, so we just won't tell her what we're doing." Adam moved his hands back to Allison's shoulders.

Allison tilted her head back and attempted to glare

at him. "There is nothing wrong with my ass. It's is neither too hard nor too soft."

"You're absolutely right. Your ass is perfect. Let's go." He kissed her cheek and straightened up. He held out his hand.

"I'll make a deal with you." She stood up and linked her arm with his as she walked him toward her office door. "If you will give me ten minutes of uninterrupted work time, I will not only feed you, I won't get you in trouble with the boss."

"If I were to get in trouble, what types of things might happen to me?" he asked. She tapped his chest and rolled her eyes again as he added, "Because I really think I need to be punished. I have been bad."

"Fine, if you go away for ten minutes, I will punish you." She smiled. "Good. I think I need to be spanked." He waggled his eyebrows.

"Then give me time to finish up." When they finally reached the door, she pushed him into the hall. "Now go."

As he started to walk down the corridor, she smiled and called out. "That's ten whole uninterrupted minutes, Adam. No phone, email, IM, texts, or even smoke signals."

He turned and saluted, then headed down the hall with a smile on his face. She shook her head and returned to her desk.

A soft knock beckoned from the doorframe.

"It hasn't been ten minutes. There is no way you're getting a good spanking," she said as Julie entered the room. Oops. "Sorry, Julie, I thought you were Adam." Allison cringed in embarrassment.

"I hope so. I really don't want to be spanked—by you, anyway," Julie said. "You're lucky I'm not easily offended." Julie attempted a smile. "So how's it going, boss? I talked to Doug Kaminski. He liked the changes you made to the designs. He placed the order today."

"That's good news. Are you okay? You seem a bit down."

"Bad day. Bad life. Take your pick." Julie sighed.

"Have you talked to your dad?"

"No, they only let the inmates call out once a week. I'm sure his phone call is used to call his lawyer, or Satan, or whoever he has found to listen to his bullshit. Lord knows no one here wants to talk to him."

"You swore. You never swear." Allison's eyes bulged in disbelief.

"It's the new me. A lot of this crap could have been avoided if I just spoke my mind. So that's what I'm going to do. I'm saying it like it is. By the way, have you heard the latest on Mörder?"

"Joe told Adam what happened. Can you believe they found him floating in the Chicago River?"

"Do they know what happened?"

"No. So far, the autopsy indicates suicide, but no one believes it." Allison smirked. "There's a reason sleeping with the fishes is associated with the mob."

"But isn't that the Italian mob?"

"Honestly, I have no idea. I'm not up on my mob lingo."

"Yeah, me either." Julie's already glum expression clouded further.

"Are you okay?"

"Yes, No. My father was such a negative influence my whole life. I don't know why I didn't see it. Well, I guess I always saw it, I just didn't do anything about it."

"Julie, he's your father. That's understandable."

"Yeah, I guess." Julie played with a loose string on her shirt. "Have you heard from Ben?"

"No, you've probably heard more from him than I have." Tears welled in her eyes.

"Not really. I used the money from the stock Herb left me to buy Ben's company, but I really haven't talked with him about it at all. He signed the papers to sell and ran out the door. Brook lives in Oak Park and said she saw a For Sale sign on his lawn. He must be leaving the Chicagoland area."

"Well, good riddance," Julie said. Despite her attempt at nonchalance, Allison saw the shadows of hurt in her eyes.

"I'm sorry, sweetie. Does he warrant ice cream therapy? Wine therapy?" Allison wrapped an arm around Julie's shoulder.

"I would, but I'm done turning to junk food for support. However, I could be talked into a little bit of girl-talk and wine therapy."

"Well, we're heading out to dinner, come with us. Then afterwards, we'll drink our weight in bubbly." Allison smiled and went back to her desk. She started shutting down her computer and moving her paperwork into stacks. There was just no way she was getting any more work done tonight.

"Shutting down already? It's only two o'clock." Julie watched her stack the papers.

"Yeah. It will be here when I get back."

"Ah, yes, after your trip. Isn't the flight tomorrow? Don't you need to pack?" Julie asked as she played with the Newton's Cradle on the desk. The *click click* reverberated through the air.

"Yeah, but I always have time for you. Come with us to dinner?"

"Who's going?"

"It's Adam and me, Brook, and Brach." Allison's lips twitched into a grin.

"Brook and Brach? Who's Brach?"

"Brach is the flavor of the month. I give it two weeks, solely based on the stupidity of their names together."

"Although the idea of a fifth wheel scenario sounds super great, I think I'll pass."

"Come on. It'll be fun. Don't leave me alone with Brrr-squared," Allison whined.

"You aren't alone, you have Adam. And I have to pick up Cody." Julie smiled in triumph.

"How is it going with Loraine watching him every day?"

"It's been really great. Today they wandered around the zoo and Wednesday they went to the planetarium. He comes home so tired. She's a godsend. Even if my dad's assets hadn't been frozen and I could afford another babysitter, I would still keep her. She's by far the best sitter I've ever had."

"That's what grandmas are for." Allison grinned. "Although it's nice that Dale sold me his controlling interest in the company, it's a shame he decided to move back to Singapore."

"Yeah. I think Cody would have liked to have his father in his life. However, it's probably better he left now, before Cody formed an attachment. One thing Dale has proven is his ability to abandon the ones he loves. Cody deserves better."

Allison reached across the desk and covered Julie's hand with her own. "Sweetheart, you do too."

"Yeah." Julie pasted a smile on her face and glanced toward the door. "You should go to dinner, start your weekend."

"Easy for you to say, you're not stuck eating with Brrr-squared."

"Stop calling us that." Brook burst into the office. "You think it's cute, but it's not."

"Stop going out with total jerks," Allison rebutted. "You think it's cute, but it's not."

"Not everyone is lucky as you are, sister dear. Some of us have to work at it. We have to pass through the weeds to get to the flowers." Brook patted Julie's shoulder as she walked around the desk. She kissed Allison on the head and sat in the second visitor chair next to Julie.

"Where did you find that saying?" Allison asked.

"I made it up. Lawyers can be very creative, you know. Come on, ladies. Dinner awaits."

"I'm not going. I refuse to be a fifth wheel," Julie said as she stood up to leave. "That won't be a problem. Brach isn't going." Brook focused her attention on a piece of lint on her skirt. She glanced up at two quizzical looks.

"What happened?" Julie asked as she grabbed Brook's hand and sat back in the chair. Allison's eyebrow shifted up as she finished shutting down her computer. She couldn't wait to hear this one.

Brook stared at the two women and sighed. "Let's just say, I think I'm going to propose we stop using female interns."

Chicago's Finest Series
    Second Time's the Charm
    Stark Raving Mad
    Stealing Vegas

Busted Series
    Busting In
    Busting Out
    Busting Through

And look for her Contemporary New Adult series:

Ritter University Series
    Major Renovations
    What Happens in College...
    Christmas Breakdown
    Rushing In
    Sophomore Slump
    The Make-up Test

Vanessa M. Knight has always enjoyed writing, and once she found romance, she was addicted. She props her laptop in the suburbs of Chicago with her husband, son, and menagerie of four-pawed claw-babies (AKA cats and dogs.) That laptop has partnered-in-crime to write contemporary romances with a dash of humor and splash of snark. When she has a few moments to spare, you can find her singing off-key (but she assures everyone it's still considered singing), reading, kickboxing, or killing a few brain cells as she stares at the many sitcoms and dramas available through the Internet and TV.

For more information on Vanessa, including her Internet haunts, contest updates, and details on her upcoming novels, please visit her website at www.-vanessamknight.com.